TIMBERDARK

DARREN CHARLTON

LiTTLE TiGER

LONDON

For Joseph.

My home.

And in loving memory of Claus.

(1976 - 2002)

'The mountains are calling
and I must go.'

John Muir

I

PROLOGUE

Some communities had islands to protect them from the Dead. Others had vast glaciers and mountains. Over in Arizona, where long, black roads shimmered like liquorice sticks out across the desert, the National Park Escape Programme was without rival. Seen from space, Grand Canyon looked like the Earth had been torn wide at the skin. It was as violent a wound as a bloody gash to the bone. Only it was a river, not a blade, that had quietly cut a mile deep into the rock over millions of years, giving those survivors living in the valley below a maze of walls to hide in and a fall from the top that made bone dust of the Dead.

To the north, Yellowstone had none of those things to protect it. The land was flat and unguarded and would have been prone to ravage from its wandering herds if it weren't for one thing. The earth held a secret.

While the air up there was so cold it glittered like finely

ground diamonds, a little piece of hell bubbled away just below the surface. Acid in the ground turned trees into tinder. It burned the grass off the land, making the soil scab with wet copper pools like freshly scalped skulls. Only raised boardwalks kept Yellowstone's inhabitants safe. They crisscrossed the park, stopping a sturdy boot from breaking through the Earth's thin crust while a series of little wooden stepping stones and moveable walkways broke the path from one cabin to the next, keeping the Dead from every door.

Yellowstone had a volcano deep in its heart, and its broiling skin was the deadliest of all the park's natural defences. And yet, when the great geysers burst, rousing plumes of hot water and chattering goshawks up into those roaming skies, this place was damned near perfect. Crying shame then, that this life beneath the doming blue was all but coming to an end.

Wyatt lifted the pan from the blue flame, swilling dregs of fizzing coffee round the rim, and watched the snow dance across the cabin window. He yawned. He scratched his butt. He considered taking a piss in the sink while Daisy was still asleep just so he didn't have to use the outhouse. He thought again. He poured the pan, taking brief pleasure in the sting of heat curling up from the enamel cups and threw another log on the fire. It popped, or maybe one of the mud pools beneath the cabin did – who could be sure at this godforsaken hour? – and he stood up on tiptoe to peek above the snow shelving the sill.

Outside, steam chugging up from the geysers broke through cracks in the decking. It was so thick this morning, it smothered the air like September snow over summer dreams. There was no sight of the surrounding boardwalks and cabins. They may as well have been up in the clouds. Only the low winter sun was visible, glowing dully inside the mist like a moon. That and the little wooden bridge reaching out from the cabin to greet it.

Wyatt jolted forward, slopping coffee across the stove. Fewer things had greater rule over Yellowstone than winter, but making sure your bridge was winched back of a night time was sure as hell one of them. Whenever the Dead came, they appeared suddenly and without warning, standing scattered across the boards like ghosts travelling up from below. Not that they took much interest in him or Daisy no more. Hell, they'd become all but invisible to them since they'd got bit. But others might, and in more recent weeks, had. Once word got round about how their kind could stop the Dead from attacking, the Escape Programme was hurried to an end.

Most people passing through on their way down from the refuge at Glacier National Park brought joy and news of electricity in some town that was already set to welcome everyone home from the parks. But others rode in on troubled saddles to recall any so-called Pale Wanderers left out here, with instruction for them to play their part leading the defence against the Dead. Now he and Daisy were the only ones who'd decided to stay back, it was all they could do to stop one of them rangers from making it right up to their front door.

Wyatt stared at the little wooden winch. "Daisy, darlin'," he called back. "Did I take a leak and forget to bring the bridge back in last night or did you?"

Daisy didn't answer. Wyatt downed his coffee and made his way through to the bedroom. The crumpled bedsheets were empty. Most likely, she'd taken a couple of eggs and a pan out to boil on one of the park's bubbling pools. Not that it was her turn. Wyatt glanced at the figurine of the silver bronco on the windowsill and sighed. He'd won more calf-roping contests than any other cowboy this side of the Tetons back in the day. And Daisy would've been Rodeo Queen too, flying the flag for them both with a thousand rhinestones blazoned across her chest like a night full of stars, given half a chance. She had what it took. Folks who thought that all it required was a vacant smile and a blouse full of boobs were wrong. It took real grit. She'd taught herself how to ride in the western style too and besides, she was unusual in her class in that she was seventeen years old back then, unmarried and without child, and you needed all those things to qualify under pageant rules. But it wasn't to be. The Dead saw to that. They saw to a lot of things.

Wyatt glanced at the old wooden fruit punnet he'd fashioned into a cot. It fidgeted. A little hand with fingers as plump as cocktail sausages poked up and Wyatt smiled. Mable was his world entire and he wanted only a world full of rushing rivers and meadow flowers for her to play in. Neither he nor Daisy would let a damn thing come along and change that, least of all a move to some town.

Something heavy landed with a thud out on the bridge. Wyatt set Daisy's cup down on the dinner table and made his way outside, but it was only a piece of carrion dropped clean from the sky. The raven soon followed. It hopped along the decking, tucking its black velveteen wings behind its back like a man bowing just before the dance, and began to peck at its kill. It gagged, parting its beak to release one of its terrible calls. That damned purr. The devil's purr. Wyatt swiped snow from the seat of the rocker and sat, pushing the chair forward with his toes to set it in motion, and watched the bird make light work of the mouse. The rodent was only small, barely enough flesh to fill a thimble, really. But it was enough to make him tremble. The raven's black beak tore shreds of raw meat from the carcass and Wyatt put his foot down to stop the chair.

"Dang it," he said. "Not now."

He set his hand across his knee to steady it, observing the grey pallor of his skin against the stark white of his cotton long johns. He cussed himself for looking at the meat. He counted to ten and hoped the feeling would soon subside. But it made no difference. Saliva goosed the inside of his mouth. His stomach yawned wide, ready to devour the mouse and a thousand more little bodies just like it.

Wyatt bolted forward, lobbing the tin cup at the bird. The cup clipped its wings, clattering across the bridge inside the steam and the raven took off with its kill. Wyatt wiped drool from his bottom lip. His hand trembled. He cussed. Being made invisible to the Dead by their bite was the blessing. Sharing their hunger for flesh was the curse.

Beneath the decking, welts in the mud bubbled and burst beneath him. But after a moment or two, the earth settled and Wyatt's hunger passed. He braced both hands on the arm rests ready to get up and fetch the cup, when he stopped.

The cup flew back. It broke clean out of the mist, somersaulting a couple of times, and smacked the cabin walls.

Wyatt smirked. "Daisy, your throw's lousier than a drunk aimin' for the piss pot."

He held his hand over his eyes, shielding it from the burn of the pale sun and waited for Daisy to walk through with those eggs. She didn't come. He called out. But nobody called back. It was only now that Wyatt noticed something strange. The sun was so much lower in the sky than it had been a moment ago. It was still early in the morning, but just as sure as he was sitting there, the sun began to set. Not slowly in real time, but fast, like a sunset dropping over a vast horizon in one of those old nature programmes. He took a step closer, aligning himself with the foot of the bridge, and the sun travelled forward. He blinked to shake off the morning grog, and the sun was closer still. Only it wasn't the sun at all, but a lamp.

Wyatt staggered forward. "Who goes there?"

Steam twisting up through cracks in the boards passed across the lamplight, diffusing the glare. Whoever was holding it remained out of sight.

"Sweetheart, don't be playin' no games, you hear me? I ain't in no mood."

The mist was still too thick for him to see anyone, but it became clear that the lamp was hovering about twelve feet off the ground. And it swayed. It wasn't being held by a hand. It dangled from a staff. Wyatt's eyes darted to the bridge's little wooden winch. He dashed forward, taking the handle in both hands, and tried to hoist it round. But it wouldn't even manage one rotation. Wyatt let go, feeling the frosted wood burn through both palms and tried again. But it was no good. The weight of the stranger on the bridge was too great. Wyatt bent double, gasping for breath, when a dark mass broke free of the folding steam.

The silhouette of a lone rider bearing a crown of antlers hung inside the mist.

The stranger was as thin as a crack in the wall, with a black robe cinched tight at the waist. There was no face to speak of, only a deer's skull for a mask. Without the skin and fur to soften it, the muzzle was nothing but ragged bone, as sharp and cruel as a beak, with empty eye sockets to watch from and two hollow nares on the ridge from which to breathe. Wyatt couldn't make out the stranger's eyes, but those blank sockets held his gaze, freezing him to the spot like an unbreakable curse.

Wyatt staggered back, reaching for the holster on his hip. He realized he'd left the gun indoors and cussed himself. But the only thing that mattered now was that the stranger thought him to be alone. He kept his eyes on the stranger so as not to alert him to the presence of another life out there in the park and willed Mable to keep quiet in her crib.

"Mornin', friend," Wyatt offered. "Now I already told you good people that I ain't interested in followin' you all into some town if that's why you're here. But there's coffee on the stove and a seat by the fire if it's a warming rest stop you came lookin' for."

The stranger showed no interest in Wyatt's nervous invitation. He lowered the lamp, setting the staff inside a metal sheath just below the stirrups with one hand and placing the reins over the bucking rolls with the other. But he never looked down.

Gloved fingers, as long as winter shadows, slipped along the side of the saddle to a velveteen bag. They fingered the drawstring, reaching deep inside, then withdrew in liquid motion as if the object the stranger sought was always within his command. He held his arm out and the gloved hand unfurled like a black flower, revealing the contents of his palm. Inside it was a gift.

The slice of raw meat was as pink as clouds at dusk. And juicy. Wyatt's heart bucked against his chest. It was so much fresher than the mouse, but he'd made a pact with Daisy not to give in to this urge. They both had. The hunger was the way of monsters and something Wyatt would have done everything in his powers to resist right now, had every pulse of his heart not strained so.

Wyatt took the piece of meat, nodding his thanks

now that the two of them seemed to have come to an understanding, and the stranger's hand withdrew. And as he brought the glistening flesh to his lips, he observed a pair of eyes beneath the skull's empty sockets and the stranger leaned in.

A thin voice, as ragged as a blade of grass shredded in the wind, broke from behind the mask. It carried with it just a single word.

"*Timberdark.*"

Wyatt didn't really catch what the stranger was saying. The promise of meat made the inside of his mouth tingle. Thrilled, he took a bite.

"Thank you, sir," he said wiping drool on the back of his hand. "Thank you."

But the stranger showed no interest in such niceties and merely repeated the word.

"*Timberdark.*"

Wyatt realized the stranger's offering came at a price and looked up. "Is that some town you seek, my friend?"

The eyes behind the deer's empty sockets blinked.

"*Timberdark.*"

"I know," said Wyatt suddenly troubled that the word was not familiar to him. "I'm real sorry I can't help you, but that's not someplace I know of."

The stranger held Wyatt's gaze longer than was comfortable. And yet he seemed satisfied that his answer held true. The rider's gloved hands slid like shadows across the reins to regain control of them and he eased back in the saddle ready to pull away. Wyatt offered a parting wave and turned to make his way back indoors. It was only then that he noticed blood as black as molasses dripping on to the bridge. The stranger lowered his hand to the side of the saddle, teasing strands of fine red hair through his spindle fingers. But the hair wasn't being drawn up from inside some satchel, but a severed head.

Wyatt recognized the frozen features of that beautiful face hanging by its hair from the saddle, staring back at him. He recognized the woman's freckles, dainty as the speckle of an egg across those porcelain cheeks. He recognized her lips. But it was no longer his Daisy. The eyes staring back at him now were as dead as a doll's.

A terrible sound tore its way out of Wyatt. A wail. A cry. One that should never come out of a man. But he didn't have time to give in to it. He dropped the meat. He turned. He ran back across the bridge, carried on by the scream for his daughter, and straight into the cabin. But he never made it to her.

The stranger's boots struck the timber boards. Wyatt heard the steady stride across the bridge towards him. His eyes scanned the cabin. Furiously. There was a knife beside the sink. A poker by the fire. There came a gurgle from the bedroom and Wyatt froze. But it was too late. The front door creaked open behind him, then shut, bringing with it only silence and resolution. There was snow at the window. There was heat from the fire. Then there was nothing.

1

Peter kicked the cabin door down. Well, he didn't exactly kick it down, more made it click open with his boot. But this was certainly more dramatic than if he'd done it by hand and some of the wood around the frame exploded into splinters, which was way more than he'd thought himself capable of managing only a short while ago. But then, so much had changed this past month. And now here he was with a pistol pointed at his face and two angry eyes staring from behind, all in the name of a daring rescue mission.

The girl they'd barged in on swivelled the cylinder to lock in a bullet and shrugged the pigtail from her shoulder. "Take another step and it'll be your last."

"I won't," said Peter raising both hands. "I promise. But we're not here to hurt you."

Cooper backed in through the door, navigating the step up into the cabin without once taking his eyes off the surrounding woods, and stood guard. And it crossed Peter's mind now, as it often did during inappropriate moments just like this, that this boy, with those ropes of golden hair matted to his face beneath a Stetson the inside of which never saw the light of day, was *his*, and how much this girl, if only she wasn't fearing for her life quite so much, would surely love to hear all about that.

Cooper doffed his Stetson. "S'OK, miss."

"Nothin's OK," said the girl.

"We mean you no harm. But you got company in them woods, so if you're gonna trust us, you better make it quick."

Peter glanced back. "Coop."

"Well, she's bein' too slow. Make her listen."

Peter shook his head to indicate his apologies for Cooper's tone. "I'm sorry I broke your door down but—"

The girl raised an eyebrow. "It's hardly down."

"Oh."

"It's ajar at best."

"Yes, but—"

"It's still on its hinges."

"Yes. All right, then, but still."

"If you boys lay one finger on me . . ."

"That's not the reason we're here."

"That's always the reason."

"No," said Peter. "We're not going to hurt you."

"Oh, I know *you* won't. Just look at you."

Peter went to defend his door-breaking abilities once more, but the girl's disdain for his heroics had already turned towards his wolfskin.

"I thought it looked menacing," said Peter.

The girl narrowed her eyes. "Looks like a onesie."

Cooper glanced back. "Quit jabberin'. They'll be here soon."

"You don't know shit," said the girl.

"Well, I know there's two of 'em comin' up through the woods right now."

"Then you'd better leave."

Peter inched a little closer. "Please—"

"Don't say I didn't warn you."

"There's a place for you nobody else knows about. A place nobody can hurt you."

"I said leave."

"But we're here to rescue you."

The girl cocked her head to one side and stared at Peter's mouth like she was waiting for a punchline. But she must've realized the joke wasn't coming because her eyes lit up with an amusement that didn't seem entirely appropriate to the situation. She placed her hand on her hip.

"Oh, honey, no."

"I'm serious," said Peter.

17

She angled the nose of her pistol up and down Peter's body. "You're like, what, ten?"

Peter clenched his jaw and said nothing.

"No, wait a minute. Twelve."

"There's movement out in the woods," said Cooper calling back. "We don't got much time."

The girl clubbed the pistol into her fist. "OK, thirteen!"

"Sixteen," said Peter. "I'm sixteen."

"Woah. You're kidding, right?"

"No."

"Then I need a minute to process that."

"I was a very light baby."

"Baby?"

"So, I can't possibly be like those men out in the woods then, can I?"

"Dunno. Maybe. Maybe not."

"I don't even weigh in at a hundred and forty pounds after Thanksgiving," said Peter. "And I wouldn't place any bets on me being able to keep the conversation going if the Super Bowl came up, or cars, or soccer, or boobs, or soccer and boobs. But I do know who won the last ever Academy Award for best actress and I do have a lot to say about the stitching on your blouse and how much I love those rhinestone flowers, even if they were put on using a glue gun. But please stop me if you still have any doubts about us or else I'll just keep talking."

The girl shook her head in a *Jesus H Christ* kind of a way and no words came out.

"Pete," said Cooper in a low voice behind him. "Super Bowl *is* soccer."

The girl raised an eyebrow. "How'd you even last this long?"

Peter shrugged. "It's a miracle, I know."

"Yeah, and I'm sure you've got a heart as big as your Care Bear collection back home, but you don't know what you're walking into. Just leave me be and go."

"Why?"

"Ain't you lookin' at me?"

Peter held her gaze. "Yeah. I'm looking at you."

"Well, you ain't looking right."

"No?"

"No."

"I mean," said Peter. "I recognize your pale skin. I can see the darkness in your eyes from the journey you've taken to death and back again. You're one of the Returned, but unless there's something else I'm missing?"

The girl looked towards the cabin window where the snow was falling softly. Outside in the wood, aspens creaked wearily, made bone-brittle by winter. Without leaves, the woods couldn't disguise the sound of muffled voices coming their way.

"They'll be here any moment," said Peter. "You don't have to be scared."

The girl smirked like his hollow words were funny somehow.

Peter cleared his throat. "You see that boy standing back there?"

The girl's eyes darted over his shoulder. A quizzical look passed across her face, followed by a strange calmness and Peter knew she'd finally clocked the pallor of Cooper's skin.

"You see that handsome man," said Peter, "with his blond hair all golden like a waterfall at sundown now he let me wash it?"

Copper huffed. "I dint *let* you, Pete. When I woke up that time, my face was hangin' over the foot of the bed with a wash tub full of water staring right up at me. I had no choice in the matter."

"You did have a choice."

"Huh? Your pa was standin' over the bed ready to pin me down in case I bolted."

Peter narrowed his eyes. "He exaggerates. Anyway, that's my Cooper. He's just like you. And I love him."

The girl raked her front teeth over her bottom lip and said nothing.

"I love him more than anything."

"We can't be trusted," said the girl. "We're dangerous."

"Is that you talking or the men who are on their way up to the cabin?"

"Men?" She laughed like that would be a relief somehow. "You don't know what you're talking about."

"Then tell me. We know the gangs that operate around these parts."

"Is that so?"

"Yes. One guy took Cooper just so he had someone to protect him from the Dead. So, tell us."

"The Harrisons."

Peter shook his head. "Sorry. Who?"

"Sweet boy, you think it's all cowboys and Indians out here."

"I don't. Cooper was traded in for medicines by our own community when he returned, so I don't think any such thing."

The girl's amusement slipped from her face as she took his words, and *him*, seriously for the first time. She gazed through the window where the sun hung low like a fireball inside the forest, as if trying to discern her fate in the darkening sky beyond, and Peter knew he'd finally reached her.

"Ray and Pat Harrison are on their way over," she said. "Our nearest neighbours. You can see their cabin on the other side of the ridge from here."

Peter made his way over to the door next to Cooper

and peered through the veil of snow to the hill on the other side. The cabin was mostly hidden, packed inside terraces of snowy pine. Then he saw the smoke wending its way up through the treetops and light from two windows glinted from inside the woods.

"Daddy's waitin' it out at their place while they come here for me," said the girl.

"Why?"

"Because he did the same for them when their boy Billy returned from death, too. I didn't know it at the time, I thought they were just paying us a visit with offers of soup and a game of cards. But the Harrisons were just waiting here while Daddy saw to him."

"But why?"

The girl shrugged. "Because they made a pact. And because nobody wants to admit to killing their own child. I guess Daddy's over there eatin' soup and playin' cards right now. Now he's made a ghost of me."

Peter looked away as if to give the girl's proclamation some privacy and Cooper almost seemed to disappear beneath the brim of his Stetson.

"The whole world's made ghosts of us, miss," he said.

"Yes. But ain't that only right?"

"No," said Cooper. "No, it ain't."

"But I coulda hurt them."

"But you wouldn't."

22

"Wouldn't I?"

"No," said Peter. "You wouldn't."

"Why not? How do you even know that?"

"Because—"

The girl shrugged. "Well?"

"Because—"

"Because" said the girl, glancing at Cooper, "if you let yourself believe I could hurt people, then so could *he*?"

Peter clenched his fist, feeling the burn of her words in the back of his throat. "I need you to trust us when I tell you that there's a place not far from here where you'll be safe and where no one will look upon you with fear. We've got two horses and a spare tent for our travels but we have to act fast."

The girl glanced at her pistol and said nothing. Peter held out his hand.

"Please," he said. "I'm Peter and this is my boyfriend, Cooper."

"You always do the talkin' and him the moody stuff?"

"Not always," said Cooper, butting in before Peter could answer. "I asked him out first. Sluiced out a bunch of guts from inside my canoe and put on a clean pair of undershorts and everythin'."

Peter smiled. "Well, they were kind of clean. But yes, he did, too."

"Told him I loved him first, too."

23

"Yeah. Well, I'm working on being better at that."

The girl narrowed her eyes and seemed to come to a decision about them. "Don't think I'm joining you. Cos I ain't. I've got some daddy issues to work through on the other side of that there ridge. But let's get this show on the road."

Peter didn't much like the idea of leaving her behind. The fifteen or so notches scored into the side of Snowball's saddle were evidence enough of just how successful their mission to offer sanctuary to as many Returnees in the region had been. But Cooper gave a reluctant nod and besides, the girl was clearly more than capable of taking care of herself.

Peter nodded and something heavy landed on the cabin roof. Footsteps scrambled and a clump of snow dropped down the chimney, smothering what was left of the dying embers.

"The chimney!" said the girl. "There's no time to light the fire if they plan on getting in that way."

Cooper shut the front door and Peter scanned the ceiling. But it went quiet. He could practically hear whoever was up there thinking what their next move should be. Then someone knocked on the door.

"Sweetheart?" came a woman's voice outside. "It's just me. Pat. I was out tracking deer this way and wondered if you might have time for a brew."

Peter held his hand up to make sure the girl kept quiet and the knock sounded again. Someone crossed the roof in a single stride and dropped past the window. Cooper edged further back inside the cabin, aiming the rifle towards the door. But somebody else popped a shot before he even had a chance to.

Peter ducked. A bullet whipped through the cabin breaking the window. But it didn't come from outside. The glass shattered out into the woods and Peter looked up.

"My name's Betty Bridges," said the girl blowing smoke from the barrel. "And is this all you boys got?"

Peter hoisted the wooden box with a plunger he had strapped across his shoulders off his back and placed it on to the floor. He stepped over the wire he'd trailed through the woods and got down on to his hands and knees. Cooper rammed a chair beneath the door handle to secure it and dropped to the floor next to them.

"I'm sorry if I honk, miss," he said looking out from behind the strands of his matted hair. "My boy and I have been out on the road some three weeks now."

Peter smiled to himself. He was never going to tire of hearing himself described as Cooper's boy. Never. Betty scrambled on to the floor next to them. Peter waited until all three of them were in position lying face down on the floor, then reached up for the plunger. He briefly glanced sideways. Cooper's dark eyes held his gaze. They said *I love you*, just as they'd done that morning beneath the warmth of the fire out on the plains. They'd been good together out here. Better than good. They'd been a team. Peter said it back without the need for words and, with a shove, pushed the plunger down.

"I guess this is where we say goodbye," said Betty. "But what in God's name is this place you boys talk of?"

The woods boomed.

The cabin shook.

Peter looked up, spitting snow and shards of sharp pine needles from his lips, and, smiling, said, "Wranglestone!"

2

They rode on towards night. Peter held his hand up, shielding his eyes to watch the red sun, low over the plains. The snow at their feet burned pink and for a moment, the Earth almost seemed to catch fire, singeing first the clouds and strands of Cooper's golden hair, then finally the land itself. The sun clipped the white plains and the horizon ignited, glimmering at the fringes of the land like embers across paper. Peter leaned in, feeling Cooper's wonder expand across the width of his back with every intake of breath. But the display didn't last long. The blazing skies dissolved into the darkness of space and soon the stars went back and back. And yet, their path remained lit.

The snow glowed blue beneath the moon, and as their journey led them off the plains into a sanctum of dark pines, snow on the ground lit the whole forest from within, transforming night into eerie day. In the summer months, when the evenings were so dark you couldn't even see the bottom of a tin cup unless you tilted it towards the fire, it was impossible to imagine that the rest of the world wasn't fast asleep too. But there was a whole other night world out there only winter could show you. The hairs on Peter's forearms bristled, alerting him to the sudden presence of life. And as they slipped deeper in among the trees, the snow gave up the whereabouts of those who lived there.

Elks' antlers cast midnight shadows across the snow. There were deer out walking the woods. Bobcats on the boughs. Snowball passed beneath a bulbous branch and a feathered face as flat as a tree stump swivelled round on hunkered claws to see them on their way. And when, some time later, Peter wrapped his arms around Cooper's waist and they left the forest behind them, the Dead wandered out from beneath the pines, spindly and black against the glow of the plains, and stood scattered, watching as they rode on by. But they didn't approach. They never did. When he survived their bite, the Dead had marked Cooper as one of their own, making him invisible to them. In turn, that sweet tang of log smoke and sweat upon Peter's skin, born of long nights wrapped up in each other's kisses, marked *him* as belonging to Cooper, and worked to keep him safe. Peter leaned in, kissing the back of Cooper's neck, and the night and all its creatures slowly slipped away behind them.

They travelled north into backcountry. Barely a single night had passed following Rider's death before Cooper insisted they got out here while Snowball could still withstand the cold. Cooper had only known Rider for the shortest time before their community had rounded on the pair of them, fearful that the same monsters they'd survived now lived inside them. By the time everyone realized they were killing the very thing that could save them, it was too late. But through the course of that single night before Rider died, the two had forged a bond. That bond then became a mission in Cooper to restore Wranglestone to the place Rider and his friends had first founded, a refuge for the Returned far away from a world that would harm them. Peter's dad had begged them to wait winter out, but as far as Cooper was concerned, they had no business cosying up in front of no fire all the while there were other Returnees out there in need of their help. But truth was, the trail had now gone cold. Every snowed-up cabin and wind-rattled trailer they'd stumbled across these last few days had been abandoned. But it didn't seem to matter. Cooper promised that this was their last search of the season. But Peter knew it was only a matter of time before he'd hear the wolves or the mountains calling from inside his arms and want to take off again.

Three more days on the trail passed without word

or incident when the landscape suddenly changed. The snow twisted up off the ground into peaks like fondant from a bowl, forming a forest of glittering stalagmites. There were trees buried beneath these snowy tombs, but if you didn't know any better, you could almost believe a child had stepped outside to build a snowman and wound up creating a whole forest instead. Peter carefully led Snowball through the maze of spires, but there were no sharp edges. Not one branch clawed at their skin. Every hackle-backed pine cone had been rounded into a ball. The air was so dry up here the snow had formed a shell, encasing the land inside a glittering crust. The only movement came from a strange mist curling up from below. Just ahead of them, bison, grazing the frozen ground for vegetation underneath, appeared like ghosts beneath their frosted coats. They seemed unbothered by the strange vapours twisting up beneath their feet, but something was different about them here. They didn't cling to the air like a mist at all, but chugged in woozy spirals, making the bison's silhouettes shimmer like reflections in water.

Snowball whinnied and three silhouetted figures appeared in their way.

"Hello?" said Peter leaning over the horn of the saddle. "Who goes there?"

The figures didn't speak.

Peter wrapped the reins around his fist before Snowball could bolt. "They're not answering."

"Nope," said Cooper. "But they ain't comin' no closer, neither."

"I suppose."

But Peter wasn't convinced. And now he was the one behind the reins without Cooper to mask him, he was suddenly unsure how much his scent could guard him. He squeezed his thighs against Snowball's side to move him along. Snowball huffed, standing his ground in protest, but Cooper made it clear he had to listen to both of them now that Peter was family and after a moment or two, he reluctantly did as he was told.

They got a little closer. The figures still didn't speak or advance. One of them had a withered arm. It jutted out at wrong angles with its stick fingers all crooked and broken. Perched on top of it, with its black eye blinking, was a crow. Peter was about to call out to the figures again when Snowball moved forward without being prompted and the bird took off into the mist.

Peter sighed. The three pine trees were dead. All that was left were their raw-boned branches, blackened once the needles had completely rotted off. Only now could he feel the heat coming up from below and he removed his gloves to hold his hands out. It wasn't mist rising from the ground at all, but steam. He withdrew the hood of his wolfskin and the earth beneath their feet rumbled like distant thunder.

"Reckon we've crossed the border into Yellowstone," said Cooper pushing the Stetson from his brow. "There's a volcano down there."

Peter retracted his hand. "Then we've come out too far. We should head back."

"We need to choose our path real careful now," said Cooper, ignoring him. "The Earth's crust is as thin as a scab on a knee in some places here."

"I don't like it, Coop. We should turn back. It feels like death here."

"Nah. I reckon the opposite's true. Pa used to say Yellowstone was one of the few places in the world where the planet can't hide itself. It might look real calm up top with its steady rivers and seasons that pass in the same order one year after the next, but just below the surface, it's all mixed up and movin' with its heart all troubled and full a fire."

Cooper's arms tightened around Peter's waist as was often the way when he sensed how dizzyingly small the planet made him feel. Out here the land had a habit of doing that. One moment you were crawling through dense woodland, the next it sprawled out into impossible distances or dropped away into impossible depths, casually reminding you of its own breathtaking enormity.

Cooper jumped down, tossing his Stetson and jacket to the ground. He stripped to the waist, tying the sleeves of his long johns around his belt buckle, and stood there bare chested with his arms out on either side, letting the heat from the rising steam curl up the length of his back. His palms tilted to let the warm vapours play across his fingers. He turned round and the darker hair beneath his armpits stirred.

"See, Pete," he said, craning his head back so his Adam's apple was strong, "the Earth ain't no different from us. It lives and breathes with a big ol' fire in its belly it can't always control."

Snowball huffed, making Peter smile. And they really should think about heading home. They had a five-day trek back to the lake at best if the snow didn't get any worse and besides, newcomers they'd welcomed to the islands might start to feel unwanted if they didn't spend more time with them. And yet Cooper was only fully alive out here. Like his whole self could breathe now it didn't have to fit into such small places.

Peter hung the reins over the horn of the saddle, taking in the blond stubble growing across Cooper's jaw after so long on the trail, the wet ribbons of blond hair lashing his face. In the last few weeks he'd learned there was so much more to explore. Just as they were taking in new lands, Peter had begun to chart a map of Cooper's body in his mind as he discovered it. And somehow, those changes brought on by the Dead only served to make the man Cooper was becoming appear stronger. The flush of pallor to his skin seemed to make that surge of dark hair about the belt buckle sprawl thicker. The tint of night across the white of his eye only seemed to offer more gaze to fall into. Peter's heart pounded. But it wasn't watching Cooper that excited him, although it did so very deeply, so much as the fact that as his boyfriend, he let him. Cooper gave him permission to see his body act in this way. A boy. A man. An animal. Nobody else got to see him like this. And the moment of them both being out in the world together was so perfect that when another part of Peter decided to break it, he was as surprised as Cooper was.

"What are we doing out here?"

Cooper's arms dropped by his sides. "You tired or summat?"

"No."

"I mean we can rest up a while if you want."

"No. It's not that."

"Need a kiss?"

"I'm being serious," said Peter. "Because, apart from Betty, we haven't come across a Returnee, or anyone else for that matter, for days now."

Cooper scratched the trail of hair below his navel and said nothing. But it was obvious he was irritated.

"And we haven't got a lot of supplies left, Coop."

"We got plenty."

"Well, it's getting colder, then."

"Anythin' else?"

"Yes. There are people back on the lake counting on us and we're not there for them."

Cooper crouched down, grabbed a fistful of snow and proceeded to wipe his pits with it. He washed his face before swiping what was left of the slush across the flat of his stomach and waited for Peter to finish his thought. Peter's chest heaved rapidly now his nerves were racing and just for a moment, he hated Cooper. He hated him for knowing him so well. For standing there so easily, arms at his side with his beauty right on show for all the world to see. Waiting so patiently for him to say what was really on his mind.

Peter took a deep breath. "Are you going to stay on the lake when we get back? For the whole winter. Without leaving me, I mean?"

Cooper's face scrunched up like someone squinting in the sun. "Huh? Why would you think I wouldn't?"

"But are you?"

"Course. But again, why would you get it into your head that I would leave you?"

"Because you don't wanna go back."

"That ain't right."

"You want to stay out here. When we're done searching, I mean."

"Nope," said Cooper. "I just wanna explore a bit more."

"But you must've spent plenty of time out here already. Before us, I mean."

"No. I never did. Not this far out."

"But I thought you had."

"Nope."

"Oh," said Peter. Then, "Why not?"

"Because of you."

Peter looked up, startled by his answer. But surprise didn't cross Cooper's face once.

"But we've only been together a short while."

"It don't make no difference," said Cooper digging both fists inside the seat of his jeans pockets. "I never could stray too far from the lake, even before we was together. I mean, I wanted to. I wanted to real bad. I knew about the Yellowstone since I was a nipper and dreamed of seeing the Earth breathin'. But even though we weren't together then or nothin', you always pulled me back to the lake like you already had a piece of my heart. I'd only get so far away. Then it just started hurtin'."

"I never knew that."

"Well, now you do."

"I just thought you were happier out here."

"I am," said Cooper.

"Right."

"But only cos I'm with you."

Cooper's dark eyes held Peter's as was often the way when he wanted to make sure that when he spoke plainly it didn't go unnoticed. Peter cleared his throat and felt a sudden lightness in his heart he realized had been missing until now.

"And when I'm with you back on the lake," Cooper went on, "and we're snowed in with nothin' much to do but kiss and crochet blankets all winter long, I'll be just as happy then too. OK?"

Peter nodded.

"OK?" said Cooper.

"Yes. OK."

"Does that take that pain away?"

"Yeah."

"Well, that's settled, then."

Cooper nodded to put a full stop to the matter and shoved his arms back through the sleeves of his long johns. "But the way you go on sometimes, Pete, is like I don't got insecurities of my own."

Peter's skin flushed with shame that he'd been so wrapped up in his own worries he hadn't been present enough to see Cooper's. Cooper swept his Stetson off the ground and held it down in front of him with his head bowed, the way people do at funerals.

"I mean, we're good, right?" he mumbled. "I mean, us is OK, ain't it?"

"Yes," said Peter. Then rushing in, "Of course. I'm sorry I got it wrong."

"Pete."

"What?"

"Don't you worry I could be dangerous? After what that girl said? Or because you saw how Rider reacted to raw meat?"

Peter shook his head. "No. No, I don't."

"Don't you worry that I could wind up hurtin' you?"

"But you haven't."

"But I could. I could do any number of things."

"What other things?"

"I dunno."

"Has something else happened?"

Cooper shrugged.

"Well, has it?" Peter's throat became sore. "Have you noticed any other changes since you were bitten?"

"No, not really."

"Not really?"

"No, then."

"Well, there you go."

"I mean, I like to wander with nowhere in particular I got to be. Like the Dead."

"But you liked that before."

"I did."

"So, there you have it."

"And I think I can see better in the dark now, Pete."

"You can?"

Cooper nodded, but barely, like he was daring to offer something new about himself but without the confidence it would be received well. He started to fiddle with the brim of his Stetson. A moment later, he looked away completely.

"Like a night owl," said Peter. "Snowy owls have orange eyes because they hunt at dusk, but barn owls' eyes are black because they hunt at night."

Cooper looked up. "Yeah," he said smiling. "That's it. Or maybe not even for huntin', Pete. Just seein'. Seein' you all wrapped up in my arms at night and knowing that you're there."

"Yes," said Peter. "For seeing."

"It's just that I never want you to have to be scared of me, Pete."

"But I'm not."

"Never?"

"No," said Peter. "I never will be. Never."

The sun burned through the steam revealing a small creek of black water between two pillows of snow. Behind it, funnels of rock, with holes in the top like chimneys, chugged out plumes of steam, spitting water like an overboiled kettle on the flame. Bison grazing nearby struggled to lift their heads up, their beards were so weighed down by the ice balls that had formed in them. But they responded to the promise of heat and light sparkling across the surface of the dashing water and slowly made their way towards it.

"I'm just scared by how much I love you," said Peter after a while.

Cooper nodded as if that was just about the measure of things.

"Peter?" he said after a while.

"What?"

"Oh, nothin'. I just wanted to hear your name is all."

Peter smiled. He watched the way Cooper put his Stetson back on brim-first to shield his eyes from the sun and loved him that little bit more for not letting him be the only one to worry about them. For some reason it was reassuring seeing him get anxious like this. Not that he ever wanted Cooper to worry. Never. But he didn't need to know that.

"Do you think we'll ever run out of things to talk about?" said Peter after a while.

Cooper pushed the brim of his Stetson up with his forefinger to reveal a raised eyebrow, and for the first time, Peter saw a bit of old Bud in him. "Don't you ever quit thinkin'?"

Peter smiled. "Come here."

Peter swung his right leg back over the saddle to dismount and slipped down on to the ground. Cooper strode forward holding his gaze in ways that told him they were about to kiss. He cupped the back of Peter's head to bring him in close and their lips met.

They set up camp. Cooper fashioned an A-frame out of four ski poles dug into the snow at cross angles with a sheet of tarpaulin over the top to form a tent, then quickly bundled their blankets and then Peter inside. Some time later, after they'd kissed, Peter found that his mind was free of all those stupid little insecurities. He lay back in Cooper's arms listening to the tarpaulin crinkle in the wind and none of them seemed to matter any more.

"Reckon we just needed to cuddle so tight you can't squeeze a toothpick between us," said Cooper after a while.

"I know," said Peter. "We won't leave it so long next time."

"It's real important we don't. We can get through anythin' as long as we stay close."

"I love you," said Peter.

Cooper leaned over, gently kissing Peter's forehead. "So much. I can't keep none of it in."

Peter slipped his hand inside Cooper's and listened to the earth below them grumble away in constant motion.

"It's breathin'," whispered Cooper. "I can hear the Earth breathin'."

"Me too," said Peter. "Why don't we set up camp here for the night and head back first light?"

"You sure?"

"Yeah."

"I want the lake to work," said Cooper. "I want the Returnees to have a home."

"Me too."

But even as he said it, Peter's thoughts turned to that town. The town that Tokala talked of when he arrived, the one only some thirty miles west of the lake where a community living in harmony alongside the Returnees had already been made. And he wondered about the pretty lights and the buildings and all the kitchen comforts waiting out there to be discovered.

"I want us to be happy on the lake, Pete."

Peter nodded absent-mindedly.

"I'm gonna paint Pa's canoe up real nice for the summer, too. Make it ours."

"Oh yeah?"

"Yeah."

"What colour?" Peter asked.

"Bright red. As red as saddle sore."

The bison moaned in quiet contentment at the grass they'd found.

Cooper went quiet.

"We will be happy on the lake," he said after a while. "Won't we?"

"Yes," said Peter putting all thoughts of the town away. "Always."

3

The mudflats hadn't been visible before now. But overnight, while the wind pummelled the tent making the tarpaulin crimp and rumple, Peter could've sworn he heard something gulp out there in the darkness. By morning, the bison were gone and the steam had blown away, revealing their position on a ridge some elevation from a basin of wet land below them.

Peter pulled a blanket across his shoulder and stood on the rim where a set of wolves' pawprints played. The ridge curved round some half a mile to form a lip like a crater. Pine trees flanking the hillside were frozen inside their snowy tombs, but the basin was completely bald of any coverage. Steam constantly churning up from below made it hard to see the ground beneath, but every now and then the wind shaved it off the surface like foam from a cup, revealing a scabby patchwork of copper pools and fizzing potholes. Here the skin of the Earth was just too thin for any life to grow. The volcano was bleeding through.

Traversing this shallow crust was a series of silvered boardwalks. They zigzagged across the land dodging every thermal feature to connect a series of little log cabins. According to Tokala, the community at Yellowstone had only vacated the park a year or so ago, but the elements hadn't wasted any time moving in. Heat rising up from the ground stopped the boards from snowing under, but most of the cabin roofs had collapsed beneath giant slabs of snow the size of refrigerators. All that was, except one. The roof to this cabin had been recently tended to. Any icicles forming above the door had been snapped off at the root. Candlelight winked from the window and there, standing guard outside, was a black horse. Someone was still home.

"Coop."

"I see it," said Cooper, appearing sleepily at Peter's side.

"Who do you suppose is down there?"

"Dunno."

"Did they leave someone behind when they evacuated the park?"

Cooper didn't answer.

"But Tokala wouldn't have left anyone—"

"Perhaps someone chose to stay behind, Pete."

Peter glanced at Cooper and wondered if that statement was meant for him. Cooper didn't speak in code or leave truths unsaid. It was one of his qualities you could count on the most. But still . . .

Cooper doffed his Stetson, indicating it was time they went down to take a look, and turned, ready to saddle Snowball again.

They packed up their things, making their way down the spine of the ridge where the snow was thinnest, then rode out on to the boards with only the clop of Snowball's hooves across the wood and the gurgling earth for company. The park was quiet. The wind had dropped too, causing steam rising up either side of the boardwalk to fold in across their path. Snowball pushed through, but no sooner had he passed than the steam drifted back into place again. The way back seemed to disappear behind them. The way ahead remained unknown. It was as if the boardwalk was being laid down one plank at a time then quietly removed again. You wouldn't even know there were homes out here. But then, perhaps that was the whole point. On Wranglestone, the islands had distance from the Dead. Here on Yellowstone, their homes could hide from them.

The boardwalk took a sharp turn left to avoid a geyser. It was only now that Peter noticed the little wooden winches and how the seemingly continuous boardwalk was broken by a series of interconnecting bridges that either raised or swung round to break the route should anything unwanted take up the path with you.

A spit of hot mud dashed Snowball's heel making him start. Peter gripped the reins, steering him back into a steady walk, when Cooper tapped him on the shoulder. Just ahead, the dull glow of candlelight broke through the grey. The cabin was still some distance away and probably further still given how the boardwalks didn't form a straight line to any destination. But there was something else at play. Every now and then the lamplight would disappear inside the mist only to reappear again, twinkling much further away.

Peter leaned over the horn of the saddle. "Do you see that? The light's moving."

"That can't be," said Cooper. "The mist's just playin' tricks is all."

They carried on, the boardwalk at once never seeming to take them any further away or bring them any closer.

They hadn't got much further when Snowball struck his hoof down sharply across the boards and stopped.

"Easy, boy," said Peter leaning forward to pat his neck. "Easy does it."

Steam folded over the boards, handcuffing Snowball's hooves. But there was nothing there. Peter squeezed both thighs to will him on, but he only whinnied, striking his hoof down with greater force this time.

Cooper jumped down, kneeling with the flat on his hand across the boards. "Pete."

"What is it?"

"Somethin's taken up the walk with us."

"Don't say that."

"But it's true."

"Maybe it's just the ground gurgling."

"Maybe." But Cooper wasn't convinced. "The vibrations in the wood are gettin' strong. We're being followed."

Peter craned round and three figures hovered inside the grey. They looked like used matchsticks. There were no limbs to speak of, just sticks with cinder heads perched on crooked necks almost too fragile to support them. It was as if the blackened trees they'd passed yesterday had followed their trail and finally caught up with them. But these weren't trees, and the shuffling sound their feet made as their twisted forms broke through the mist had haunted Peter's dreams since he was a child. He rubbed the back of Snowball's ear to calm him.

The Dead were no longer of any concern to Cooper, though. He didn't even reach for his machete. He just strolled a little further back along the boardwalk, doffing his Stetson as one traveller might another and made his presence known.

The three figures stopped just short of Cooper. Their faces were quite without features and completely flat now the cartilage of their noses had rotted away. But light glinted inside the inky mulch of their sunken eye sockets. Just as Cooper was looking at them, they were looking back. If you didn't know any better, you might almost believe they were thinking.

Peter had watched Cooper turn the Dead dormant simply by standing beside them, many times over the last month. Somehow, they recognized the kiss of death inside his blood as one of their own. But it didn't matter how many times he'd witnessed it, it still had the power to unnerve. Cooper always took a moment, as if to pay his respects to the poor souls who'd once occupied these bodies. But it was the moment of strange connection he made with them that troubled Peter most. Perhaps Cooper knew something of their midnight world. Perhaps there were lessons about life in death only the Returned could understand. But as time went on, they began to belong to a set of feelings and experiences Peter could never know or be a part of. And for some reason, Cooper never reached out to share them with him so that he could be.

Further out across the basin, the steam stirred and another boardwalk came into view. One of the Dead drifted across the deck. Its skeletal feet were so nearly invisible against the white steam that black rags hanging from its meatless frame appeared to hover above the boards. It was just a shadow, peeled up off the ground. Peter watched this apparition float by and tried to let the sudden intrusion of his separation from Cooper pass. He ran his fingers through Snowball's mane. He'd never known it was even possible that two people who loved each other could also feel separate. And yet, there it was. But something else caught Peter's attention and he was suddenly brought out of his thoughts. The cabin. For a moment, he thought it was different to the one they'd spotted up on the ridge. The black horse was no longer waiting outside. There was no light coming from the window. But the roof was clear of any snow and there, quietly coiling up from its chimney stack, was smoke.

Cooper didn't show any signs of breaking away from the Dead, so Peter swung his leg over to dismount and walked a little further out. He continued to make his way along the boards when he stopped.

The boardwalk ended abruptly. Boiling mud at the foot of the boards bubbled in blisters, bursting across Peter's boot. He took a step back, wiping his toecap on the back of his shins. But before he could work out how anyone living here managed to cross the basin from this point, the steam shimmied across the land to reveal the way.

Beyond the boardwalk was a timber stepping stone. Behind that were three more. Four simple stepping stones close enough for almost anyone to navigate safely, but far enough apart that the Dead would lose their balance and fall. Peter held both arms out either side of him and strode each one in turn until he crossed the boardwalk on the other side. Pumped by this little triumph, he looked back to tell Cooper. But he and Snowball were now faint inside the rising steam so he turned back.

A wooden bridge jutted out from the main boardwalk to connect to a timber disc that would become a complete circle with a moat once the bridge had been winched round. Set in the middle, at a safe distance from the bubbling pools below, was a tiny log cabin turned driftwood grey by the elements. It was small, just a cube really, with one square window framed by a single gingham curtain. But it had been made into a home. Three woollen stockings hung from moose antlers above the door. Two were a matching pair with brightly stitched holly and red beads for berries. The third was a tiny knitted bootie. A baby's. Peter felt a sudden tug in his belly. In the fifteen years since the Dead first walked the planet, the lake had lost count of the days and only had the seasons to guide them. But perhaps it would be Christmas soon. Peter crossed the bridge, smiling up at that little symbol of joy, and lifted his fist to the front door ready to say his hellos. But he held back from knocking.

The door was ajar. Peter thought to call out so as to alert

the family of his friendly presence here. But something stopped him from doing that also. Warmth radiating from the hearth broke across the doorway. Someone had been here a short while ago. But the cabin was empty now. For some reason, he was sure of that. He stepped away from the door, uneasy. There were no signs of a disturbance. The door wasn't splintered and showed no signs of forced entry. The little square window to its side was completely intact. But something bad had happened here. And recently.

Peter gently pushed the door aside, praying that two shocked faces would bolt from their rocking chairs in anger at his sudden intrusion. But no one came. Beneath the window, steam curled from a tin cup to mist the glass. The fire crackled. Peter glanced down, picking a small wooden ball on a stick up off the floor. He shook it and it rattled. Another door led off to the bedroom. A crib made out of an old wooden fruit punnet was suspended by a rope from the beams so it could swing. The crib was perfectly still. Empty, perhaps. Peter thought to make his way through to the bedroom just to be sure, but the silence surrounding the crib was heavy and unnatural. His eyes scanned the base of the crib for the tiniest signs of movement. A jolt. A wriggle. Anything. But it didn't come. Perhaps it was just empty. But he'd grown to recognize the moments darkness hid inside a place or object. He'd felt it when he stared at the crate in the boathouse the night he found the Bearskin's pelt, and he could feel it now.

He stepped backwards towards the front door, setting the rattle down across the sill. Cooper had taught him many things over the last month, but always knowing your exit route was paramount. He turned away to leave, but the silence emanating from the crib crawled out of the bedroom and sat heavy across his shoulders. The cabin was lifeless. But the crib wasn't empty. He was sure of it now. Peter braced both hands across the doorframe. He should go back. He should go in and make sure the swaddling was drawn over the little one's face so their eyes weren't left staring up at the spot above the crib where their parents' faces once smiled. But he couldn't.

Peter staggered outside, pulling the door to, and the dreadful grumble and spew of the geysers drowned out the silence festering inside.

Something popped. Peter grabbed his waist, feeling for the gun Cooper insisted he kept there. A welt of bulbous mud splattered over the bridge and he loosened his grip. It was just a geyser.

Across the way, a pillar of steam broke from the ground, launching gallons of vaulting water some twenty feet up into the air. But Peter's eye was drawn further back across the boards by a light. It was no doubt the same one they'd followed earlier, mistaking it for the cabin. And now it was clear that it really had been moving. The dull glow glinted from inside the steam and continued to drift further out across the park. It was lamplight. But it wasn't held out at arm's length. It was higher than that. On a pole, perhaps. Or a horse. Peter remembered the black horse they'd seen from their vantage on the ridge. He looked back towards the cabin noticing now that there was no stable. The horse belonged to a visitor. Worse, an intruder. Peter's hand reached for the holster, more out of instinct than decision, and a flush of surprise broke across his skin. Cooper had told him that survival instincts would work their way into his bones sooner or later, but he never thought it possible. He stepped out on to the bridge, following the light, but his attention was disturbed by a gurgle at his feet.

To the side of the bridge was a small pool. Earth around the rim had been so traumatized by acid in its bubbling waters that a copper scab had formed around the edge like blood drying across a wound. The hole was deep. It burrowed right down into the earth. It looked so abnormal, it wasn't really like a hole at all, but a gaping mouth with fleshy walls disappearing down inside a gullet. Staring up from inside were two terrible screams.

The faces looking back at Peter probably would have stood at the cabin door to welcome him only an hour before. But what was left of their severed heads had mostly dissolved now. Grey skin flailed from the skulls like tattered curtains caught in the wind. The eye sockets where bubbles of boiling water broke were hollow and raw.

Panic burrowed under Peter's skin. Then into the heart. Into the skull. Into the damned stupidity of separating himself from Cooper when they'd promised to stay close at all times. He couldn't be sure the greying of the couple's skin hadn't just been caused by acid in the pools. But their home hadn't been raided for goods or food. No. This family was dead simply because they were Returnees.

Peter staggered back, pulling the gun from its holster. He aimed it this way, then that. At the cabin. At the bridge. Back at the intruder out on the boards. He closed one eye over the barrel, ready to aim and fire. But there was no need.

The lamp travelled further out across the boards. Clear at first, swaying in steady rhythms with the horse's gait, then finally, and to Peter's relief, faint until it was swallowed by the mists.

"*Keep going*," he whispered to the intruder. "*Don't look back.*"

Peter lowered his arm to his side. After a few moments the glow had almost disappeared. He started to make his way back across the bridge, when Cooper suddenly called.

"Peter? Pete!"

The lamplight stopped moving. It hovered in place. Predatory. Patient. A hawk on the wind, alert to the sound of prey on the ground below. But for a moment at least, it didn't seem too interested in taking the bait and stayed exactly where it was, faint inside the mist. Then it turned.

The intruder brought their horse back around and the glow brightened. Peter held his breath, paying little attention to the burn of sulphur in the back of his throat, and watched the lamp take shape. It was an orb of some kind, swinging from the end of a staff. Cooper called out for a second time and the orb lowered, leaning into the sound, deeper into the direction of his voice this time.

Peter's throat tightened. "Be quiet, Cooper," he whispered. "Just be quiet a damned minute."

Quickly, he ran on soft feet back along the bridge to the timber stepping stones. He strode out on to the first and the light stayed where it was. He crossed the third, went on to the fourth and turned back again. The orb held its position. Reassured, Peter leaped back on to the boardwalk and turned. Steam folded across the stepping stones behind him, covering his path. The cabin had gone. He swung back round to look for the orb. The intruder had gone too.

"You better quit runnin' off like that," said Cooper,

emerging through the steam holding Peter's wolfskin out. "Here. Put this back on before you catch your—"

"Ssh." Peter raised his forefinger to his lips. "We're not alone."

"Nah, they're fine. I sent 'em on their way."

"No, not the Restless Ones. Something else. Coop, there are two dead bodies near the cabin back there." In his mind's eye, Peter saw the crib hanging in the silence, but chose not to amend the number and quietly cleared his throat. "Coop, I think they were Returnees."

Cooper withdrew, lowering his head so spills of blond hair partially covered his face. He just stood there in silence, the dark pools of his eyes glowering. It hurt him. Learning of another Returnee's death always hurt. And it didn't seem to matter that they'd made it in time to help every other person before this. For the first time since they'd set out in Rider's name to tell people of a place called Wranglestone, they had come too late.

Cooper cleared his throat. "We should bury 'em."

"No," said Peter. Then, much softer this time, "That won't be necessary."

Cooper looked up, his face noticeably bruised by such a statement and what it could mean. Peter gently shook his head, willing him not to press the matter further, when two plumes of smoke emerged just above Cooper's head. Except it wasn't smoke at all, but breath. One plume for each nostril of the black horse behind him.

The horse stood like a shadow inside the steam. The clop of hooves across the boards hadn't even broken once to alert them of its arrival. It was as if the beast had simply appeared, carried in by the mist. The velvety sheen of its black coat shimmered beneath the orb of light hovering above it. But nobody was holding the staff. The saddle was empty. Before Peter had time to realize that the stranger was already standing there, his eyes were drawn to Cooper's waist.

A gloved hand, with fingers as slight as smoke, moved across the wolfskin still folded over Cooper's arms, making the grey fur bristle like a snake creeping through grass. They didn't carry a weapon or draw blood. The hand hadn't even alerted Cooper to the presence of a stranger standing there. He remained lost inside his troubled thoughts and the hand was free to withdraw back behind him as silently as a shadow.

Peter drew the gun from his side, feeling the hammer flex against his thumb, and Cooper's eyes widened. He responded to the threat of danger now that Peter had alerted him to it and turned, the ribbons of his hair whiplashing his face. But Peter had it covered. He brought his second hand up to the handle to steady the gun from trembling and brought the muzzle into position.

"Cooper, get down!"

"But—"

"I said get down."

Peter released the hammer.

His other finger pulled the trigger.

There was a crack. Cooper dropped to the boards, hands clasped over his head, and the stranger flew back inside the mist. Peter winced. The shock of the bullet bolting the barrel reverberated into his shoulder. And it stung. He staggered forward, shaking his arm out furiously. But only one thing mattered. He stared into the mist. The sound of the stranger's body hitting the boards should come any moment now. Any moment. But it didn't.

The silhouette of a man with a crown of antlers rose up from the horse's back, at once becoming one with the beast. Breath chugged from the steed's flaring nostrils and the horse reared. It turned on silent hooves, dashing back across the boards inside the mist and was gone.

Cooper spat hair from his mouth and held Peter's gaze. First his eyes told him that they loved him. Then they told him, this wasn't done.

4

They chased the intruder out on to the plains. Snowball made the steep climb up the ridge from the basin, lurching through mounds of banking snow. He stumbled to the top, wearied and whinnying. But the snow grew thinner on the spine of the hill and as the intruder's horse made pace across the flat lands beyond, Snowball came up to speed. A sudden jolt, a jump and they left the fires of Yellowstone behind them and took up the hunt.

Cooper leaned into the horn of the saddle, whip-cracking the reins. Strands of golden hair lashed Peter's face. The snow too, which came twisting out of the sky to strike his skin. Ahead of them, the black horse was a shadow moving at speed out across the plains. Every now and then it took a sudden turn, veering left and right, navigating tufts of frozen grass and hillock. But nothing broke its pace. It leaped across a cleft in the ground, clearing a grove of pines and ran on. An owl took off from its vantage point inside the woods. Snowball galloped beneath the boughs and Peter glanced back, watching the bird's white wings take flight. A ghost with a moon for a face, travelling out across the frozen wastes.

The plains howled, driving shards of whisking snow from the earth. The sun vanished beneath the blizzard and the stranger's horse increased its gallop. A black bullet, streaming through the dizzying vortex. Cooper flicked the reins, geeing Snowball on, and tightened the distance between them.

The stranger's horse maintained its lead. But it hadn't gone much further when a grey mass broke from inside the slaughtering snow. The horse recognized the huddled mound of ashen flesh and bone for what it was and reared up, quickly changing its course again. It struck down with clashing hooves, galloping deeper across the plains. Cooper tugged on the reins and Snowball made the adjustment, arching round to keep clear of the herd, then carried on his pursuit.

"They followin'?" Cooper hollered.

"No!" Peter cried, craning around. Then, "Yeah. They're coming."

A wall of featureless sludge surged across the pristine snow and the Restless Ones took up the chase.

Snowball pushed on, increasing his pace. But the plains were as endless as the sky and Snowball was beginning to tire. Peter held on a little tighter to Cooper's waist and leaned out. There was no sight of a forest or river ahead of them. Nothing to break the race. Nothing to break the stranger's increasing lead. But just when Peter was about to call out for Cooper to give up the hunt, something changed.

The black horse had gone. Peter leaned into Cooper's shoulder, furiously scanning the blizzard for a black spot. He craned round just in case the stranger had doubled back somehow and was now in pursuit of them. But there were no signs of him, and nothing he could hide behind. No hill. No trees. Nothing. One moment the horse was right there in front of them, the next it was gone.

"Coop, where did it go?"

Snowball ran on, now chasing nothing but the horizon.

"Cooper?"

Cooper turned his head into profile, his eyes startled and unsure. But he didn't have time to answer.

The ground gave way beneath them. Snowball reared up on his hind legs, whinnying wildly, and Peter lost his grip. His fingers slipped from Cooper's waist. His body left the saddle. And in the moment before the back of his skull struck the frozen ground, he saw Snowball's neck twisted round. His body contorted so monstrously, there was no semblance of a horse any more, just neck and hoof and mane and eyes. And as he toppled backwards, taking

Cooper down with him, Peter saw it. A cornice of snow snapped just ahead of them, dropping away sharply into the valley below.

5

Snowball landed on his back, legs flailing, head thrashing, left and right and left again, carving out a trench in the snow with every twist of his neck. The brown of his eye reeled back in terror that something as stable as the ground should fail him. He rolled over on to his side, staggering to his feet and bolted from the ledge as fast as his legs could carry him.

Cooper was lying just a short distance away from Peter, face down with ribbons of wet hair splayed across the snow. He pushed himself up, spitting a lump of snow from his mouth, but his hands started to sink, seemingly deeper than the surface of the ground. Peter got to his knees, feeling the reassuring hardness of the frozen earth beneath him. But Cooper hadn't been so lucky.

The plains ended abruptly to form a rugged plateau that towered some two hundred feet high, forging a natural barrier to the wilderness below. And the rim was so white against the snow-strewn sky, it wasn't even visible until you were right on top of it. Cooper was several inches away from the edge, but it was only now Peter realized he didn't have any ground beneath him. He was balancing on an overhanging cornice completely clear of the cliff.

Peter drew the snout of the wolfskin back over his shoulders to release the sweat pouring across his scalp and whimpered Cooper's name. It barely broke across his lips to even register. But it didn't matter; Cooper already knew he was in trouble. He peeled his chest from the snow, spitting matted hair from his face, and looked up.

"I can hear the river, Pete," he said, eyes wide and full of tears.

Peter's eyes darted to the rim, realising he could hear the thundering pummel of rapids too. "Don't focus on that."

"I can hear it dashing over the rocks below me."

"I said don't—"

Something cracked, like wood splintering, and a hairline fracture appeared. It drew itself in the snow right in between them like a pencil line on blank paper. A moment later, the line began to thicken.

The cornice sank. Cooper's eyes widened. It would give way any moment now. Peter scrambled to his feet, helpless to do anything, but Cooper obviously didn't dare risk doing the same. If he placed all his weight on one spot, the cornice would simply drop right out from underneath him.

The fracture widened further. One side had the solid foundation of the whole cliff beneath it, the other nothing but air and a river some several hundred feet below.

Peter heard snow on the underside of the cornice starting to give way. It dashed like dry sand over the rocks below. The snow beneath Cooper's fingertips started to withdraw. He lifted both hands, trying to gain better purchase on the surface layer, but the snow only continued to recede underneath him.

There should have been a mad scramble. Panic. Instead, there was calm. Cooper's eyes searched Peter's. *Don't*, said Peter, without saying the words. *Don't you dare tell me you love me.* But Cooper insisted. And somehow those dark eyes smiled, carrying the memory of their adventures together and the new worlds they had shared, not just out here but inside each other, in those places that belonged only to them.

The cornice gave way. But in the moment it broke free of the cliff, Cooper pinned himself flat, distributing his weight down the length of his entire body, and rolled like a log towards Peter. Peter grabbed hold of his arms, his waist, his belt, his jeans, hoisting his body and legs back up on to the cliff until he was completely sure they both had solid ground beneath them, and toppled backwards clear of the rim.

The shelf of snow dropped. The cornice cracked across rock, exploding into plumes of white powder into the valley below. Then there was silence. Peter rolled into the crook of Cooper's arm, frantically wiping off all the hair and snow that had smooshed into his face, and kissed his cheek.

"Coop."

"I'm OK, Pete."

Peter kissed the other cheek, his lips, his forehead and nose. "Cooper."

"I'm right here."

"I know but I—"

"And I can't breathe."

Peter recoiled. "Why, what's wrong? Did you swallow some snow?"

"Nope." Cooper winced. "Nope, I think that'll just be you squeezin' me too hard."

"Oh, sorry."

They hugged for a moment just to be sure of each other. Behind them, snow continued to break off in sections along the rim. But with the cornice removed, they could finally peer over the edge of the plateau all the way down to the bottom.

In the shadow of the valley floor, white water roiled over rock and boulder. Buckled pines beaten down by the spray lined the bank opposite the cliff. There, dashed across the shallows, the black horse lay bloodied and broken. But the stranger was nowhere to be seen.

"Where do you suppose he is?" Peter asked.

"Dead in the water, carried downriver with any luck."

But Cooper didn't sound convinced. Peter scoured the forest for any signs of movement in the shadows. What if the stranger was still out there? Perhaps he was down there looking up at them right now.

"Who do you think he is?"

"Dunno, Pete."

"And why would he be this far out looking for Returnees?"

Snowball whinnied, so Cooper scrambled back off the cliff to inspect his legs for injury. Snowball did as he was told, raising each leg in turn when Cooper patted it. But nothing was broken and Snowball didn't seem to be in any pain. Peter held back, watching the two of them together. Snowball just needed to feel the weight of Cooper's arms around him. Peter sighed. Perhaps Snowball would find the same comfort in him one day. Then they would be a family.

Cooper leaned into Snowball's neck, nuzzling his mane for a hug. But he whinnied again as if to draw their attention to something and Peter looked back across the plains.

A band of grey separated land and sky. It travelled silently across the frozen waste like a storm scoping out the land before deciding where to strike next. But this dark mass wasn't made up of rolling cloud and thunderbolts. It was flesh and limbs and jaws and death.

Peter staggered to his feet. "Cooper."

"I see them."

"There's too many of them for you to shield me."

"Reckon I can manage. It worked on the lake, dinnit?"

"Yes. But there's far more of them this time."

"Nah."

"Cooper, I'm telling you."

Cooper scooped his Stetson up off the ground, toying with the brim. "Then we better get off here before we're cornered."

But he'd missed the point. The rim of the plateau stretched out for a mile or so on either side of them. Snowball might've had a fighting chance of outrunning the Dead if they'd left a few minutes ago, but as the earth began to rumble beneath their feet now, the blundering herd closed in on either side like ranch hands rounding on cattle.

Peter looked back over the cliff edge. "We don't have time to run."

"Then what?"

"The Dead will drive themselves over the cliff. But we need to hide down there."

Further along the plateau about five feet below the rim was a shallow ledge protected by overhanging rock. It only jutted a couple of feet out from the cliff, but it was long enough for the pair of them to stand on and be protected from anything falling past.

Peter turned back. "Coop."

Cooper's hand fell away from Snowball's neck and he just stood there with his back to Peter, saying nothing.

"Cooper."

"Yeah. I heard you."

Cooper turned round and his dark eyes searched now as was often the way when he was looking to connect with the part of Peter that belonged to them. But there was something else this time. A sudden pain that hadn't been spoken.

Peter shook his head. "You blame me for not killing the stranger when I had the chance. I tried my best, I did. You're angry at me, aren't you?"

But that wasn't it.

Cooper shrugged. "What about Snowball?"

"He's OK, isn't he?"

"Where's he gonna go, Pete? There int time to get him out of the way."

Peter's throat tightened. "Cooper, I'm sorry. I wasn't thinking right."

"He won't leave me."

"Course he won't."

"He won't even try runnin'."

"Then we all leave together," said Peter. "I'm sure we can make it in time. Maybe I got the distances wrong."

But even as he said the words, the grey mass coming their way started to have features. All raggedy hands and rolling eyeballs. The herd was close now and Cooper was left with no choice but to say his goodbyes.

Cooper walked forward, taking Peter by the hand. He leaned in so their foreheads touched and kissed him softly. And they stayed this way for a moment, but soon he quietly made his way back to Snowball, placing both arms around his neck, and stroked him. But to watch the pair of them any longer was an intrusion, so Peter made his way along the rim of the plateau, sitting with both legs dangling over the edge, and looked down.

The ledge was just a short jump down. It only seemed so much deeper because Peter's eyes were further away from it than his feet. But nothing would break the fall into the valley if he misjudged it. He gripped a tuft of frozen grass and shuffled forward. His legs became pendulums, heavier than the rest of him now gravity had a stronger pull. He edged forward just a little further and his body slipped from the cliff.

He landed, arms flailing to propel his body away from the edge. He thrust them forward until he could feel the heels of his boots touch down, and planted his back against the cliff. He ducked beneath the rocky overhang and Cooper's boots struck behind him.

"Pete," he said flatly. "They're comin'."

Peter nodded. He tried to make eye contact with Cooper so he didn't get lost inside his own pain. But Cooper wouldn't let him in. Instead, he ducked beneath the rock, carefully removing his Stetson so the overhang didn't knock it off, or maybe just out of respect for Snowball, and stood there gazing into the river's dashing waters. And as they stood, with fingertips touching but each of them locked inside their own private goodbye to that trustiest of friends, the Dead came.

The first thing to fall was a tiny rock. It skipped across the overhang, toppling past them into the valley below. Further along the plateau, a cornice of snow snapped, breaking across the rocky outcrops to form a waterfall of cascading plumes. Then Peter heard them.

The herd rumbled towards the edge of the plateau like a thunder of wild horses. Cooper braced his hand across the flat of Peter's stomach to steady him and another rock bounced off the overhang. A deer, drinking from the shallow waters below, looked up. It started, bolting this way and that, heading back into the darkness of the forest beyond, and was gone.

Another cornice cracked. A shelf of snow as long as a canoe plummeted right past them. It remained intact all the way to the bottom then exploded across the rocks below.

The first of the Dead followed, all jangling limbs like a rag doll from a child's hands before hitting the shallows below. Another body fell. Then another. It somersaulted past them, freewheeling in mid-air before dashing across the rocks in bloody ribbons. Then came a baying scream from above. It was so disturbing it was all Peter could do to stop himself from covering his ears. Over the years, he'd heard animals being taken by the Restless Ones out on the mainland, from his safety at the foot of the island. But this sound, this wretched sound echoing across the valley was so unnatural, it was hard to imagine that any creature could make it.

Peter took Cooper's hand. "Close your eyes, now. Cooper, close them."

Cooper lowered his head so the spills of his hair shielded his face and a bulky white mass dropped right past him. Peter looked away. But it was too late. He'd already seen the writhing mass of gnashing teeth and clawing fingers clambering across Snowball's body to dominate him even as he fell. They struck the valley floor with force and there was silence. Peter squeezed Cooper's hand. Then the rest of them followed.

An avalanche of snow toppled across the overhang, all the way along the length of the plateau. But the white soon turned grey. Ashen bodies tumbled past and the avalanche transformed into thick sludge. Peter closed his eyes, listening to the leaden slop of those wretched bodies dashing against the rocks. But the onslaught was short lived. A final boulder of snow cracked overhead, exploding into powder across the forest below, and it was over.

In the darkness of the valley floor, the river started moving in unnatural ways. It undulated. Those skeletons and limbs that had survived the fall stumbled up from the riverbank, passing like shadows through the water into the woods. The pines quaked. Snow on their spires shivered then broke free. It took a few minutes for the Dead to spread out into the forest, but soon pine trees further back juddered, and the herd moved on deeper into the wilds until eventually they were gone.

Cooper didn't once look out from inside his own thoughts, even to notice they were safe. And not for the first time, Peter wondered if he alone was enough to comfort him. But as sunlight struck the back of the forest, breaking in beams through the pines on its way into night, other thoughts grew stronger: that perhaps Snowball's death would finally be enough to keep Cooper home. Wherever home was. Wherever home could be.

6

Cooper looked so small out on the lake. Just a speck passing from one snowy island to another, not so much carrying himself on his own two feet as drawn home by his shadow which crawled out long across the golden ice this late in the day. Peter clambered the rope ladder up to the tree house, stopping on the bridge in among the bundled pines, and watched him for a while. Cooper hadn't spoken once these last few days during the walk home. He hadn't even taken his hand. He'd cut a lock of white hair from Snowball's mane before he fell and spent the journey caressing it between his fingers allowing his thoughts to drift elsewhere, most likely to those days spent roaming beneath the sky when it was just the two of them. Once or twice, Peter placed his palm across the small of Cooper's back or tried to initiate conversation, but he remained locked inside his own thoughts and Peter didn't dare intrude by asking him to share them.

Stretching out from the middle of the lake, the watchtower's shadow struck the eastern islands like the hand of a clock announcing sundown and Cooper's shadow dimmed. Sunlight that had dazzled like liquid gold across the cabin windows of Old Pappy only moments before began to fade, until only the island's treetops were left clipped by gold.

A loon bird wailed like a wolf in the night. The snow on the mountains glowed. And soon a host of little lights twinkled out across the lake from inside the island's woodland chambers and Peter was glad to be home.

He waited on the bridge for a while just in case Cooper turned back to look his way. He never did. Peter already longed to be back in Cooper's arms. But he would wait. He hadn't seen his dad in weeks now.

Lamplight from the tree-house window winked through the pines beckoning Peter indoors, so he quickly crossed the bridge, stubbing snow from his toecaps as he went and quietly turned the door handle.

His dad had helped bury Darlene and Henry's bodies out on the mainland so memories of them wouldn't linger nearer home. But he'd mostly been inactive in the weeks that followed, waiting for his ribs to heal. And he looked kind of small tucked up inside his long johns beside the log burner. His stubble had started to grow back into a beard. But the truth was, being locked inside Henry's bedroom that night while the others perished out on the lake was probably the thing that had saved him.

"Pete."

"You haven't drowned in dust yet, then," said Peter.

His dad set the piece of wood he was busy whittling down across his lap and raised an eyebrow. "Oh, hi, Dad. And how are you doing since I dumped all the newbies on you and went out shopping for more? Well, son, I've still got a broken rib but I'm doing just swell, thanks for asking."

Peter glanced at the pair of boxers draped over the antlers that were used to hang mugs from and his dad pressed back into the rocking chair. "Go on," he said tilting forward. "Say it."

"Say what?"

"It looks like we've been robbed."

"That would be a blessing," said Peter. "Then at least some things would be missing."

"Well, I'll tell you what is missing."

"What?"

"A hug. Come here and give your old man a kiss."

Peter mustered a smile. "You've gotten skinny," he said, bending over the back of the rocker to kiss the top of his dad's head.

"Yeah. Reckon I lost some muscle mass sitting around so long."

"But you're OK?"

"Better for seeing you. And Cooper?"

Peter quietly hung his wolfskin on the back of the door and stood at the window. A blue jay popped out from beneath a bough, shaking snow dust from its rump. It screamed to ward off an intruder and disappeared back inside again.

"Snowball's dead."

"What?"

"I'm fine."

"No, you're not," said his dad. "You're shivering."

"I'm fine."

"Peter, come here."

"No. I need to find Tokala."

"Pete, come over here where I can see you properly."

"Dad, I said I'm fine."

"At least tell me what happened."

The blue jay popped his head out again, angrier this time.

"We went as far as Yellowstone."

His dad's tools clattered to the floor. He didn't speak, but his disapproval of them travelling out so far became a silence beating across Peter's back that was somehow more unbearable than any amount of shouting. Peter placed his forehead to the glass, but after another moment or two, he couldn't bear the silence any longer.

"Cooper's scared of leaving any Returnees out there alone."

"But—"

"He knows what it's like to be taken."

"Yes, I know that. But now he's got Snowball killed. Jesus, Pete, he could've got you both killed. It's too cold up there."

"It wasn't the cold."

"Then what?"

"We came across three bodies. A young Returnee family."

"Peter, you and Cooper have brought so many people back to Wranglestone these last few weeks, but you can't be expected to—"

"The child was only a baby."

His dad's eyes widened in wild ways that only someone who'd parented their own child could harbour.

"You shouldn't see such things."

"Dad."

"No. I don't want you boys going out there any more."

Peter perched on the foot of the bed, watching the logs on the burner glimmer, and explained how they'd chased the hunter out of the park and over the cliff. But his thoughts never once strayed from the memory of that silent crib.

"Dad," said Peter after a while. "Tokala told us that the

Returnees and the rest of the community at Yellowstone had lived in peace up there."

"Yes. But that family put themselves at risk by choosing to stay back the second everyone else left."

"But why? Who would even know that anyone had been left behind, let alone decide to go looking for them?"

"I dunno, Pete. But if people weren't safe up there then who's to say we're safe here any more?"

"Don't say that."

"Well, it's true," said his dad, chucking a log on the burner. "And besides, you and Cooper haven't been here. You haven't been the one answering that goddamn door every five minutes to everyone you rescued but haven't bothered sticking around long enough to make welcome. You haven't been the one getting told how scared they were out there and asking if I can fix an extra lock on their cabins or put more people on watch. They're sick of it out here, Pete, and they want to go back to some kind of normality. So, perhaps you'll think twice now before discouraging everyone from leaving for West Wranglestone."

Peter sat upright. "I'm not stopping anyone."

"But you've made a stronger case for staying here."

"We can make a good life on the lake. That's what Rider always wanted."

"They might have a good life waiting for them there."

"I know, but—"

"But you're scared Cooper doesn't want that."

"No, I—"

"Pete, you're scared that Cooper doesn't want that. Doesn't want some town."

Peter stood, making his way back to the window and wondered what it'd be like if Cooper appeared at the front door now with tickets for a double bill at the movies that night and enough money for popcorn and soda for two. He wondered this. He wondered this so much. But only for a moment.

"He loves it out there," he said, looking off towards the mountains. "I'm not even sure I can keep him *here*, let alone in a town."

"No one's for keeping, Pete."

"I know."

"That's not love."

"But—"

"And it's not love giving up too much of yourself for someone else either."

"I should go."

"Pete," said his dad, leaning forward. "Look at me."

"I'm OK. I just need to find Tokala to tell him about that family in case he knew them." Then, "In case he knows something more."

"Cooper loves you. It won't matter to him where you

are, but you can't spend your whole time fighting to keep him."

"He won't like it there. He'll feel suffocated."

"And what about you? What do *you* want? You've dreamed about the world that was before the Dead your whole life. And now you're finally close to getting just a tiny slice of it, it's as if your own dreams don't even matter any more."

"I don't care. I just want to be with him. And I want to make this place work for Rider, like he always hoped it would."

"And Rider would love you for that gesture, I'm sure," said his dad. "But what's done is done and staying here will never make up for what happened here."

"Won't it?"

"And you and Cooper are sure everybody's safe here?"

"Yes."

"You're sure that hunter's dead in the bottom of a river somewhere?"

Peter saw Snowball in his mind's eye, toppling over the cliff swarmed by clambering limbs. Nothing could survive that fall. But he didn't answer the question. Dad picked the tools back up off the floor to resume his woodwork and set the rocker in motion.

"Pete," he said after a while.

"What?"

"Why *do* you think someone knew to go looking for Returnees in Yellowstone?"

"Because they'd been told that the family had decided to stay back when they weren't meant to."

"And you think we're not meant to?"

Peter nodded. "Maybe."

Flames surged inside the burner, making the stovepipe howl like the wind had got inside it. His dad pushed the rocker down with his foot and the weight of that thought lingered in the air between them.

"Then go find Tokala," said his dad. "He's pitched a yellow tent next to a fishing hole round the back of the Whistles."

Peter took his wolfskin down off the hook. "I don't want to leave the lake."

"I know, Pete. But you're acting like it's your decision. You have other people to think about now. Other considerations. Without Henry, we don't even have a doctor here any more. And what about medicines? Have you even thought about how you expect to replace dwindling supplies without Returnees to make trade with?"

"Then, tell me what to do."

His dad offered a weary smile. "No. If you and Cooper have taken the decision to lead, then lead. But I think you be should clear in your own mind that you're not putting everyone at risk just for Cooper's sake. You also need to speak to Becky. You can't ignore her forever."

"Can't I?"

"Pete, she risked her life crossing the ice to help me. She hasn't forgiven herself for what she did to Rider and she won't be able to either. You'll have to do it for her. If you can find her, that is. The last I heard, she was sitting on the waiting bench beneath the falls. But no one's seen her since."

Peter took his staff from behind the door and struck the floorboards with force, once, just to be sure of it. "And what about you, Dad? What do you want?"

"You know I'll be wherever you need me to be."

"That's not what I asked."

"I know."

"Would you be happy in a town?"

"I'll be happy just as long as I'm close to you and Cooper."

"But—"

"I love you. That's all that matters."

Peter stood at the door and his dad resumed his work. There was something he wasn't saying. But whatever it was it hovered just out of reach of the conversation, so Peter let him be and quietly made his way down on to the frozen lake.

The Whistles were made up of two steep forested islands, separated by a tight ravine where the rock had split in two. In the summer months, fisherfolk took smaller canoes down there in search of a day's catch. The black waters bristled with scores of breeding trout. But winter was another matter entirely. In the dark months, it became the place of lost voices. Once, a deer hoping to make the leap from one island to the next had misjudged the distance and failed to make it. The speed of its fall into the converging walls was so great that when Bud went down there to put the poor beast out of its misery, he found the animal stuck halfway down, back snapped in two. Head over hind.

The nearest of the two islands wasn't far once you'd reached Boulder, but it was exposed to the western woods. Soon, wolves would come wandering down from the mountains. The Restless Ones too, who were prone to drifting out of the darkness to stand in scatters across the ice, transfixed by the moon. Peter pushed the hood of his wolfskin back to improve his peripheral vision and briefly glanced round. Above the tree house, the sun was a fireball breaking across the mountains. High up on the ragged peaks the snow was pink, scorched by the bright burn of dusk. There wasn't much of the day left. He jockeyed the staff, feeling for the right balance until it was horizontal inside his fist, then fixed his sights firmly on the nearest island and ran.

He made it to the halfway point then bent double,

bracing both hands across his thighs to steady his breathing and stared at the ice. His shadow had all but gone now. He glanced back towards Boulder where lamplight from Darlene's porch would've once lit the way. But it was dark now. Henry's island too. Peter became aware of a nagging pain in his stomach and cussed himself for missing them both.

"Go away," he mumbled. "Go away."

Further out, way past the watchtower towards the top of the lake, there was no light at Cooper's window now, either. This struck Peter as being strange, but he was pulled from his thoughts by another feeling. He wasn't alone. He swung round, thrusting the staff forward. But it wasn't a Restless One making its way towards him.

Two black plaits, poking out from inside a red hood, swish-swashed across the shiny breast of Tokala's ski jacket as he approached. It struck Peter again just how gaunt his features were. His cheekbones were so sharp that his face couldn't hide the framework of the skull beneath it. But even though the whites of his eyes had become dark pools after the journey his soul had taken from death and back, they showed something most grown men lacked. His boyhood. It was almost impossible to imagine someone like Bud or Henry being anything other than their current age. But not Tokala. The twinkle in his dark eyes told you he'd once been five. Then thirteen. The boy he'd started out as wasn't lost in the man he'd become. They'd taken that journey together. And for a moment, Peter was so happy for the company, he completely forgot the matter at hand.

Peter smiled. "You've been fishing?"

Tokala hoisted his catch aloft, slapping the trouts' golden bellies. "Yes. There's good weed under the ice down by the Whistles. The waters were teeming."

"How do you even know that? Is that a Cheyenne thing?"

Tokala's eyes narrowed. "*Fishing World* magazine."

"Oh."

"The *Oh My Cod!* Thanksgiving Special."

Peter offered a smile but said nothing. The subject of sports magazines lived in that same huge box marked '*Awkward*' as topics like football, beer and the attractions of girls. It'd been some time since he'd stumbled into one of these conversations, where he was at a loss to know what to say to men who would only like him if he talked about the same things they did.

"Salmon," said Peter for no good reason. Then, "Bream."

Tokala raised an eyebrow. "Are you just naming fish, Peter?"

Peter searched for other words. Better words. But found nothing. And Tokala seemed to take the same dull amusement in this that Bud or any number of other men on the lake had taken over the years when toying with him for sport became a decent enough substitute for the real thing. But Tokala didn't let Peter stew for long.

"My *Neho eehe* taught me how to fish, Peter."

"Sorry?"

Tokala's eyes warmed into a smile. "My father."

"Oh, but I thought you just said that—"

"Have you always been this easy to wind up?"

Peter curled the corner of his mouth into a weary half-smile. "Cooper's dad used to say I was easier to wind up than a dog chasing its own tail."

"I think dogs know it's their own tail, Peter. I think they just like to play with them."

Peter looked off towards the twinkling lights of Six Little Fishes and let that happy thought grow inside him. "Yes. Maybe."

Tokala hooked his catch on the top of one of his ski poles. "It's good to see you again, Peter."

"Yes," said Peter. "You too."

"I saw Cooper cross the ice a short while ago."

"He's just gone home for a little. We're both fine, but the last trip kept us away so long that he said he wanted a bath before he forgot what one feels like. And I'm the last person to discourage him from doing that. Before we got together, the bath tub had been left hanging on the wall outside his cabin so long, the wood underneath it was a completely different shade to the rest."

Tokala held Peter's gaze and said nothing.

"But," Peter went on, "I'll see him tomorrow. I'm having dinner with Dad tonight. And there'll be plenty of food if you want to join us. Me and my dad, that is. If you wanted, I mean. If you had no other plans."

"Why do you act as if nothing has changed?"

Peter shook his head. "I don't know what you're talking about."

Tokala blinked once, deeply, as if to absorb Peter's lie. But he didn't break eye contact.

Peter looked back across the lake towards the boathouse with its sunken roof as weary as an old nag's back. Not even two months had passed since he and Cooper first shared a kiss in there. Barely any time at all given the years spent waiting. Of course, they'd kissed many times since then. Out on the trail, whenever their kisses came, they arrived as passionately and numerously as the snowflakes dancing across their skin. But they'd only kissed as boys that one time in the boathouse, before their picture-book vision was stolen.

"Everything's changing," said Peter.

"And you won't let anything else change."

"I can't."

"And you're scared of Cooper changing further."

"He won't cope in a town."

"Or perhaps it is you who's worried you'll cope too well, and then Cooper will change his mind about *you*."

Peter looked up, a sting right in his belly. "No. That's not it." Then, "I don't know."

"Peter."

"It's OK."

"Peter, listen to—"

"Why did you make out it's our choice whether we come with you to that town or not?"

Peter winced. That'd come out sounding sharper than it meant to.

"It is your choice," said Tokala.

"But you told us Yellowstone had been evacuated."

"And that is so."

"Except we found a family of Returnees out there."

"Daisy and her partner Wyatt, yes. When Terri and I brought news of the town in West Wranglestone to the community living there, they chose to stay back, as you and Cooper may indeed choose to stay back, also."

Peter nodded. "They're dead."

Tokala's eyes widened, the effect of such news so instantly visible that Peter almost took grim pleasure at seeing alarm overtake such calm features.

"Someone must've known they were still out there," Peter went on. "Yellowstone is so remote, why else travel up there? And now they and their baby are dead."

Tokala closed his eyes. "They must have sent someone out after us."

"So, is that how it works?" Peter asked. "Is that the choice we're left with?"

"No. Not this. Not to deploy Ghost Rangers to kill anyone who refuses to come back. They promised us they wouldn't do this."

Peter stepped away and the words Ghost Ranger seemed to harden from mere words into a cold presence standing there.

"They?" he whispered. "Who's they?"

But his whispers went unheard. The burning flush of pink across the mountains faded into blue and Tokala gazed up, seemingly unburdened by the troubles Peter had brought to him.

The day had died. Only wisps of cloud and the downy breast of the snow goose passing overhead remained dipped in pink. All around, carried down by the inky darkness, came the stars.

"Can you sense the night is coming, Peter?" he said.

Peter followed the snow goose, feeling the deep beat of its wings in his chest as it travelled out across the islands towards the forest.

"We're not quite there yet," Tokala went on, "but there's a space that exists in the exchange from day to night where everything stops. Birdsong. The animals. Movement. Time, even. It's barely a beat, really, like the moment you throw a stone up in the air and it hangs there just before it falls. The world hovers in space. But life is so present here, you can almost feel the scales of a pine cone closing. We're inside that moment right now. Can you feel it?"

A lone deer, perched beneath the pines at the lake's edge, lifted its head from the ground and paused. Its front hoof hovered. Ears flicked forward then held still. Peter set his staff down across the ice, drawn closer to the world by a strange sense of arrival, and the world was still.

"I felt this just before daybreak once," Peter whispered.

"Yes. That too."

"What is it?"

"Tranquillity," said Tokala.

Peter followed Tokala's gaze and the cold mountains glowed.

"The Earth," Tokala went on. "The universe. Mysteries that let your imagination wander."

He wasn't watching anything in particular and yet his eyes were somehow travelling great distances now, at once passing over mountains and seas, deserts and vast forests.

"We had everything we ever needed, Peter."

"Had?"

"I'm only sorry I can't make this moment last forever."

"What did we have?"

"I am truly sorry."

"What did we have?"

But Tokala didn't answer. The deer's ears flicked back, alert to movement behind it in the woods. Its hoof struck the ground and it turned away, bolting.

"Nineteen of the former United States have re-formed," said Tokala. "With government, business and infrastructure. The group of people Cooper and I belong to now can help stop the Dead from attacking, Peter. They are no longer the threat they once were, and so the government are standing poised ready to recall everyone from the national parks back to the real world. West Wranglestone is only the beginning, a gateway town before full integration back into the modern world. The Escape Programme is over."

Peter looked out towards the tree house he'd called home for so long, and suddenly that golden world he'd only known in bedtime stories and magazines rushed in to take its place. And his heart skipped at the thought of all those pretty little towns with their white church spires poking up above the trees. Where streets were alive with the sound of tinging bicycle bells and lawn sprinklers going *chucka chucka* over carpets of glossy green grass. Where children bundled into bright yellow buses and the mailbox sat cockeyed on a post with a flip-down lid like the sole of one of his dad's busted-up shoes. He saw it all so suddenly and clearly. Every sight. Every sound, except one. He couldn't picture Cooper there. He looked for him in among those weaving bicycles. He tried to find him out on that pristine lawn. In the garage. The bedroom, perhaps, where the scent of log smoke and sweat might still linger. But he was nowhere.

Peter's throat tightened. "Why didn't you tell us this before?"

"It's a lot to take in, Peter. And I wanted so deeply for the choice to be yours."

"Even though it never was."

"I'm sorry. Truly."

"And no Returnees can stay behind?"

"No one can stay behind."

"But mainly them."

"I didn't say that."

"You didn't have to," said Peter. "But if the Returnees have been accepted as some kind of ally, why has a bounty hunter been sent out to kill them?"

"I don't know. I wish I did. Perhaps the ranger was provoked. Daisy or Wyatt must've instigated violence for them to have taken such action."

But Peter wasn't convinced.

Tokala wandered across the ice a few feet away from

where they were standing and scanned the darkness of the woods. "Are you and Cooper sure no one followed you back?"

"What?"

"Are you sure no one—"

"Yes," said Peter. "Yes, of course."

"Peter."

"I said yes. We chased the ranger over a cliff. But even if he'd survived, Cooper knows the rules. The lake might not have any faith in me, but he'd never be so stupid as to let anyone follow. We waited in the tunnel behind the falls for three hours before clearing the other side. No one took up the trail behind us."

Tokala looked back. "Very well."

"And you haven't given Wranglestone's whereabouts away to anyone?" Peter asked. "Before you came for us, I mean."

"We have not."

"To your town or the people outside it?"

"We came straight here when we saw your flare that night."

Peter nodded as if to put an end to the matter and looked out across the lake towards the twinkling islands. He should think of getting home. They were in for a cold night and besides, there were things he had to talk over with Cooper that he didn't have the words for right now.

He dug a fist inside the pocket of his wolfskin, feeling for one of his gloves. He reached for the other. But as well as the glove, his fingers found something else.

The object was smooth to the touch and rounded like a pebble worn soft by water. It was attached to a keyring. Peter pulled it free and held it in his palm. The black plastic pebble had a tiny red light in the middle. And the light was blinking. It was only now Peter realized the Ghost Ranger's intentions. He thought back to Yellowstone. In his mind's eye, he saw that gloved hand withdraw like a shadow across the coat in Cooper's arms. Peter's heart pounded like a fist against a door. He went to shove his hand back in his pocket before Tokala had time to notice the device. But it was too late.

Tokala's dark eyes widened. "Drop it."

"I'm sorry," said Peter.

"I said, drop it."

Tokala prized Peter's hand open, wrenching the tracker from his grip. He dropped it on to the ice and with one swift move, stamped the light clean out of it.

"I'm sorry," said Peter. "I'm sorry. We—"

"Retracing your steps to what could've been matters little right now."

"But—"

"He's either dead or on his way."

Peter staggered round, taking in each one of those

vulnerable little islands in turn.

"He could be anywhere."

"Yes. And we need to get off the ice."

"He could be watching us right now."

"Go home, Peter."

"But we need to warn the others. I need to warn Cooper."

"Yes," said Tokala. "But let me."

"But—"

"Let me take care of it. We must act fast. We're already as exposed out here as a mouse beneath a hawk-filled sky. Now go. Take refuge in the cabin perched on the rock back there until I come for you. It's closest."

Peter glanced towards Darlene's old place on Boulder. Perhaps he could take his chances out on the ice and make a run for it to Cooper's. If he could just get as far as the watchtower, he could make it the rest of the way. But Tokala had already made a run for the snowy islands of Six Little Fishes where most of the newcomers had settled. He called out one last time.

"Peter, go back!"

Peter ran, slip-sliding across the ice to Boulder. He jumped up on to the wooden jetty, causing the snow to spring from the boards, and dashed up the steps on to the porch. He flung the mesh screen door open and bundled inside.

The chalet was dark and it was cold. Peter watched his breath plume across the hearth, but that was practically all he could make out. The plaid couch that he and Darlene had spent so much time snuggled up on over the years was just a dark mass against the light stain of the timber floorboards. He ran his fingertips over the back of the couch feeling for the familiar bristle of the weave across his skin. But it was a stranger to him now. The hours they'd spent here together chatting, gossiping, and then, when Peter was older, talking endlessly about Cooper, seemed to belong to another lifetime.

The screen clattered back into place. Peter returned to the door, feeling for the notches in the frame that had scored his height since he was a toddler. But even they seemed smoothed over. Erased somehow. Everything that had once been good here had faded. Only the white of the animal skulls mounting the far wall were clear inside the darkness like the moon at night. It was quiet, too. Peter's throat tightened and for the darkest moment, a small part of him wished he'd never unearthed the truth about the Returnees so that everyone could've carried on being happy, living inside the lie and a home that was never meant to be theirs.

Peter parted the crack in the curtains to look across the lake. One by one, the lights over at Six Little Fishes went out. Tokala had made it. And a short while later his little red ski jacket broke free of the snowy pines and dashed off towards the northernmost islands. Peter let the curtain go and felt the dread of the wait burrow deep inside the pit of his stomach.

He noticed that one of the many skulls Darlene had mounted on the far wall wore strange antlers. The animal's own pair had been replaced by the bones of two human arms which jutted from the moose's skull, with fingers that fanned like winter branches. She'd probably yanked them from the arm sockets of a Restless One. But now he thought on it, he had no way of knowing who they might have belonged to.

Next to the moose was another skull. A deer. The forehead was tilted forward so the ragged bone of the muzzle pointed down. The beast's hollow eye sockets seemed to glare. Next to it, with its shaggy head mounted on a board, was some poor bison. But Peter's eyes returned to the deer skull because it did something it shouldn't have. It stepped away from the wall.

Only now did Peter see that the deer's head was attached to a body. The gown the intruder was wearing was as black as the darkness filling the chalet. The skull's hollow sockets fixed their empty gaze on him. Footsteps broke across the boards. The Ghost Ranger was already here.

7

There was only one place to hide. The ravine. Peter flung the screen door open. It clattered violently against the chalet wall on broken hinges, and he ran. He leaped down the steps, taking out three at a time, missing the jetty entirely and skidded on to the ice. He heard the screen door clatter open again behind him and ran on towards the Whistles.

Halfway across, he bent double, wincing at a stitch in his guts. He hunched over, hand clasped at his side, heart pounding like wild horses, and hobbled on. But he didn't look back. He didn't turn to see the Ghost Ranger make easy work of the ice on his way towards him.

Boulders littered the frozen lake at the foot of the black cliffs below the Whistles. Half of them were above the water line. The other half, below. It was as if winter had caught them mid-fall and stopped them from sinking by clenching them inside its icy gums. Over time, the rocks had become steepled with towering pines. Some of them were young of branch and plump with fresh snowfall. But not all. Some had been worn down to the bone, their spindle branches so blackened by rot that the wood was spongy to the touch. Peter's hand sank into the mulchy wood, but he got purchase and pulled himself between the boulders, out of sight of the lake, and collapsed.

He glanced back. The ranger was standing on the lake a short distance from Boulder, scoping out his choices, and for a moment Peter thought he might have lost the trail. The skull rotated towards the islands of Six Little Fishes. Then seemingly decided against it. The watchtower, perhaps. Not there either. The ranger looked down at his feet so the ragged muzzle dug into his chest and those two hollow sockets scanned the ice. He spotted Peter's footprints and the antlers turned his way.

Peter felt a sudden rush of blood. To his head. To his toes. To the tips of his fingers until they hummed like every part of him was raging to get out of there. He stumbled up to the island, furiously patting the black rock to find the entrance to the ravine. Except, here, in the dark, there was no sign of it. At a glance, the two islands seemed to continue unbroken. But Peter knew this wasn't the case. Directly above him at the top of the cliffs, the pine trees bowed in opposite directions like hair parting across a fractured skull. He stumbled along the length of the cliff, looking again for the slightest fissure. But before his eyes could separate the black rock from the inky night, the islands called out to him.

His dad used to tell tales of how the pine trees cowering over the cliff edge bowed inland away from the ravine so they didn't have to face the monsters waiting in the shadows below. The truth was that winter winds whisked right through the ravine, twisting the trees back that way, giving the islands their name.

The island whistled like a restless wind at the door. Peter glanced down and the silver fur of his wolfskin coat bristled backwards. The mouth of the ravine was right there in front of him. He approached, bracing both hands against the tight entrance walls. At his feet, an ice path dusted with snow shot straight through the rock like a sliver of lightning into darkness. Halfway in, a giant rock had broken away at one side of the ravine crushing into the other to block the path. But just when Peter thought he'd backed himself into a dead-end, he crouched down feeling the frozen surface of the lake where the winds were most keen and there, beneath the hanging rock where the snow came scurrying through, was height enough to scramble under. If he could make it, no one would even know he was hiding in there.

Snow came skittering out of the darkness.

The islands whistled.

Peter stood, angling the tip of the staff forward and quietly made his way in.

8

The ravine gripped. Peter hunched a shoulder to the rock and thrust himself forward. A push. A scrape. Something gave, releasing his shoulder, and he slipped inside. High above him, a raggedy strip of stars between the islands mirrored the path of ice below. But the darkness inside the ravine was so complete, you could almost bump into it. Peter inched one foot in front of the other and quickly made his way through.

At the fallen rock, Peter set his staff down. He kicked it beneath the overhang, clambering down on to all fours to watch it. The staff disappeared into darkness until there was only the echo of the wood skittering across the ice left to follow its movement. It reappeared, faint against the glow of the path on the other side, and Peter lay flat on his front. Reassured that there was nothing down there waiting for him, he scrambled under.

Halfway through, Peter braved a quick look round,

half expecting to see the deer skull with those two hollow sockets staring back at him. But there was nothing there. Just darkness and fear and the back of the wolfskin pelt tugging at the heel of his boot. Reassured, he reached for the staff and scrambled out, relieved to see the stars above him again.

From here, the far end of the ravine was still out of sight just around a corner. But he figured that if he heard the ranger coming from that direction, he had time to duck back and leave the way he came. Snow started to flurry over the ravine, highlighting tangles of root and blackened branches jutting from the rock face as it slowly began to dust them. Peter wiped snowflakes from his lashes. *You're OK*, he whispered clambering back up on to his feet. *You're going to be OK*. But his relief was short-lived.

Against the rock face, a short distance from where Peter was standing, the snow seemed to settle in mid-air as if falling over the darkness itself. First, it formed a mound about six foot up off the ground, then it gathered further, forming two more just below it on either side. The darkness bristled, disturbing the snow starting to settle there, and something stirred.

The Restless One was featureless against the blackness of the ravine. Down here, where moonlight couldn't touch it, it was more of a shadow torn from its body.

Only this shadow had bulk and the stench of ripe flesh weighting it to the ground. But its invisibility wasn't what was most disturbing. The thing must've smelled Peter standing there. It must've craved him. But it didn't move. It just stood there. And its inaction only gave rise to darker thoughts. What if the Dead knew how to hide. What if it was watching. Or worse, waiting for Peter to get closer. Peter jostled the staff, reassuring himself of its place squarely inside his fist, when there was sudden movement.

Something skidded across the ice from the other end of the ravine to where Peter had entered and landed at the Restless One's feet. An animal carcass. One side of the deer's leg, the one with the fur still attached to it, was dull in the darkness. The other side glistened. The thing lumbered forward and its vast mass, as big as a grizzly, distinguished itself from the surrounding darkness. Peter held his breath. The wet glint of the Restless One's eyes were sharp like starlight against the shadow of its face. And keen. They darted to the ice, fixating on the meat, but the thing stopped short of stooping down to retrieve it.

"S'all right," came a voice in the darkness. "Ain't nobody down here but us. And I won't hurt ya."

The thing hesitated.

"S'all right," came the voice again to encourage it. "You can eat it. I reckon that deer is tenderer than a sow's teat when it's suckling twenty piglets."

Peter's heart pounded at hearing that voice again. That voice as warm as sunlight on driftwood. The only voice in the world that could transform his stupid name so magically so that all he ever heard was *love*. But his heart also began to beat in other ways he didn't recognize. There was the familiar thrill of his own body recognising its proximity to Cooper's. But for the very first time, there was something else knotted up inside that. Danger.

Peter had heard Rider talking with the Restless Ones the night they met out by the falls. Years of loneliness and isolation from other people lost deep inside the woods had driven him to make friends with the Dead and led him to believe they were making friends back with him. But this was different. There was a madness in Rider, while Cooper sounded completely calm.

"Reckon you musta lost your herd or somethin'," Cooper went on. "But it's OK. Why don't ya eat? Then we'll see if we can find 'em."

The thing got down on to its haunches, hunched over the meat. There came a terrible crunch and the deer disappeared inside it. Blood, black in the night, seeped across the ice and something else rolled out towards the Restless One. A ball.

"Wait," came Cooper's voice.

"What are we waiting for?" came another.

"Ssh."

"Don't shush me. I was quite happy at home until you pulled me down here."

Cooper tutted. "Well, quit bein' impatient, then."

"Such a brute. No wonder Pete's so besotted."

"Is he?"

"Oh, please. He fucking loves you. I mean, thank God we don't have shops any more or else that tree house would be covered in cushions and mugs with your face plastered all over them."

"Tell me that wasn't a thing."

"I can't tell you that."

"Jesus."

Two bottles clinked together and Peter drew back further against the ravine wall. Cooper was with Becky. Peter hadn't been to see her once since that night on the lake. He couldn't even bring himself to look at her after what she'd done to Rider. But hearing her voice now, he realized how much he missed her.

Becky kept chatting away to Cooper. They'd never hung out together before. Not once. In a way, it was one of the things Peter liked most about their friendship. Having her all to himself. Cooper had always been popular. Always. Even when he was young, offering to canoe people home in the middle of the night when they'd had too much whisky to know a paddle from a floorboard. They'd always invite him up for a nightcap and a cup of hot cocoa. But not Peter. The lake pretty much left him alone. All of them except Becky, that was. Until now. Apparently, she had Cooper instead, and a friendship where one had never existed before.

A fist, the size of a paddle, emerged bloodied from the Restless One's hunkered form and nudged the ball back in the direction it had come from.

"See?" said Cooper. "When they don't got regular people in their way, they act different."

"Amazing."

Peter smiled to himself. He missed hearing Becky's eyes roll.

"It is," said Cooper. "They're part of us. We can do whatever we want with 'em. Just think what that means. Just think what that could mean for us."

Peter drew further back into the ravine and the word *Us* hung inside the darkness of the night.

"He hasn't even spoken to me since that night," said Becky after a while.

"Who, Pete?"

"Yeah."

"Give him time."

"I'm not sure time will do anything other than make us grow further apart."

"Then let him come to you. You only know you got a

horse's true trust when you let 'em come to you."

"But has he said anything to you?" Becky asked after a while.

"He don't say much."

"But—"

"He don't say much, Becky. And I'm here, ain't I?"

Cooper called the Restless One away. "Come on, big fella. Let's get you back in the woods before somebody finds ya."

The thing rose like a bear, with the folds of its weight unravelling, back up to its full height and slowly made its way towards the other end. Relieved, Peter released his grip on the staff and peered around the corner.

Becky stood at the mouth of the ravine. The strands of unruly hair that weren't held back by her bandana were tugged forward by the vacuum caused by the whistling wind, making them stir like reeds in water. Moonlight clipped the bridge of her nose and hands, making them luminous. And it was possible that this bleaching of her usual complexion by the moon was what gave her appearance a certain strangeness now. But when she tilted her hands into the moonlight as if to contemplate the unfamiliarity of her own pale skin, Peter saw the change.

Becky had left Essie to die in the truck out on the ice that night, then risked her own life by racing back through the Restless Ones to rescue his dad. And perhaps if he'd been to visit her even once this last month to thank her, he'd have known she'd been hurt. Worse, bitten. But he hadn't. He hadn't been a better friend. And, for a moment Peter stood there wondering why. But any shame he felt was swiftly replaced by an altogether different feeling: irritation that Becky now had access to a range of Cooper's feelings he would never understand.

Cooper wandered a short distance from the mouth of the ravine following the Restless One back out on to the ice. But he never once broke his connection to Becky. He nudged the Stetson from his brow with the nose of the beer bottle and stood gazing up at the stars. The other hand he held out for her to join him.

"Tell me what you see," he said after a while.

Becky wandered out to take his hand. "The stars," she said. "The stars. I can hear them burn."

Cooper nodded like no further explanation than that needed to be spoken. His hand gripped hers. Then their eyes travelled across the sky like all four feet weren't even on the ground any more. Peter stared at those clasping fingers. They held on to each other so tightly, he couldn't even tell whose belonged to who any more. They'd just spent the last three weeks out on the trail sleeping together beneath the night sky, but Cooper never once took him by the hand and showed him the way. Not like this.

Peter glanced up at the strip of stars caught in between both islands. He couldn't see much so he focused on the black patches of sky because the stars were always brighter when you didn't look directly at them. He could make out a few, and a cluster of them in his peripheral vision if he concentrated hard enough. But he couldn't see what Cooper and Becky could, or the way they could. He looked back across the ice, clearing his throat like all he had to do was call out to them. But he couldn't. Like hushed conversations taking place in another room, they were completely out of his reach now.

Further across the lake, the Restless One stumbled on towards the woods at the lake's edge. But before it reached the first of the pines, it stopped. Its head slipped from its neck. It toppled sideways, bouncing across one shoulder and dropped. But the head didn't roll across the ice. It collapsed in on itself. Mulch, too rotten to hold its shape. In its place above the severed neckline, hovered a new face. A deer skull with two skeletal antlers like reaching hands. The Restless One's body dropped and the Ghost Ranger stepped forward. Cooper recoiled, pushing Becky behind him, and the ranger approached.

A gloved hand reached for a pouch hanging from his belt. But he didn't need to look down to loosen the tight drawstring. His fingers dipped effortlessly inside, reaching for the contents of the bag. The empty hollows of the eye sockets held their gaze. The ranger produced a piece of flesh, offering it like an owner might to an obedient pet. Peter watched Cooper's shoulder blades flex beneath his jacket as the power of temptation rose inside his body. But he'd done well this last month, learning how to control it and how to quell the thirst by sitting with the carcass of that night's meal before roasting it on the spit.

One of Cooper's hands gripped Becky's to still her own urges, the other reached for his holster. He took a wide stance so his body could withstand the shock when the bullet bolted from the barrel, and took aim. But before he could fire, the ranger lowered his hand.

"*Timberdark*," came a thin voice from beneath the mask.

Cooper's hand wavered. His aim was always as sure as a compass finding north. But as the power of that strange word passed between them, his arm seemed to buckle and the ranger's crown of antlers bowed.

"*Timber-dark*," intoned the voice once more.

The click of the *k* was sharp at the back of the ranger's throat. Like an exclamation mark stamped at the end of a terrible sentence. Peter gripped hold of the ravine walls. He'd never heard that word before. But it was no stranger to Cooper.

Cooper tried to steady the pistol with both hands.

But somehow, this word had power to overtake him. His breathing was out of control now. He started to pant wildly, like an animal looking for a way out but knowing full well that the teeth of the trap had already killed it. But this trapper only wanted this catch's secrets.

Peter had watched Cooper without him knowing many times before now, through the gap in the door while he was taking a pee, brushing his teeth, or dozing on the couch with his hand shoved down his undershorts for safekeeping, and hundreds of times in the years before when they were just strangers to each other from across the other side of the lake. But it was something else to watch someone you love outside of your time together. The only thing that should've mattered right now was how Cooper knew that word and why he'd kept it secret from him. But it didn't. Peter stepped out of the ravine and the world forced him to know something for the very first time. That a person you loved so much, and who loved you, was also someone outside of your life together, and that someone had nothing to do with you.

Becky glanced over her shoulder. "Cooper."

"Don't say nothin'."

"Shit, Cooper. What's *he* doing here?"

"Don't say *nothin'* about that word."

But it wasn't the ranger Becky wanted Cooper to notice. She nudged him. Cooper wiped drool on the back of his hand, the lure of the meat still keen across his lips, and finally noticed Peter standing there. His dark eyes shifted beneath the ropes of his matted hair. Wide. Wild. Spiralling with boundless secrets. But the wildness wasn't just the adrenaline of being caught out, but of being found to be something else entirely.

"What are you doin' here?" said Cooper. Sharp. Like they were suddenly strangers. "You shouldn't be here. This int for you."

"Cooper, what's going on? Why do you know what he's talking about?"

"I said this int for you."

Peter's heart trembled. He'd said that twice now. Cooper might have convinced himself he was only protecting him when he said that. But it wasn't that. What he really meant was that this part of him wasn't meant for Peter.

"Cooper, don't talk to me like that."

Cooper's dark eyes blinked. But no apology flickered across them. And there was a blackness there Peter had never seen before. A coldness where he couldn't even see the part of Cooper that belonged to the pair of them inside him any more. Peter inched forward mumbling Cooper's name, but before he could even try another way in, Cooper turned away.

"Go home, Peter. Go home."

Peter dug his nails into the staff. All at once, his name sounded as dumb and small as it had always done. It was like it'd never even lived inside Cooper in the first place. Fear and fury swapped places in a heartbeat. Peter looked to Becky for support. But she was no help. She nodded gently as if to tell him to be a good boy and do as he was told, and quietly turned her back on him.

The Ghost Ranger's skull cocked to one side, seemingly intrigued by the promise of the boys' differences, when a single gunshot ricocheted out across the lake.

Tokala walked towards the ranger, aiming the rifle his way. "You have no business being here. Who sent you?"

But the ranger was quite untroubled by Tokala's intervention. He dropped the piece of meat on the ground and produced something else from the pocket of his gown. A black wallet bearing a silver star.

Tokala lowered the rifle. "Then, you're a U.S. marshal. The government has sanctioned your being here."

The ranger withdrew the wallet as if doing so was answer enough. But his attention never once left Cooper. Snow came twisting out of the night sky and Cooper briefly looked back.

"Pete. Peter, look at me."

But Peter didn't want to hear his name spoken tenderly any more.

"Don't," he said hardly mustering the words. "It doesn't

matter now anyway. We're leaving. We're leaving the lake for good. They're closing all the parks and we're never coming back. The Escape Programme is over. Sorry. Didn't I mention that?"

Cooper's eyes burned. Whether that was in pain at the thought of losing the lake or losing him, Peter couldn't tell. But it barely seemed to matter now. There were secrets and secret parts of Cooper he'd decided not to share. And for the very first time, Peter realized something, that two people, no matter how much they might love one another, were only ever two separate people.

II

9

Snow drifted between the gap in the blinds. Peter didn't part them to take a look outside. The plastic slats were filthy. But he could hear voices out on the street. Voices in the corridor just outside the office talking about him, too. They kept saying how someone should go in and be with him. They just didn't know who yet.

Peter tucked his legs beneath the chair where he'd been waiting this last hour and stared at the sheriff's desk. There was a square pad of acid-yellow paper. Seven plastic stacking trays toppling sideways because some of the metal rods supposed to prop them up were missing. There were pens in a mug with a boss-eyed moose on it yelling, *'You don't have to be crazy to work here but it helps.'* In the corner of the ceiling, a stub of old Christmas tinsel stuck behind tape where the garland had been ripped from the wall. A stuffed marmot getting dusty on the filing cabinet. A computer. Dust on top of that, too. A keyboard with bits of food stuck in the tiles. A fan in the ceiling with a pulley thing and eighty-two white square ceiling tiles, last time Peter counted. There were a lot of things. He'd heard of some of them, too. He used to spend whole afternoons getting Darlene to walk him through every department store and boutique in her memory until he could practically reach out and touch the world that was before. But now that he was here, in some police station on the outskirts of a town called West Wranglestone with barely any memory of how they got here or when he last saw Cooper, he realised he didn't want any of those things.

Another ten minutes had passed when the people in the corridor suddenly stopped talking. Peter looked round. The door opened and a boy carrying a mug of hot drink scurried in. He couldn't have been any younger than Peter, but he was working so hard to prove he could keep quiet that he tiptoed over to the desk like a child pretending to creep through a spooky mansion. His Hawaiian shirt drew too much attention, too. It was so loud. You wouldn't think it was possible for flowers to scream at you, but, there it was.

The boy pulled a square of yellow paper from the pad, setting the mug down on top of it so as not to make a ring stain on the desk, and held back a moment. He was conscious of his weight as he kept yanking the bottom of the shirt away from his belly so it didn't cling. Peter focused on the snow falling between the slats in the blinds and felt the boy staring at him. Growing up, he was used to being the one to break any awkward silences. Men like Bud back home weren't disposed to small talk at the best of times.

He was about to say hello when the boy cleared his throat.

"I'm not supposed to talk to you before my dad does," he said, "but I'm Teddy."

Peter nodded. "OK. Hi."

The boy seemed to get a kick of confidence out of Peter saying hello, even though he couldn't have sounded any less interested if he tried, so he took a seat on the other side of the desk and sat there beaming at him.

"And you're Peter."

"Uh-huh."

"I'm the welcoming committee. Ta-da!"

Peter stared at the desk and said nothing.

"Because I chat."

"OK."

"I get real chatty."

"I can see."

"And people think I'm a card just because I like to wear fun shirts. But the truth is, I carry a bit of weight down there and nothing disguises it quite like a floral. Not even a Christmas sweater."

"OK."

"And Christmas sweaters are as busy as they come."

Peter shrugged. "Are they?"

"Sure are. You get a lot of good coverage from reindeer antlers and wreaths and a big pile of presents, but nothing covers a belly quite like a Christmas pudding."

Peter creased the corners of his mouth into a weary half-smile and nodded.

"But I get real sweaty in them."

Peter sighed. "Do you?"

"Yeah. Especially if the sweater's got a ton of viscose in it. Scratchy, too."

Peter looked up. The boy was keener than a dog looking for treats. "I don't think you carry too much weight."

Teddy beamed. It was like no one had ever said anything nice about him before, and suddenly Peter felt bad that he hadn't been friendlier.

"Tea," said Teddy.

"What?"

Teddy pointed at the mug. "It's a cup of tea. You probably haven't seen one before."

"Oh. I have, but only the home-made kind."

"It's OK. There'll probably be a lot of things you haven't tried and a lot of things you won't know the name of and don't know what to do with. It's especially like that for us.

People born after."

Peter stared into the tumbling snow. "I guess."

"But don't worry. I can show you around if you like."

"OK."

"But only if you want me to."

Peter nodded along. He could feel the gap Teddy left him, the one where he was supposed to jump in excitedly to take him up on the offer. But when he decided to ignore it, Teddy bolted forward in the chair and filled the silence for him.

"But only if you—"

"No." Peter cleared his throat. That was a bit harsh. "No. It's OK."

It was just that everything was suddenly all so new and so overwhelming. He hadn't even seen Cooper since they got here. They were separated on arrival and now it felt like he didn't even exist any more. Peter stared at the stuffed marmot. Back home, every single corner of the lake had seen them together and witnessed what they shared. When they crossed the lake on a bed of stars, the watchtower looked over them. The canoe knew their kisses. But not that marmot. That marmot didn't have a clue who they were. None of this place did. The two of them no more existed here than they did in the ravine the moment Cooper looked back and saw Peter standing there. That look. The horror in Cooper's eyes, to be seen as somebody other than the version of himself he showed to Peter. That look. Just one, and everything they were together had changed.

Teddy smiled. "It gets easier."

"What does?"

"This place."

"Oh, that," said Peter. "I hope so."

"I didn't even know how to turn a lamp on until a year ago."

"Is there electricity in the whole town, then?"

"Sure. But no TV or cell phones. Nobody's got those back yet."

"But how is it all working again?"

"The government. They want this place to be as real as possible so we can practise before the move back into the real world."

"Like a show home?"

Teddy jumped up in his seat. "Yes! You know about those?"

Peter had seen plenty over the years. River traders, whenever they came hawked, were full of magazines telling you how to stage a home for maximum impact. He just wasn't in the mood to encourage Teddy any further.

"No," he said. "Not really."

Peter stared at the steam rising from the mug and

let Teddy scramble for another way in. He was so desperate to keep him talking, he could practically hear him thinking of the next thing to say. He didn't have to wait long.

"I can point at things and tell you what they are too, if you like."

"No," said Peter, "I'm fine."

"Oh, OK."

Teddy sat on his hands like that'd keep his mouth shut somehow. But his eyes were burning a hole through the back of a small metal object on the desk and a moment later his hands popped out from underneath his lap and pointed at it.

"Pencil sharpener!"

"OK."

"For sharpening pencils."

"Right."

"Ceiling fan."

"Yes."

"For fanning the—"

"And those?" said Peter pointing at the pad of yellow paper.

"Post-its."

Peter shrugged.

"For making notes and sticking them on things."

Peter picked the pad up and smiled. "Nice."

"Aren't they? The low-tack adhesive allows the notes to stick and unstick real easy. All you've gotta do is press!"

"You can reuse them?"

"You sure can," said Teddy. "Well, kinda. They tend to curl and drop off after a while."

"All the same, I wish I had some of these back at the tree house to tell my dad where things are supposed to go."

"Is he here in the station, too?"

"Yes," said Peter. "He's having a medical."

"Well, now you can leave notes for him all over the place. You can stick one on me too if you like, just so you don't forget I'm Teddy and that I'm here to show you around."

Peter looked across the desk and smiled. Teddy was all right. Or he might be, in small doses.

The door flew open and Teddy bolted from his seat.

"If that boy's walking around the office pointing at things and naming them, you can leave *him* a rotten review on TripAdvisor, not me."

The man was chunky looking and worn-in like an old couch. His voice had the kind of booming warmth that'd charm chocolate out of a kid's hands and it was clear from his position as the town's sheriff that Peter wasn't the only one to think so. The man kicked the door shut with his heel and collapsed back into the chair. Peter glanced at the sheriff star pinned to the breast of his cable-knit cardigan and wondered if the weight of the thing would eventually damage the wool.

"Sheriff O'Hurn's my dad," said Teddy.

"Yeah," said the sheriff wiping coffee foam from a thick handlebar moustache, "but only when I need to wheel you out so we seem real friendly to the newbies, and don't you forget it."

Peter sat up in his seat and smiled. "He just brought me a cup of tea."

The sheriff winked. "Talked you through his Christmas knitwear collection, dint he?"

Peter didn't contradict him so the sheriff gently patted Teddy on the butt. "Skedaddle."

"See you later," said Teddy.

"Yes," said Peter. "OK."

The sheriff tugged on a couple of pulley strings next to his seat, making the blinds close. He waited until Teddy had shut the door behind him before dropping a folder with Peter's name on it.

"You scored high in math and reading," he said lifting the mug to his moustache. "Higher than the average for those born after. Tuition of our youngens has varied from park to park so it's just good to know what any one person might need before final reintegration."

Peter sat forward. "My dad taught me."

"Tom?"

"Yes. Thomas Nordstrum."

"Nice fella. And what did he do before?"

"He worked for a bunch of lumber firms."

The sheriff turned the page, running his finger down the list of scores. "And it says you sew."

"Yes, sir. I used to trade deer hide for old cotton reels with some of the river traders back home and although I wouldn't really want to showcase a pair of white socks with black stitching if I can help it, I made it work. And besides, Cooper's usually covered in so much blood, you wouldn't even know his socks were supposed to be white in the first place."

Peter looked down at his lap, suddenly aware just how reassuring it was to refer to Cooper in the present tense.

The sheriff wiped foam from his moustache and turned a page.

"Cooper's reading's not so good," said Peter. "But he can walk down the length of a canoe on a rapid without even rocking it and I could never do that. Never! Does reading matter so much?"

"It will do, yes."

"Why?"

"The world we're walking back into won't have much need for balancing on canoes, now, son, will it?"

"I guess not. But he can also pop a tin can with a single shot from fifty yards away."

"I see."

"And wrangle a whole herd of the Dead away from the lake. Sorry, I should've mentioned that first."

"And now?"

Peter shook his head. "Now?"

"Yeah," said the sheriff turning another page. "What does he do now he's Returned?"

"He does the same."

"But how does he behave?"

"Behave?"

"Yes. Is there anything else?"

Peter glanced at the blinds, irritated that he could no longer see through them to distract him from what he could still see in the ravine that night, and heard the cool tone of Cooper's voice telling Becky how easy it was for them to control the Dead.

The sheriff cleared his throat. "Peter."

Peter became aware of a clock ticking in the office. He supposed it must've been there this whole time, but he hadn't noticed it before now.

"Peter, does Cooper do anything else now he's Returned?"

The ticking got louder.

"Peter."

"Yes. He loves me."

The sheriff's attention lifted from the page. "Son, look at me."

Peter scanned the office for the clock. Where was that damned thing?

"Son."

"Where's Cooper? Where is he?"

"In interview room seven down the other end of the corridor with Tokala, but he's fine, Peter."

"And—"

"And your dad's just outside waitin' for you."

Peter held the sheriff's eye longer than was comfortable just to see if he'd look away. But he didn't. His eyes were warm with reassurance and there was a kindness in his voice that didn't leave just because his son was no longer in the room with them. Peter noticed the back of a picture frame beside the sheriff's computer and quickly changed the subject.

"Is that your family?"

"No," said the sheriff, tilting it so it lay face down on the desk, "I guess it's the family of whoever ran this town before all this. And this here sheriff badge ain't real neither. I looted it from the toy department in the supermarket on the other side of town when we got here. I just grew the tache to fit the bill nicely, but Mandy who runs the Lone Star across town reckons it makes me look kinda porno."

"What would she do if you got rid of it?"

"Kick me out of bed probably. But don't tell Teddy I told you that. It's secret until we know it's a sure thing."

Peter smiled.

The clock ticked.

The sheriff set his mug down on the desk, easing back into his chair. "Peter, what do you know of Timberdark?"

Slices of sunlight breaking through the slats in the blinds dimmed, dulling the shadows around the objects littered across the desk. And yet the office became brighter somehow. Luminous, even. Peter recognized the grey glow of heavy snowfall from many a day spent trapped inside the tree house. He parted two slats to watch it tumble down in thick drifts across the window. The last time the snow had fallen this heavily had been in the days following his very first kiss with Cooper in the boathouse. He'd spent so many hours pressed against the tree-house window longing to see him again, he thought that snowstorm would never end. Looking back now, the only thing standing between him and Cooper had been the days. Now there was a word. *That* word. And now the sheriff had brought it into the room with them, it stood directly over Peter watching, knowing full well its secret was so powerful it made the truth pitiful, that there was something about Cooper he had no access to.

"I thought Cooper was supposed to be invaluable now he can help stop the Dead from attacking," said Peter after a while. "But it doesn't sound like it."

The sheriff's eyes smiled sadly in ways that told Peter he completely understood his instinct was to protect him. But the matter still stood. "Drink your tea, son."

"I don't want it."

"Teddy made it with more love than a damned cup of tea has any right to. He'll be offended as all hell if you—"

"I said I don't want it."

"Then at least take a breath and realize we're just tryin' to help you. Of course Cooper's invaluable. All Returnees are. With so many of the Dead left roaming the land, our reintegration is utterly dependent on them. Utterly. We just need to keep the government on side is all."

"But—"

"And stamp any worrying words like *Timberdark* out before they catch fire."

"He'll tell you when he's ready to."

"Are you tellin' me that, son, or are you simply tryin' to convince yourself?"

Peter let go of the blinds. The plastic slats thwacked back into place.

"It's OK if you don't know, Peter. It's OK."

But it wasn't.

The sheriff took a sip of coffee. The sound of the clock ticking seemed to mark the time between either one of them saying anything. After a while, the grey glow in the room became stronger, bringing with it thicker snow, and eventually the sheriff sat back in his chair.

"At the beginning of a relationship, you think you'll know everything about a person there is to know," he said. "It's all ahead of you to learn like a book you've not read yet and the other person is just itchin' to pass theirs over to you. When I met my Judith, her favourite colour was yellow and her favourite movie was anything with Patrick Swayze. Take your pick. She got on well enough with her brother, but he'd stolen from her family once and so I always knew to keep his visits short. Christmas made her sad. Halloween brought her joy. She wore no-frills double D sports bras and preferred her eggs over easy with toast on the burned side. But you know what? I never knew she struggled with her eating until it took her from us."

Peter looked up. The sheriff's candour was so surprising, he had no choice but to hold his gaze.

"What I'm tryin' to say, son, is that it's OK if you don't know what that word is. We can't know everythin' about our loved ones. We never do."

"But why not?"

The sheriff sighed as if to say if only everything was that easy, and Peter felt the familiar prickle of his own naivety being reflected back at him. "Sweet boy. Because people have the right to their own secrets, and the right to guard their own demons."

"Don't say demons."

"I didn't mean—"

"I know. But don't say demons."

The door to the office opened behind Peter. The sheriff glanced up, raising a finger to whoever was standing there as a sign to give him a minute, and the door quietly closed again.

"Son."

"I know. You need to go."

"Peter, the marshal ranger you first encountered at Yellowstone has shared the government's concerns that *Timberdark* may be a code or acronym for a plan being prepared by the Returned against the wider population."

Peter sat forward. "No."

"No, why?"

"Just no."

"Then tell me."

"Because this is why the Returned made a sanctuary at Wranglestone in the first place. To escape people who assumed they'd be monsters."

"Son, nobody's talkin' about anybody bein' a monster."

"Aren't they?"

"No. They're talkin' about what any people will do to

protect themselves when they're threatened or scared."

"Why?" Peter asked. "Have they got a reason to be scared, then?"

"No. Well, only if the government has."

"What? So, somebody's got to be the first to say they're not scared of each other, now? That they won't do anything to defend themselves as long as the others don't. Is that it?"

"In their defence, Peter, the Returnees' concern for their own safety does come with some historical precedents."

"Yes. I know that."

"And Cooper knows what happened to the original community on the lake and what drove them to live there in secrecy in the first place."

Peter nodded. "Our friend Rider told us that when he was bitten and went to the hospital, that the government were using admissions to detain Returnees. He only got out because an ally was there to warn him."

"Right. And knowing that is reason enough why any Returnee might want to avenge past mistakes made against them. And why someone in Cooper's position might begin to harbour separatist feelings against the general population."

"I don't know," said Peter. Then, "I guess."

"Then surely you can understand why that makes the new government very nervous right now."

Peter looked away and the clock kept ticking. "I suppose."

The sheriff sighed like *suppose* was as good a place as any to start negotiations and leaned back into his chair. "What matters is that the government won't make those mistakes again."

"Even though the ranger just killed a family."

"We haven't proved that yet."

"But—"

"You have my word that any wrongdoing will be properly investigated."

"Well, then someone needs to tell Returnees they have no reason to be scared."

The sheriff shook his head. "That's the same reassurance the government are seeking."

Peter slumped back in his chair.

"I know," said the sheriff. "I know. And that logic would be crazier than a box of frogs had it not been for that damned word. With it, I'm afraid the fact remains that when the time comes for us to all leave here, the government simply won't let Cooper or any of his associates in while those doubts hang over him."

Peter looked away. "What's so special about going back, anyway?"

"Now, Peter, come on," said the sheriff, yanking the pulley string on the blinds back. "You don't mean that.

From what I hear, this is the moment you've always dreamed of. And there's so much to look forward to. Look."

Cooper had told Peter, from his time looting the stores for medicines and firearms all those years ago, that the town was just a gap in the wilderness. That the winding road broke clean out of the woods, straightening out on to Mainstreet with its movie theatre and diner, a general store and bar, and how, when you got to the other end, the buildings just stopped and the road disappeared back inside the pines on the other side. And he was right. But what he'd described was a ghost town.

Hills of snowy pines rose up sharply behind the red brick of Mainstreet. But somehow you barely even noticed them. Because below was nothing but magic.

Neon lights flashed. From every store. From every window. And in every colour. Above a store called the Old Western Outfitters, a giant neon cowboy rode a bucking bronco. The lights switched and the cowboy launched his Stetson into the air. Over at the old movie theatre, scores of amber light bulbs rippled beneath the marquee, turning snow on the sidewalk beneath it gold. A neon Budweiser sign fizzed. Twinkling fairy lights had been coiled around every lamppost. More lights were strewn above the road, crisscrossing the length of Mainstreet on thin cables. Snow hurried over the little town and the brightly coloured light bulbs jangled. And high above them all, burning red like a branding iron in the sky, swung the town's largest sign.

Coca-Cola ™
Proudly Sponsors Your Welcome Home

"It's just a darned show town really," said the sheriff, coming to stand by Peter's side at the window. "As Walt Disney as Mainstreet, USA, except the rocks don't play goddamn 'Zip-A-Dee-Doo-Dah' all day long. But it's a glimpse of what was, Peter, and what could be again in the cities and towns. If they let you in."

Peter pressed both hands to the window in wonder. It was a toyshop, the most beautiful toyshop in all the world. Only he was on the inside looking out.

"And it's safe, too," said the sheriff. "You won't have to live in fear no more, son. You can always call on one of our Returnee friends to chaperone you door to door if you feel safer that way, but we got two of 'em on watch down either end of the street, night and day, come snow or more snow, so folks never have to worry."

Peter stepped back from the window and the sheriff's reflection came into focus in the glass.

"I'm sorry your boy's got himself mixed up in something, son."

"Then tell me what I have to do."

"Just do what you can to find out what Timberdark is. If we can get there before the government do, then we might, just might, be able to keep this whole thing from blowing wide open."

Peter gazed through the sheriff's reflection, watching the snow flurry over the brightly coloured town, and resolve settled deep inside him. "OK," he said. "OK."

10

Cooper's head hung low over his lap. The window to interview room seven wasn't frosted like the one to the sheriff's office. Anyone passing down the corridor on their way back to reception could see in. But perhaps that was the point. The room was just a box with two chairs in it. The walls were so bare that the one missing carpet tile almost became a feature. Cooper sat with his back to the window facing Tokala, answering a series of questions. Tokala was leading the registration process for all Returnees so they were probably having the same conversation he'd just had with the sheriff. Only it didn't look that way and there was no desk dividing them. Tokala sat with both hands flat across a clipboard. His dark eyes were so unblinking that his entire being seemed distilled to focus on Cooper. There was a voice in the room asking questions, but Tokala's mouth wasn't moving. He just sat there with his long hair unbound across the chest of his zip top, studying Cooper and on occasion smiling warmly, like he was eagerly receiving everything he had to tell him even though he wasn't the one doing the asking.

Voices broke further down the corridor. Peter glanced back and a woman with a swinging ponytail and a file in her hand marched out of one door and disappeared through another. The door slammed. When he turned back, Tokala was looking up at him. Peter mouthed the word *sorry* and moved away from the window. But Tokala smiled, as if the intrusion was welcome, and indicated for him to come inside, so Peter quietly let himself in and crouched on the floor beneath the window.

Cooper remained hunched over. He glanced up towards the corner of the ceiling where a small mesh box had been fixed. The box crackled and a dull voice entered the room.

'*What's your favourite food?*' came the voice from inside the box.

Cooper tucked his hair behind his ears. "Racoon. They never quit stealin' stuff."

'*What's your favourite colour?*'

"The sky just before it snows."

'*What's your earliest memory of being embarrassed?*'

"Takin' a piss all over Essie Morgan before she could get me outside in time."

'What's your most recent memory of being embarrassed?'

"Honkin' of guts when I shoulda worn a fresh T."

'Why?'

"Cos I was trying real hard to impress Peter."

The mesh box crackled.

Peter looked down at the carpet tiles and his stomach churned a little.

'What makes you feel big?'

"The mountains."

'What makes you feel small?'

"Here."

'Do you wish you'd lived in the world that came before?'

"No."

'Are you glad the world before is gone?'

Cooper shifted about in his seat. "No."

'What's your favourite colour?'

"The sky just before it—"

'Do you have strange visions or dreams?'

"No."

'Do you ever have intrusive thoughts?'

"No." Then, "Wait, what does intru—"

'Are you ever scared you might harm yourself?'

Cooper shook his head.

'Are you ever scared you might harm yourself?'

"No. No, I ain't never—"

'Are you scared you might harm someone else?'

Peter looked up.

Cooper shoved his head in his hand. "No. I—"

'What's your father's name?'

"Bartholomew Terrence Donaghue."

'What's your mother's name?'

"Mattie Donaghue."

'Do you—'

"Mathilda May Donaghue. That's her name in full."

Peter watched Cooper's shoulders expand as he drew her name inside him for a moment. He never talked about his mom.

'What's your favourite season?'

"Fall."

'Do you think the Dead were brought down by God to destroy humankind?'

Cooper looked up for help, but Tokala urged him to do his best.

"No," said Cooper.

'Do you think the Returned are agents of the Dead sent to help them wipe the living from the planet?'

"No."

'What's your happiest memory?'

Cooper clapped both hands down across his knee. "I dunno. Hell, I can't even think straight no more."

'What's your saddest memory?'

Cooper looked down.

The mesh box went quiet.

'*What's your saddest memory?*'

'*What's your saddest memory?*'

"Peter lookin' at me like he dint know who I was no more."

Peter's heart pounded. He was so sure he would've said Snowball dying.

'*What's your favourite animal?*'

Cooper said nothing.

'*What's your favourite animal?*'

"Moose."

'*What's your favourite plant?*'

"Pine."

'*What's Timberdark?*'

Cooper's shoulders expanded to draw in the enormity of the question or maybe the enormity of the answer, Peter had no idea which. But he didn't answer.

'*What's Timberdark?*'

Cooper lowered his head even further so his hair spilled across his face. The mesh box crackled. It waited. But Tokala pre-empted any further questioning. He glanced up towards another box in the corner of the room behind Cooper and shook his head. A little red light on the side of the machine faded and Tokala turned towards Peter, leaving Cooper alone with his thoughts.

"I'm sorry Cooper had to suffer those questions," he

said. "So, I thought it best to sit with him while he did. Peter, it's good to see you again."

"You too."

"We didn't get a chance to talk on the journey over. Are you well?"

"I guess." Then, "West Wranglestone is very pretty."

Tokala nodded in agreement.

"The lights."

"Yes. They've gone to great efforts to make it welcoming. But I'm sure the town must fill you with a hundred questions."

Peter glanced at the empty square in the carpet and smiled. "I met Teddy."

"Ah. He means well."

"I expect he'll have all the answers."

"Most likely."

"He told me what a pencil sharpener was."

"I see."

"And told me that they were used for sharpening pencils."

"I have no doubt."

"And—"

Tokala smiled. "You survived. That's the most important thing."

Peter offered a smile of his own, but when it didn't last, silence took its chances, destroying what little opportunity there was for small talk until all that was left was the truth, that this hurt.

Tokala stood. "I should give you two some space."

Peter looked up, at once relieved and frightened to be left alone with Cooper.

"Your father has been offered an apartment across town, Peter. He thought you and Cooper would both appreciate your own space, so we've allocated the studio above the Lone Star for you both if you'd like it."

"Yes," said Peter. "Thank you."

"That's settled, then. I'll get the keys for you now."

Tokala's dark eyes held Peter's, an invitation to talk to him whenever he needed to. But he didn't linger. Peter nodded his thanks and Tokala quietly left, closing the door behind him.

Cooper didn't turn round. And in the moment of the two of them being alone again, it almost seemed impossible to Peter that so much separation could exist where not even a gap between two kisses had existed before. But there it was. He didn't even feel he could look at Cooper any more. The most he could manage was the space surrounding him. The chair. The carpet beneath his feet. The air above his head. But no closer than that. He didn't have permission for any closer than that. And right there and then, he realized something else. If it went on like this, if it never got any better, then it wouldn't just hurt because he no longer had access to Cooper's heart, but to his own heart and those parts of it that forever lived inside him now whether he liked it or not. But perhaps that's how it was. That when two people ended, neither one got the part of themselves that once belonged to the other person back again.

"Did they treat you right?" came Cooper's voice low inside the silence.

"Yes. Everybody's been nice."

"And your dad?"

"He's OK. He's waiting for us in reception, I think."

"Us?"

"Yes," said Peter quietly. "Of course, us."

"No *of course* about it, Pete."

Cooper stood, scuffing the corner of the empty carpet tile with his toecaps, trying to lift the edges, and the space between them got a little wider.

"Reckon I'm more nervous of you now," he said, "than that night I made a mess outta askin' you out."

"I love you," said Peter.

"Pa said I'd held out longer waitin' for you than a dog staring at a cookie jar. But he made me put on a clean pair of undershorts that night of First Fall. Well, kinda clean. I only wore them inside out once before then. And you know what he said?"

Peter shook his head.

"He said, *Coop, a patient fisher always gets the bigger catch.*"

Peter's stomach turned, startled that Bud would ever have regarded him as anything other than a liability, let alone a catch. "Did you hear what I just said?"

"I got to thinkin'."

"Cooper, did you hear—"

"My brain lost count of the times I used to canoe past your island, tryin' to rummage up the courage to come talk to you. I'd only get so close and my nerves would just about quit on me. I was out on the lake one day, right near the bottom by your place. We was probably only about fourteen or somethin' but I remember how clear the water was that day cos I could see minnows swimmin' in the fizz my paddle made through the water. The water was so clear I remember seeing the shadow of the canoe passing over the shingle below, too. And then I saw something that weren't no shadow. A great white sturgeon, Pete. Hell, it was the biggest darned thing I ever did saw. It had whiskers longer than bootlaces and spines on its back like some dinosaur. A real fifteen-footer. And you were back on the island somewhere you wouldn't even have noticed it and it made such a splash when its tail smacked the water, the canoe just about rocked over on to its side like a toy in a tin bath. And . . . and, I dunno. I just wished I coulda shown it you, is all."

Cooper scratched his pit and stood there staring at the missing carpet tile and nothing more came out of him.

"Why are you telling me all this?"

Cooper shrugged. "The ravine."

"What about it?"

"I don't want you to think of me like that, when you think of me."

"Think of you like what?"

"Dunno. Talking with the Dead. Not lookin' at you right." Then, "Bein' secretive."

"Then help me not to."

Cooper's dark eyes glared from behind the ropes of his matted hair.

"Their questions won't go away, Cooper."

"And what about yours?"

Peter stood. "What's Timberdark? Where did you even get to hear that word?"

"I said it int for you. That should be enough."

"And I'm begging you and *that* should be enough."

Cooper's chest heaved, seemingly inhaling every bit of fury coursing through his blood and bones rather than have it pile on to Peter. But he wouldn't budge. "Is this gonna split us?"

"I don't know any more."

Cooper nodded as if he'd simply respect that decision rather than challenge it, and somehow that was so much worse than if he'd kicked the chair over and fought back. Peter inched closer to the door and the pain of Cooper's resignation burned across his skin.

Voices further down the corridor came and went.

Doors opened. Others closed.

A minute passed, or maybe longer, when Cooper cleared his throat. "Reckon holdin' hands is underrated."

Peter looked up, startled that he'd managed to read his heart so deeply. And it was true. Although nothing could beat feeling Cooper's kiss, kissing was still a whole lot of wanting and needing and trying to make two separate things turn into one. Holding hands when all else failed? Well, that always put you back together again.

Cooper's fingertips reached for Peter's. Peter took his hand, and the pair of them stood in the room with the missing carpet tile for a moment, neither one of them feeling the need to say anything further.

11

The apartment above the Lone Star was strange. The main room had a bay window at the front overlooking Mainstreet with a kitchenette in the back corner and two other doors leading off to the bedroom and bathroom. The entire apartment was clad in wood panelling to give the illusion that it had been built of something sturdy. But unlike the thick timber of the tree houses back home, the panels were as thin as cardboard and the walls behind just plaster. Peter rapped his knuckles across the panels and felt the hollow space of the apartment next door just behind them. Nothing could disguise the fact that you were only ever inches away from your neighbour. Someone could be standing there on the other side from you looking back, right now. And the missing furnishings didn't help.

Darker rectangles on the panelling not bleached by sunlight highlighted where picture frames and mounted animal heads had once hung. Next to the couch was a little side table stained with a series of circles where a mug had been repeatedly set down without a coaster. A table beside the front door had an island of glossy wood surrounded by dust where a lamp once stood. They were just empty spaces now, but they told a story. Memories of a household; a coffee break; a light to welcome you home. Fingerprints of a life once lived. Peter ran his fingertips along the top of the oven extractor fan, grinding a ridge of dusty grease into a ball with his thumb and forefinger, and wondered what happened to the people who used to live here. Maybe they made it to the refuge at Yellowstone. Maybe they wandered the Earth in a herd with the rest of the Dead. Maybe they didn't even make it that far. He let the ball of dust topple from his fingers and stood in the middle of the room watching the snow tumble across the bay window. It was getting dark now. Flashes of neon coming up from the street below struck fronds of frost crawling across the glass, turning them red and then green.

"Whoever lived here before liked a lot of wood," Peter offered. "So that's a good start."

Cooper tossed his Stetson across the table. "This wouldn't look like wood if I straddled it in a plaid shirt with a pickaxe."

Peter smiled. "But would you do that for me anyway?"

"It ain't wood."

"It is a bit orange."

"And cold to the touch. How'd they even manage that?"

"Teak varnishing," said Peter.

"Huh?"

"Teak varnishing. *Enhancing the natural charm of your home with timeless beauty.*"

"Jesus. Tell me you didn't trade good meat for those darned magazines."

Peter cleared his throat and proceeded to pick the welcome pack up off the dining table. Cooper made his way into the kitchen area, yanked a drawer open and quickly shut it again.

"What was in there?"

"Just a bunch of whosits," said Cooper opening the refrigerator. "And this won't fit a deer carcass in it."

"We're not storing a whole deer in the refrigerator."

"We could if its head sat on the top shelf."

"Why don't you make yourself useful and go fill the bath tub? It's the big empty white thing in the middle of the room, if you're not sure."

Cooper grumbled. "You int funny."

The Coca-Cola™ Welcome Pack had everything in it you could possibly hope for. Peter started to read all about silk washes and the microwave standing on top of the refrigerator and how it cooked stuff from the inside out and went *ping* when it was done and where all the utensils were stored while Cooper explored the other rooms. There were vouchers with discounts on food shopping once you spent over a hundred dollars and things called loyalty cards where you could get a free coffee after twenty other coffees. Towards the back of the folder was a blank budget form with two columns so you could keep an eye on the money you had coming in compared to the money you had going out. There was a checklist for your bills, details of where you had to go to pay your rent and a full list of support groups where you could learn how to manage money and budget for bills in preparation for re-entry. Finally, at the back of the folder was a list of all the current vacancies in town plus a hundred dollars to keep you going until then.

"There's a mandatory reintegration meeting coming up in a few days' time."

Cooper mumbled something from the bedroom.

"It means you've gotta—"

"Yeah," said Cooper calling back. "I get it."

"What job do you think you'll take, anyways?"

"Pete, the beds have got some dumb fancy curtain around the base."

"Yep. A valance."

"Huh?"

"A valance! A stylish skirt so you can't see the base of the bed."

Cooper poked his head round the door. "Why wouldn't you want to see the base of the bed?"

"Did you hear what I just said?"

"Yeah. I start at the supermarket tomorrow."

"Oh. Since when?"

"Since I decided. And Becky's working at the diner. Tokala talked to us about it when you was in the sheriff's office. I'll be working there when we're not taking shifts lookin' out for the Dead."

Peter offered a smile. "Why didn't you tell me?"

"I'm tellin' you now."

"I guess. Well, that's good."

Cooper shrugged. "Is it?"

"Well, it's a start."

"And you?"

Peter looked at the list. But he couldn't really concentrate. "I thought we'd go through the jobs together over dinner or something."

"It's just a job, Pete."

"I know, but—"

"Why don't you try out the movie theatre?"

Peter nodded. "Yeah. Maybe."

"Anyways," said Cooper leaning into the bedroom door. "What are we gonna do with ourselves when we're not at work?"

"We need to get our grocery shopping done."

"What then?"

"Well, then we can start filling the place with things."

Cooper shrugged. "What things?"

"Well, if we each have a toothbrush we'll need somewhere to put them. So, we could buy a cup to put them in and then maybe that cup will need a shelf so it doesn't get in the way on the sink. Then if we've got a nice shelf, we'll have more room to store a few extra things like the toothpaste and deodorant and scissors and wash foam. Maybe put a mat down on the floor so our feet don't get cold standing there. You know, start building up a home."

Cooper dug his hands down the seat of his jeans. "Deodorant?"

"Really? Is that your takeaway from all this?"

"OK. But once we've got all the things, then what do we do?"

"I don't really know how long we'll be here before we make the permanent move. Nobody's mentioned it yet."

"After that, though. In the long run."

But Peter wasn't too sure. "Did Bud ever say what he used to do with your mom in an evening?"

Cooper shrugged. "They watched TV. Yours?"

"Same."

The largest dark rectangle in the whole apartment was on the wall directly opposite the couch. Two holes were left in the panelling so it must've been where the television set had been displayed. The rectangle was huge. Bigger than a window. It was empty now but Peter flicked through the back of the welcome pack and there they were. Televisions. Right at the top of a *Coming Attractions* list.

Peter stared at the dark rectangle. "Well, that'll be something when it arrives."

"I guess."

Cooper made his way back into the bedroom so Peter proceeded to flick through the rest of the welcome pack trying to work out if he had any right to be angry that Cooper had already spoken to Becky about stuff before he'd had a chance to.

A clock was ticking. Peter turned around and spotted one on the wall next to the extractor fan. He was sure that sound hadn't been there before, but just like the sheriff's office, now he was aware of its presence in the room, it wouldn't leave.

Someone next door cleared their throat and Peter stepped back, alarmed by the sudden intrusion. He set the welcome pack down on the dining table, unsure which was worse, having your privacy invaded this way or invading someone else's by overhearing them when they don't know you're there, when Cooper opened the front door.

"Where are you going?"

Cooper swept his Stetson off the side table. "Out."

"But there's a pre-made meal in the refrigerator for us. It just needs re-heating. The microwave goes *ping* when it's done apparently, so that should be fun."

Cooper dug his fists inside his back pockets and said nothing.

"We've only just got here, Coop."

"I need some air is all."

"But—"

"I might go and see if the night watch need an extra pair of hands."

"But—"

"Or see if Becky's OK. Seeing as you ain't thought to ask after her."

"Cooper, I—"

Cooper squeezed the dent in the brim of his Stetson. He did this while he chewed over the other things left unsaid. But he'd clearly made up his mind to say none of them. He put the Stetson back on, doffing the brim as had been Bud's way, and quietly let himself out with an "I won't be long".

Peter heard the front door downstairs slam shut followed by the crunch of footsteps in the snow outside and ran over to the bay window. Snow flurried over the town, making the brightly coloured lights strung across

Mainstreet bob and jangle. Cooper squeezed between two cars lining the sidewalk, flicking his jacket collar up around his neck, and made his way out into the middle of the road. If he glanced back now, they'd be OK. But he didn't. He leaned into the wind, pulling his collar in even tighter and set off up the road. Peter rapped the glass with his knuckles. But Cooper didn't hear, or pretended not to, so Peter grabbed his parka jacket off the back of the chair and ran out on to the road after him.

Cooper neared the top of the street, too far away to hear Peter calling. But now he was out here, he didn't seem particularly irritable any more. He ran his hand over the hood of a car, scooping a thick wedge of snow into his hands, then turned off into one of the side streets, dashing a snowball across a car window, and was gone. Nobody makes snowballs when they're unhappy. Cooper was buoyed, whatever he was up to.

Fat snowflakes tumbled into the town's neon signs like moths drawn to the light, making them fizz and flicker. The fairy lights bobbed in the wind. Peter dug his fists into his pockets and stood there listening to the soft tinkle of glass overhead. But these were the only sounds. The window of the Lone Star was dark. The laundrette across the street was empty. He stood over Cooper's footprints wondering what he was up to, and another thought presented itself. He could take a look inside Cooper's bag while he was out. Peter gazed up towards the apartment window when he felt the weight of someone watching him and turned round.

The deer's skull, with its reaching antlers like skeleton hands, seemed to hover in the darkness. The Ghost Ranger stood out of the light in the middle of the road at the edge of town. Perhaps he had been there all along, but he stood completely motionless as if he hadn't walked up, simply appeared. But his reasons for being out here were the same. The ranger nodded, making himself complicit with Peter. He'd been watching Cooper, too. Peter nodded back, more out of politeness than anything else, then regretted it immediately. He dashed back indoors, closing the door firmly behind him and ran upstairs. He stood in the corner of the bay, careful not to be seen, and the clock ticked. Peter wondered how it was even possible for a sound to be at once constant and yet able to fade in and out of a room like that. He pressed his hands to the glass and peered out, but the Ghost Ranger had gone. Snow flurried over the town smothering Cooper's footprints, and soon they were gone too.

12

Cooper didn't come home. Peter took one of the two twin beds and lay facing the wall waiting to hear the creak of the other mattress behind him, followed by his name being called tenderly from the darkness. But it didn't come, and somehow the empty bed became an emptiness inside him, the cold across his back keeping him awake no matter how much he pulled the blankets over him. In the last month on the trail, when wild winds ripped across the tent, the two of them had been able to lie in their sleeping bags watching the snow tumble across the gauze window and never once feel the cold. The steady rhythm of Cooper's breath across Peter's neck was warm. The heat radiating from his palms as they held hands was warmer still. And they could lie like that, talking, sleeping, stirring to kiss, listening to the storm, but somehow in another world of their own making, the heat between them never once dipping lower than a glowing ember. But not now. The space between the two beds was a cold chasm. Peter rolled over, gazing into the darkness where Cooper should've been, except if he'd come back and not called out his name, that would only have been worse. Not a chasm, but a canyon so vast that love, struggling to breach the divide, would simply fail and plummet into the bottom and be lost.

Peter shoved the duvet aside and rummaged inside his bag for one of Cooper's old T-shirts. The pits of the old white crew neck were yellowed. He pulled them to his nose, inhaling the sweet tang of Cooper's body and longed for it to be his. He sat there for a while, with the coarse crust of the carpet at the soles of his feet, nuzzling the T-shirt just so Cooper's presence wasn't entirely missing from the room. After a while, Peter put it on and made his way into the front room where he sat quietly at the kitchen table waiting for first light to crest over the hills above town.

The clock made itself heard again. It broke into the apartment like a cat without any invitation and sat behind Peter in the kitchenette where it ticked constantly, pestering him for attention. Peter huffed. He'd take the battery out next time it did that. *See how you like it, then.*

Sunlight struck the snow on the rooftops across the street from the apartment and Peter lifted his arm up to catch Cooper's scent. But the smell of his body on the cotton had already started to fade, so he gently slipped it off, careful to fold the armpits well inside the middle of the garment, and stuffed it under his pillow for safekeeping. Peter placed his hand across his bare chest, running his fingertips down across his nipple. But they were too soft for him to make-believe they were Cooper's and suddenly the tender coarseness of those hands seemed harder to remember.

The person in the apartment next door coughed then cleared their throat. Rushing water followed. But it wasn't coming from a tap. Peter stared at the wall and the sound of pee splashing into the toilet bowl on the other side echoed behind the plasterboard.

A minute passed, or maybe longer, Peter wasn't too sure, when the neighbour's toilet flushed and the tick of the clock crept back in.

Ticking.

Always ticking.

This was its final warning now. But there was something else in the apartment calling for his attention. Something stronger and even more persistent. Cooper's rucksack. Peter stared at the rucksack and the rucksack stared back.

The main compartment was stuffed full of Cooper's clothes. But not the side pockets. And the rucksack had plenty of those. A dozen little compartments with room for a dozen zipped-up secrets. Peter ran his teeth over his bottom lip and the word *Timberdark* seemed to strain beneath the rucksack, teasing to be found. Anything could be in there. A plan. A map. The location of a government building Cooper planned on targeting.

Peter stood over the bag. He could shake out its contents. He could scramble on hands and knees for the thing that was keeping them apart and put an end to this right now. He didn't know what he'd be looking for, but it was likely to be small. Small things to hide big secrets. A slip of paper. A note. Peter crouched down, hungry to tear the bag apart. But it was no good. Whatever it was, that word was stronger than he was. And it would win. He'd merely drag it out by the scruff of its neck and a whole other life, the life Cooper lived parallel to the one they shared, would look up at him grinning and quietly tell him to go away.

The microwave pinged. Peter didn't even recall turning it on, and yet there it was. His porridge. He pulled the bedroom door to, just so Cooper's stuff would stop looking at him and quietly made his way back into the front room. When the clock finally reached nine, the time listed in the welcome pack that the supermarket opened, the porridge had hardened into cold sludge. Peter pushed it aside and quietly made his way out into the snow.

166

The supermarket sat beneath the foothills at the edge of town. A parking lot, vast and white like the lake in winter, stood between Peter and a long glass window where a row of cash tills had been stationed. Cars, domed with snow, sat in gridded formation across some of the lot. Peter supposed that most of them had been here since the world before. Icicles caked their exhaust pipes with banks of snow that flanked the wheels right up to the chassis. Further out across the lot, a pack of shopping trolleys stood stranded and exposed. They were huddled one inside the other, the way buffalo do out on the plains when finding warmth in each other's bodies. A short way away from the pack, one of the trolleys had come undone. It lay on its side all alone with the ribs of its metal carcass completely buckled. Pawprints led away from its skeleton. Bears were in hibernation. Wolves, perhaps. The prints led back across the lot up into the hills beyond. Peter looked up, taking in those dark places beneath the snowy pines where any beast could be watching him, and for a moment recalled the roughness of Cooper's hands touching him. He could see them now too, reaching back from his place on the saddle, with those blond hairs flat across the back like dry summer grasses, to stroke his inner thigh as they rode. Rising blood flooded Peter's body, making his racing heart pump. He ran across the lot, swinging his arms about him to gain good traction in the snow, and stood gazing up at the hills, panting. But he couldn't chase that memory to make it come any closer. He scoured the pines for a wet muzzle or a pair of turquoise eyes, pierce and hunting. But there was nothing, and a moment later, the blood drained from his limbs and all memory of Cooper's touch had gone again.

The double doors to the supermarket opened all by themselves. Just when Peter was looking for something on the glass he could push, they parted in the middle, and simply let him in. Peter crossed the threshold, stamping snow from his boots on the large welcome mat that lay beyond the entrance, and smiled. The window at the front of the store was easily ten cash tills wide, with as many aisles opposite it running the length of the store all the way to the back. A set of shiny cardboard stars dangled over the tills, highlighting the store's many discounts. Their glossy sheen struck like headlights every time they spun towards the window. Peter unzipped his parka to release some of the heat and noticed a girl in a green tabard seated at one of the tills looking at him. Peter offered a smile and waved, but the girl's face was unmoved by either joy or disdain. The smile dropped from Peter's face and the girl looked back down again. It was only now that he heard the music. He'd only ever heard live stuff before, sung or played by a fiddle on the lake. But this was different. 'Jingle Bells' was playing on speakers, but the store was so cavernous, the notes seemed to swim, colliding into each other woozily like an echo.

Peter took a step back, suddenly unsure of how he felt being in a room so big you wouldn't even call it a room any more. He turned back, watching the snow tumble in thicker drifts now against the large front window. The greying sky was luminous over the parking lot, making daylight at the front of the store seem harsher somehow. Fringes of black clouds glowed like silver. A blizzard was coming, he overheard an old couple say as they scurried in through the double doors shaking the snow from the ears of their trapper hats. One of the women was angry with the other for making them go outside in this weather. She rolled her hooded eyes at Peter, seeking solidarity with him, then broke into a gruff smile. Peter smiled back, taking comfort in that fleeting exchange, and quickly made the decision to stay. But the music changed to a tune he didn't recognize, so he turned into the aisle lined with multicoloured cereal boxes and started to look around for Cooper.

The welcome pack boasted of the supermarket's fully recreated 'Shelves Galore Just Like Before'. And they weren't kidding. There were as many things stuffed inside boxes all stuffed up on shelves as there were lights over Mainstreet. Just above Peter was a row of cereal boxes decorated with a cartoon of what looked like a chipmunk wearing a sheriff's outfit. *Kellogg's Sugar Pops.*

The chipmunk, or whatever it was, was called Sugar Pops Pete. His candy stripe pistol blasted a bowl of cereal, filling it with milk.

What had been looted all those years ago had surely been replaced three times over. There was vegan, gluten-free, sugar-free, completely free of colourings. Half-cal, low-cal, no-cal and finally *All-cal, Go Treat Yourself, Extra Maple Syrup Sugar Pops*. Peter drew a deep breath and quietly nodded to the chubby little chipmunk. Enough.

He made his way along the back of the store, passing among the cooler cabinets full of beer and soda, checking each aisle in turn. What if Cooper didn't want to talk to him? Perhaps he should've run out after him last night. Maybe that was the only reason he didn't look back. He was testing him and Peter had failed.

Peter cleared the back of aisle three, passing rows of tinned mullet, but there was still no sign of Cooper. Perhaps he hadn't even checked in for work this morning. He'd probably been up all night with Becky. That girl knew how to drink and now she had a drinking buddy and a place to find the stuff. Maybe they'd found a station wagon somewhere and driven it up into the hills where they sat on the hood popping beer cans off a fence all night long the way his dad always described in movies. Or perhaps it was none of those things. They were just indoors somewhere they couldn't be overheard, talking about what to do next now the Ghost Ranger was on to them.

Peter ran his hand across the back of his neck to catch a bead of sweat before it could drip any further and considered taking a bottle of Budweiser from one of the cabinets to cool himself. But it was only now he realized that the store had gone quiet. He hadn't really taken much notice of the squeak of the shopping trolleys as their wheels turned a corner, or the clatter of baskets being stacked down by the main entrance until they weren't there any more, but the silence they left behind was powerful enough to make you stop and listen. Storm clouds hanging over the parking lot were reflected in the glass-fronted doors to the cooler cabinets. Peter watched them pass behind his own reflection and the store darkened further. The cardboard stars dangling over the cash registers suddenly drifted sideways as if pulled by an invisible hand. They swung back into place and fell still again. A draught was coming from the front doors, no doubt. But something heavier than a passing wind hung over the store. He pressed his fingertips against the cabinet. The glass was shivering. The beer bottles started to jostle and clink. Peter turned round, looking down the length of the aisle at the snow driving into the store's front window. A moment later it came.

The blizzard leaned into the building, blasting it with snow. Peter dropped to his knees, pressing his back to a cabinet. Snow clouds hurtled over the building and the light and the dark swarmed across the ceiling.

It roared.

It blasted.

Outside, shopping trolleys hurtled past the front window, snaking out across the lot in their chain. The chain broke and the ones left behind clattered on to their sides, driving nose first into one of the cars. The sky over the parking lot was so luminous now that the snow appeared grey like ash inside it. Snowflakes as thick as leaves pummelled the glass, and soon you couldn't even make out the cars on the lot or the little red-brick buildings of Mainstreet beyond. But just as quickly as the blizzard had taken hold of the supermarket, it stopped.

The cardboard stars spun violently in place. Round and round. Then nothing.

There was sudden silence. Snow continued to pummel the large front window, pushed by the wind, but the blast subsided and a moment later the clink of the beer bottles butting into each other stilled. Peter pressed his hands to his knees ready to stand when a tin can rolled out of the adjacent aisle and bumped into the base of the cabinet next to him. Peter leaned over to pick it up. The label on the front said it was one hundred per cent quality salmon caught in

Alaska, and a natural source of omega-3, whatever that was. The pink salmon painted on the front of the label certainly looked one hundred per cent leaping over the mountains, but Peter wasn't too sure you could say that about the poor thing squished up inside. Still, it must've slipped from someone's shopping basket, so he made his way towards the next aisle when someone behind him cleared their throat. Peter turned. The two elderly women in the trapper hats were huddled into the corner at the back of the store. Peter offered a smile, glancing up towards the ceiling to reassure them that the storm was passing. But the one with the gruff face nervously shook her head to indicate it wasn't the storm she was afraid of, but rather something else behind him. Peter looked round. There was nothing there. Just the empty supermarket. When he turned back, the two women had gone.

There were hurried whispers coming from the front of the store. The sound of people running on soft feet. The double doors opened. The cardboard stars stirred. People ran back out across the lot in hurried numbers and the doors closed. They didn't move again.

Everyone had fled the building. The store was completely silent now. But inside that silence was a presence. Peter had felt it once before, that night Bud first took him out on to the mainland, when the deer fled the woods and all birdsong vanished from the boughs. The pines held their breath for the thing that was walking among them. Peter did the same now and quietly acknowledged the presence of death on the other side of the aisle from him. But he'd learned a lot since then, and more on the trail this last month with Cooper, and even though he knew the town borders were patrolled by Returnees, his fingers felt for the sheath he kept in his parka pocket and withdrew it. Reassured, he quietly turned into the aisle.

Cooper stood motionless in the middle of the aisle facing the shelves like a toy that had wound down midwalk. His head was low on his shoulders so his blond hair spilled across his face. He'd been stacking shelves with the same tinned salmon as the one that'd rolled away. But his arms hung heavy at his sides and he made no effort to retrieve the lost can. He didn't do anything at all. Cooper's fingers twitched and Peter's heart bucked against his chest. There were the same beautiful coarse hands that had held his. There was the same chest, defined beneath his white T-shirt, rising and falling. The same forearms with their fleecy blond hair. Peter had kissed and touched them all in turn to tell each and every part of Cooper that it was beautiful, the way he'd done for him. Only now they were attached to something he didn't know.

Those two dark eyes peered out from behind the tendrils of hair. But just like back in the ravine, something was wrong with them. On a starry night out on the trail, Peter only had to gaze down at Cooper to see the night sky. Those two dreaming pools were fathomless mirrors, full of stars. Now they were as dead as fish eyes.

"Cooper," Peter whispered. "Coop."

Cooper's fingertips twitched. But it wasn't at hearing his own name being called. More like a dog dreaming. Peter inched forward. But something changed. Cooper's jaw clenched and the skin shielding it moved in knotted rhythms following the grinding bone beneath. Peter attempted to whisper Cooper's name again, but the word stayed inside his lips and all desire to reach out and touch him was replaced by an altogether different sensation. Fear. Peter glanced down, watching the white of his knuckles burn across the handle of the blade, and the blood came pumping to his temples.

He was so close he could smell Cooper's scent now. And it was so sweet and familiar that his heart ached to find something it recognized so deeply. But it was the only thing. Everything else held danger. Those hard hands, like the blades of a paddle that had held him so tenderly, were no longer his. That beautiful face that knew only their kisses, was no longer his. Peter shuffled forward and Cooper's name broke across his lips.

"Cooper," he called. "Cooper, don't."

But Cooper was completely unmoved by Peter's voice.

An appalling amount of drool poured from his lips. The chest started to heave in quick succession and his breathing accelerated.

Panting. Panting. Panting. Panting.

Peter stepped forward. "Stop it."

Panting. Panting.

"Please, Cooper. Stop it."

Panting. Panting. Panting. Panting. Panting.

"I said, stop it!"

Enough. Peter reached out, clasping Cooper by the shoulder. But something other than Cooper struck back. There was a sudden convulsion. Abrupt. Violent. Like every blood cell had come rushing to the surface of Cooper's flesh to expel the sudden intrusion.

Cooper struck Peter.

Peter tumbled backwards striking first the shelving, then the floor. Tin cans tumbled. A bottle smashed. He tucked his knees up under his chin making himself as small as he could and braced both hands across his head. The thought of looking up to see Cooper standing over him with those dark eyes all bottomless and unseeing was unbearable. And he should run. Peter scrambled to his feet, bolting back down the aisle. He didn't look back. He didn't dare. The double doors flung open and he ran back inside the flurrying snow.

13

The blizzard came in from every direction. Peter leaned into the wind, holding his hand up to shield his face, and staggered on to the lot. But the air was so thick with pummelling snow, it smothered any features that could guide him back through, and soon the cars and all the shopping trolleys vanished inside the white and he had no way of knowing which way was forward and which was back.

He staggered on. He stopped. He yanked the hood of his parka up over his head, swiping snowflakes from his eyelashes and waited for the silhouette of a car or building to give up its location. There was nothing. But the darker skies must've activated the streetlamps across town. A tiny light appeared in the distance, pulsing from inside the snow like a fallen star. Peter recognized it as being one of the streetlamps at the end of Mainstreet and was about to set off towards it when something heavy landed with a thud directly in front of him.

A speckled wing stuck up from the snow. Peter couldn't tell if it was twitching because the bird was still fighting for its life or if it was merely flailing in the wind, but it was almost as if the little wing was waving for him to come help it. He ran up to the bird, cradling both hands ready to lift it to safety. But it was no use. It had struck the ground with such force, there wasn't enough of it left intact. The poor loon's body was pulp.

"I'm sorry, little one," said Peter. "I'm so sorry."

He crouched down, trying to get purchase on a substantial enough part of the body that he could put it somewhere more private, when it happened again.

Another bird struck the lot. It dropped from the sky at such speed that its body imploded on impact. Snow on the ground surrounding the buckled wings was smattered with bits of gore. Then the poor bird's feathers loosened from the carcass. Without enough skin or body to hold on to, they simply let go, cast away with the wind. Peter stood over the carcass, but again, all semblance of a bird was gone.

There was a sudden *swoosh* and another bird drove into the concrete. And another. They seemed to disappear right inside it.

Another bird landed directly on top of one of the

shopping trolleys. Its beak jutted through a gap in the metal frame and the body fell still. Peter staggered back, gazing up into the clouds spiralling above him.

Clouds whipped and surged in luminous swells, transported by the scourging snow. It was so bright, Peter had to squint as if looking directly at the sun. There was a spot in the middle where the sky was grey and smudgy, like storm clouds full of rain just before the downpour. In a matter of seconds, the grey mass was closer. Then, Peter could make out individual bodies. It wasn't rain at all, but birds. And not just a few of them. Hundreds.

Panic ripped through him. There was nowhere to hide. Nowhere to scramble. Parked cars were banked with snow, making it impossible to crawl underneath them. Shopping trolleys that had rolled out across the lot were nowhere to be seen. He turned back, looking for the entrance to the supermarket, but there was nothing but the blizzarding snow. Peter spotted the streetlamp at the edge of town and was about to make a run for it when a shaft of light broke across his feet, followed by a loud screech. A car door opened. Footsteps pounded. Someone grabbed him by the waist and before Peter knew it, his feet had left the ground and his body was dragged backwards.

Sheriff O'Hurn bundled Peter into the Jeep, his eyes all ablaze with hurried expressions like *Move!*, *Scooch over* and *Brace yourself.* But there was no time for the actual words or any niceties. He shoved Peter across to the passenger seat, clambering in after him, and quickly shut the door behind them. He grabbed the steering wheel. But he didn't reach for the ignition to drive them away to safety. The keys jangled in place and the sheriff closed his eyes. Peter fell back into his seat, staring out across the bonnet, and the rest of the birds followed.

A hundred loons drove into the concrete. Peter recoiled and a dozen bodies pummelled the hood. Blood splattered the windscreen. The Jeep jolted on its chassis. But the attack was over in seconds. In one swift move, the birds plunged to their deaths and the parking lot fell still.

14

The figurine of a little girl in a grass skirt with flowers in her hair jiggled on top of the dashboard. The motion of the car caused the toy to move at the hip, and even though she was only made of plastic and her painted features had been applied too crudely to be pretty, her little dance had a kind of enchantment about it. Peter watched her for a while, wondering what magical land she had come from and, if it were real, how they'd coped with the Dead, and for a few moments at least he forgot his worries for Cooper. But after a while, the girl stopped dancing, making her smile seem even more fixed, and Peter became aware of a sharp pain in his hand. He looked down, releasing the tight grip he had on the door handle, then remembered to breathe. The sheriff leaned forward, pulling the trapper hat from his head to wipe condensation from the windscreen, and gazed up into the rolling skies.

"Well, I'll be."

Peter cleared his throat and said nothing.

"You all right, son?"

"Yeah."

"You sure?"

"I think so. Is it over?"

"Yup," said the sheriff. "I reckon they're just about cooked, all right."

"They just came clean out of the sky."

"That they did."

"But why?"

"Well, they ain't called loons for nothin'."

"They came for us."

"Now, don't be getting all jumpy on me."

"But—"

"Birds seeking shelter from a storm try to find open water is all."

"But they—"

"They weren't to know the parking lot weren't no lake," said the sheriff, pulling a Thermos flask out from under his seat. "Especially when the cars are under so much snow. Accidents like this used to happen all the time in urban areas."

"They did?"

"Yup. As if it wasn't enough that we took up so much of their space, we made parking lots as big as Lake Titicaca to confuse the hell out of 'em. It's sad but it's no reason to be scared. Bears don't wander into folks' swimming pools because they're looking to attack us and birds don't divebomb parking lots because they're coming for us neither. They're just confused about where their home is."

The sheriff unscrewed the Thermos, setting the lid upside down on the dashboard to make a cup, and Peter looked out across the lot towards the supermarket where the cash tills were visible again behind the drifting snow. Perhaps Cooper had the same problem: he just didn't know where home was. Peter started to fiddle with the car lock, pulling and pushing the plastic stick from its hole, and let the thought that Cooper might just be lost in new surroundings comfort him when the alternative was too much to even contemplate. And even though he didn't voice his worries, the sheriff sighed, like the matter at hand was already known somehow, and quietly sat round in his seat.

"You've seen it, then?" he asked. "You've seen the trance."

Peter clenched his jaw and pushed down on the lock again. Great. They already had a word for it.

"What is it?" he asked after a while.

"Nobody knows, son. But he's not the only one. It's happening across town to a number of our Returnees, and although folks are doing their best not to be alarmed when they've had no reason to be before now, I'm sure you can understand it's hard for them not to be. It's hard for everyone."

"Everyone?"

"Yes. Everyone."

Peter nodded and the snow continued to fall. "The government."

"Yes, Peter. Them too."

The sheriff poured some coffee into the cup and passed it over. "Here, get some of this down ya. I reckon you're in more shock than a cowboy's crotch on rodeo day."

"He was just standing there, though."

"I know."

"He wasn't hurting anyone."

"I know, son. But—"

"He wasn't hurting anyone."

"No?" said the sheriff. "And yet you ran out here."

Peter touched his neck, rolling spots of oily blood between his fingertips where Cooper had nicked him. He shoved his hand under his lap and said nothing.

"All we know is that they haven't hurt anyone yet. And I know how that sounds, Peter. Believe me, I do. But I also know that the government have got a job on their hands keeping their civilians safe. And, yes, I also know that the Returnees are civilians too, who, if what happened to them over at your place is anything to go by, need protection more than anyone else. I know all these things. I know all these things and I don't have the answers. Not a damned single one of 'em. I just have a flask of coffee and a lot of people to keep happy and safe here while we try and figure it all out."

Peter stroked the back of his hand, finding strange comfort in that touch, even though it was only his own, and the pair of them sat in silence looking out over the lot. The smile on the little dancing girl didn't fade once.

"She's from Hawaii," said the sheriff watching him. "Well, that thing's probably from China but you get the idea."

"Hawaii's in the sea, right?"

"That's right, son. A whole bunch of islands out there in the Pacific. They were the last territory to become part of the United States."

"What united them? The states, I mean."

"Oh, the same stuff that usually unites places."

"Love?"

The sheriff let out a short laugh. "War."

Peter looked away, feeling the familiar prickle of embarrassment to have been the one not to have understood the joke. But the sheriff cleared his throat, as if the shame at having found amusement in a word as precious as *love* was all his.

"War from other countries?" Peter asked after a while.

The sheriff toyed with his handlebar moustache like that would've at least made sense somehow. "No, just war," he said. "War among ourselves. There were territories still left outside of the United States that the United States wanted, so we did what we always do. We came along and took 'em."

"Like my people did to Lake Wranglestone."

"I guess." Then, "Yes, son. Something like that."

Peter blew on the coffee to cool it and took a sip. It tasted bitter. Not half as nice as he'd expected it to, given that half the world had been taken over by coffee shops, before. But that many people couldn't be wrong, he decided, so he took another sip and tried to find a way into liking it.

"Now," said the sheriff, screwing the cap back on. "Teddy likes you."

"Oh."

"And there's no point me being coy on the matter, so I hope you can forgive his poor old dad for saying so."

"Yes, but—"

"And I know his constant pointing and naming things ain't gonna be to everybody's taste when I'm sure most folks don't need toilet-roll holders spelled out to them, but he's got a heart of gold and he sure could do with a friend in this town."

Peter offered a smile. He just wasn't sure how much more of Teddy he could take. The sheriff shuffled round in his seat and sat there looking hopeful and after a while, there seemed to be no way out of it.

"Maybe he could show me the sights of Mainstreet?" Peter offered.

The sheriff beamed. "Crackin'. That's his favourite."

"Great."

"Followed by dinner at our place?"

"Err—"

Peter left a beat, a pause big enough for the sheriff to clock his reticence and realize the decent thing would be to spare him any further impositions. But the sheriff didn't take the hint and a moment later the pause became so big that Peter's reluctance to accept the invitation just seemed plain rude.

"Sure. I'd love to."

The sheriff winked. "Dandy. Well, that's all settled, then."

The sheriff wound the window down, shaking dregs of coffee from the cup. Snow fell so thickly over the parking lot that most of the dead birds had already been rounded off into rows of little white graves. The sheriff leaned into the door and for a moment Peter thought he was watching the lot transform into a graveyard, too. But his gaze had settled on the supermarket window and Peter felt the mood in the Jeep shift somehow.

"But what if, Peter?" said the sheriff darkly.

"But what if what?"

"What if the trance is only the beginning?"

Peter looked off into the hills, to those places beneath the pines where the boughs grew dark, and for the first time wondered what else Rider would've done that night if the lake hadn't acted against him. Would he simply have regained control of himself to push that plate of meat aside, or would something else have taken over those dark and boundless eyes and transformed his friend into a monster?

Animal. Beast. Fiend. Monster. Peter turned the words over in his head, finding a nauseous thrill in exploring them. Another word presented itself. A word no one ever used. Not even a word, just a single letter, the one banished to the very back of the alphabet and for good reason. Peter dug his fingernails into the palm of his hand, feeling shame to have made the same connections that Darlene and Henry had once made. He didn't want that thought. He didn't want that word anywhere near Cooper. But nobody else had put it there.

15

Peter wandered back down Mainstreet. The sheriff had offered him a ride back to the apartment, but Peter decided to take a walk and made his excuses before he could press him any further. At least, he presumed he'd done that. He had no memory of leaving the Jeep or crossing back across the parking lot. His feet had carried him so he could be left alone with his thoughts and he was halfway home, with the neon signs burning dully inside the veiling snow, before a set of rippling lights called out from the other side of the street and stopped him.

The marquee of the old movie theatre thrust out over the sidewalk. The underside was studded with hundreds of golden light bulbs that rippled in waves towards a glass-fronted ticket booth and two sets of double doors on either side. Like a hand beckoning you to come closer, it was as if the lights were tempting you to leave your troubles outside and join them. A billboard sat above the marquee. It was illuminated so the film's title, spelled out in big black capitals in front of it, seemed to announce itself. *IT'S A WONDERFUL LIFE*. Peter had never heard of it. It wasn't one Bud had told Cooper about as far as he was aware, and yet a whole world of possibilities lived inside those words alone. High above all this, a host of tiny amber light bulbs chased each other around the *Wranglestone Roxy* sign. Peter gazed up, wiping snowflakes from his lashes and smiled. It was easily the tallest sign in town. And merry. The little lights couldn't get enough of chasing each other, round and round. Round and round. Perhaps he and Cooper could come here one night. Call it a date. Apart from that night in the boathouse where they'd first kissed, they'd never had a date. Now, they could sit at the back of the movie theatre kissing and walk back home in the middle of the street hand in hand with neither one of them having the faintest clue what'd happened at the end of the movie, but with a neck full of hickies.

Peter looked back up the road towards the supermarket. They hadn't even said *I love you* since they got here. Or Cooper hadn't said it back, and sometimes, hearing it back was better than being the one to say it first. Hearing Cooper say *I love you too* was like hearing the mountains echo your own voice. What bounced back was always so much bigger.

A sign on the door said to make all work enquiries in the manager's office next to the old popcorn stand. Peter shook snow from the trim of his hood and crossed the darkly lit lobby to the door on the other side. He gave a good *rat-a-tat-tat* and a flat voice, which didn't seem entirely appropriate to the occasion given the enthusiasm of his knocking, told him to come in.

A large woman, with a big doughy bosom squeezed up against her desk, gave a cursory glance and continued eating her popcorn.

"I've come to enquire about a position, miss," said Peter. "I don't have any direct experience working in an establishment like yours, but back on the lake where I come from, I used to chaperone islanders to the falls, so I know how to make people feel at ease even if I don't know them that well. I think I could transfer that skill to showing people to their seats in a warm and friendly way that'd make their custom here feel appreciated."

The woman picked a piece of popcorn off the shelf of her bosom and said nothing.

"And," said Peter, taking a seat, "if that's not enough for you, I know how to have conversations about movies even though I've never seen one because Cooper used to tell me all about the ones from before. So, there's that too."

The woman looked up, narrowing her eyes like she was in an incredible amount of pain, and said nothing.

Peter set his hands down across his lap and smiled. "I'm Peter. Peter Nordstrum."

"Kid, I just need someone to sit in the ticket booth and take out the trash once in a while."

"I'm good with trash too. But more than that, I—"

"It don't need to be more than that."

"Oh. Only I've got an eye for things looking tidy. I noticed that the carpet in the lobby's gotten threadbare. I can stitch that up. And I'm so used to my dad making a mess of things in the tree house, I'd have no problem going into the restrooms to clean them. I know what men are like when they're aiming for the tree and hit the grass."

"It's just a job."

"Oh, I know."

"It won't get you into the damned movie business."

Peter laughed, but he didn't know if he was being made fun of now. "No. I know that."

"You always talk too much or can you sit and be quiet?"

"No. I can do that too."

"For long hours at a time in the ticket booth?"

"Yes."

"Alone?"

"Yes. I'm a team player but I know how to motivate myself as an individual."

The woman picked more loose popcorn from her shirt and ate it. "Jesus, kid. Where'd they get you from?"

"Wranglestone."

"Yes, I—Look, never mind."

The woman sank back into her chair and not for the first time in his life, Peter felt the presence of another person tolerating him.

"I'm Peter."

"I'm exhausted."

"Sorry. I've already said that."

Peter cleared his throat, hoping the woman would remember her manners enough to share her name with him. But she merely glanced at her chest to point out the sheer stupidity of introducing herself when a name badge was there for all to see, and hoisted herself up out of the chair.

Peter smiled. "Hello, Marge."

"Come," said the woman, leading Peter back out through the lobby. "I'll show you the ticket booth."

"Do I get to wear a special uniform?"

"If a T-shirt with a dickie bow printed on it is special."

"And carry a torch?"

"And serve ice creams from a tray around your neck during intervals?"

"Really?"

Marge raised an eyebrow.

"Oh," said Peter. "You're joking."

A thin red curtain masked the ticket booth which

was barely bigger than an upright canoe and fronted by glass that bowed out on to the sidewalk beneath the marquee above. Marge stood to one side, holding the curtain back so Peter could squeeze in next to her and take a seat on the high chair. The curtain fell back into place behind her. It smelled of cigarettes. It must've been years since someone had last smoked in here, but the stale scent of nicotine had worked its way into the skin of the curtains as strongly as an old smoker's fingers. In fact, once you were sealed in, the booth was so airless and unchanged, with its clump of old gum stuck to the metal base of the chair and bits of food stuck in the cash register, it was hard to imagine that any time had passed at all.

Peter swivelled the chair around from the register, pushing his fingers through a small slot in the glass to pretend he was exchanging money for tickets. He swivelled back again repeating the action a few more times when Marge cleared her throat.

"There are only so many times people can watch the same movie," said Marge. "So, don't expect it to be busy."

"Oh," said Peter. "OK. So, what do I do?"

"You sit here looking open."

"Do I take a note of how many people come in?"

"Sure. Whatever you want."

"I'll do that, then."

Marge gave a cursory nod. "You do know this is all there is to it?"

"What, the job?"

"Sure."

"Yes. I know."

"Trick is to keep yourself busy."

"Why is that a trick?"

"You'll need to know how to pass the time."

"It'll probably be more exciting when the theatre's open."

Marge shrugged. "Sure."

She reached up to a shelf just above the curtain and her belly grazed Peter's knee. She passed Peter a mug and a scrunched up old T-shirt and stepped out of the booth. The T-shirt was dusty and wrinkled so Peter placed it across his lap and started to iron out the creases with the flat of his hand. He felt Marge watching him.

"You're real excited for this, aren't you?"

Peter looked up, suddenly unsure of why there was any embarrassment in saying yes.

"I've always wanted to work in a movie theatre."

"No, not that. Life before."

"I guess." Then, after a moment, "Yes, so much. But I know some of the people I grew up with loved it on the lake. When my dad didn't know I was there, I'd catch him standing outside the tree house, or down by the

195

water's edge, looking out across the water into the forests, wondering what was out there, what was coming, never knowing from one day to the next whether the Dead would find us or just the wind, and I think part of him secretly enjoyed it. Not just him either. Bud in his rocking chair. Mr Schmidt in his canoe. My dad never talked about it, no one ever did, and I guess admitting such a thing would disregard Mom's memory and all the other people the Dead took away from us. But underneath it all, there was a gladness for it. To be there on the lake, I mean. I don't know why. But not me. No. I was never cut out for it."

"And what are you cut out for?"

Peter shook his head. "A quiet life, I guess."

Marge mumbled something under her breath.

"You know?" said Peter. "Qualifications, prospects, a job and a home with nice things to show for it."

"Is that right?"

"Yes."

"Sounds like you got it all figured out."

"Maybe." Then, "Yes. I've thought a lot about it. Why?"

Marge shook her head. "No reason."

But there was an edge in her tone, a distaste for his excitement even, that Peter couldn't place. He continued flattening the T-shirt across his lap and an awkward silence passed between them. Perhaps Marge had lost loved ones back then as most people had at the advent of the new world and the thought of returning to normal held too many ghosts for her. Peter swung his chair round, looking out on to the street. As far as he was concerned, the world that was before had always been a fantasy, stolen away from him by the cruel timing of his birth. But for many, he supposed, the past must just be a graveyard.

Peter turned back. "I hope I haven't said anything to offend you."

"Your excitement gets wearing."

"Sorry, I was just trying to—"

"You get sixty dollars a day after tax. Half an hour for lunch; unpaid."

"OK."

"You won't do nothing either side of that lunch but you'll sit here just the same."

Peter nodded.

"And then you'll come back again tomorrow and do it all over again."

"Yes, but if you do want me to do more. . ."

"It won't be more than that."

"But—"

"I said it won't be more."

Peter looked away. He wanted to point out that the offer to stitch the lobby carpets back together was still there just in case Marge had thought he was only trying to impress her for his interview. But he thought better of it.

"Thank you for taking me on."

"Sure."

"It's a wonderful oppor—"

"Kid, take a break, will ya?"

"But I've only just started. Oh, you mean from talking. Yes, but if I have any questions I'll know where to find you."

"I don't doubt it."

Peter offered a smile. But the induction was over. The curtain swished back into place and Marge's footsteps schlepped back across the lobby. Peter stared at the red curtain for a moment. She probably just needed a nice invite for dinner. Most people were nicer when they were made to feel wanted. But he needed to get on so he told himself he would work on her later.

Peter folded his parka and sweater neatly under the chair and started to change into his work T-shirt when he stopped.

He swept the curtain aside. "Do you think I'm stupid for being excited?"

Marge stopped just short of her office. Her hand fell away from the door handle and the weight of her entire body seemed to exhale every last bit of patience she had left in her.

"No," she said without turning round. "Now go back inside."

"Why do you think my dad was glad for the lake?"

"It isn't for me to say."

"But—"

"I ain't never met him."

"No," said Peter. "But in your opinion."

Marge stood with her back to Peter a moment and her thick shoulders heaved heavily beneath the strain of her shirt like the question had more weight to it than was necessary.

"I can't speak for your father," she said. "But maybe, when death is coming for you, you live."

"But fighting the Dead was never living, it was survival."

Marge's hand paused over the door handle. "Survival don't just look like a bloodied knife in your hand."

"Why, what else does it look like?"

But Marge didn't answer that. She made her way back inside her office as if to draw a close to the conversation and quietly shut the door behind her.

Peter corrected the T-shirt so it fell neatly around his waist and stepped back inside the booth. Marge was wrong. Living wasn't waiting for the ice to form a scab around the edge of the lake knowing that when it'd completely sealed over, anything could reach you. The Returned had put an end to that kind of living, of just surviving, of just making it through. Now they had a chance to live. Peter sat with that idea for a little while when difficult thoughts of Cooper crept back in. Difficult thoughts followed difficult words. Not even a word. Just that one letter he'd banished to the back of the alphabet again. His throat became tight so he looked at the black slushy snow on the sidewalk outside the booth. It made the entrance seem dirty. A bucket of water would probably turn to ice if he tried to sluice it away, so Peter had a look inside the alcove beneath the cash register and found a cloth for the window instead.

It took some effort to remove the clump of old gum on the base of the chair, but eventually he got that off. Bits of food stuck inside the register fell away with a good shake too and eventually the booth was as clean as it could possibly be without washing the curtains or stitching the piece of ragged carpet beneath the base of the chair, torn by too much friction. Peter shuffled in the chair and swivelled around. He didn't manage to complete a full circle so he pushed off with a heavier shove and it spun all the way around. He was about to have another go when he noticed that one of the rippling light bulbs underneath the canopy had bust. He stared at the bulb and the bulb stared back. How annoying. There was probably a spare one and a ladder somewhere inside the theatre, but he thought better of wandering off to look for one and instead angled the chair so the bulb no longer caught his peripheral vision.

An hour passed before anyone walked by. But the old lady in the trapper hat wasn't on her way to the movies and walked directly in front of the ticket booth without even noticing Peter sitting there. He lifted his fist to the window to say hello.

He'd make Cooper a tasty dinner tonight. That's what he'd do. There was some cutlery back in the apartment, plates and placemats for the dining table too. He'd make it look nice. Set the scene. Then, if there was time, he could wander out of town a little, not too far, but just enough to find some pine cones and fir branches so the place felt like home. There was probably a vase in the apartment somewhere. But a bottle would do. And then they'd sit across the table from each other and share their news. He'd tell Cooper all about his exciting first day in the theatre with Marge, then Cooper would tell him all about his, about the trance, how frightening it was at first when he could feel something else inside him take him over. Then, how he fought it away. They'd take a walk after dinner. Kiss beneath the sparkling lights, then hurry back to the apartment and pounce on the couch. Their bodies. Their scent. All tangled up as one, kissing.

Peter stretched out a yawn, peering round the side of the booth to watch the old lady pass by. But she'd gone. It was darker outside now too. Snow covering the road was all blue in the twilight. But he'd only been smiling at the old lady just a few seconds ago, he was sure of it. Peter sat back and caught his own reflection in the glass. He looked anxious, drawn, even. He turned the corners of his lips up and watched his own face smiling back at him. But it was strange, like somebody else reassuring him of his own existence sitting there. He huffed on the glass to obscure the other Peter and swiped the mug up in his hand.

He made his way across the lobby to the tiny kitchenette next to Marge's office. He found a plastic kettle perched on top of the refrigerator because the lead was too short to place it on the work surface. There was some brown grit in a jar labelled *Coffee*, and one spoon sitting in the sink underneath a soggy teabag. Peter fished it out and ran it under the tap. Then he made his way out to Marge's office while the kettle was boiling and quietly knocked on the door.

"I don't mean to bother you," he said, "but I'm making a cup of coffee if you'd like one."

He held back at the door a moment. Nobody answered. Marge must've have gone to inspect the auditorium or something, so Peter made his way back towards the kitchenette when he briefly glanced back.

Marge's shadow passed beneath the gap under the door. For a moment, Peter thought she was crossing the office ready to join him. But she wasn't. Her shadow didn't move again. It just lay there. Peter felt a sting in his stomach and stepped back. Marge was just standing on the other side of the door waiting for him to go away. Peter glanced back across the lobby to the path of bare carpet between the entrance and the auditorium where feet had worn the pile down over the years. The auditorium. How he'd longed to see inside an auditorium. Ever since his dad first told him about the movies. Every time Cooper told him one of the stories. Every time other than now.

Peter's stomach started to ache. He didn't know he was so annoying that people would choose to hide from him. He didn't know he was one of *those* people. He didn't know he was a Teddy.

The kettle clicked.

Someone might be waiting to buy a ticket.

Peter made his coffee, hurried back to the booth and drew the curtain aside.

No one was there and Mainstreet was empty. He took his seat and sat a while beneath the ripple of the marquee lights, quietly watching the steam rising from his mug, and waited for a customer.

Shoulder deep, the canoe drifted among the tall grasses at the lake's edge. Peter drew the paddle up and water beaded down the length of the wood to gather in sparkling baubles at the blade. He plunged the paddle back down and pushed on.

Sunlight glittered across the golden water.

Warm winds whispered among the trees.

At the middle of the lake, where the air was thick with gossamer and purring dragonfly wings, something stirred. Cooper's bare buttocks and toes breached the surface and Peter pushed on into open water.

16

Cooper sat across the table from Peter in silence. Dad had taken pity on them for being two boys left alone to fend for themselves and kindly stocked the fridge up with a few home-made meals until they had a chance to settle in. Cooper's hair spilled in ropes over a plate of brown stuff called nut roast where he'd been hiding for the last ten minutes. They hadn't spoken since he left last night and he'd only offered a few grunts since he got back from the supermarket. Peter sat across the way from him wondering if this was how it all started going wrong. He'd been invited over to the Carmichaels' home on Bear Island on more than one occasion over the years. They used to make out they liked having young company around the place on account of them never having had children, but it became obvious in time that his being there gave them more than just another body to focus on, but someone to do all the talking for them when they were clean out of anything left to say to each other.

Peter lowered his knife and fork. "Do you want some water?"

Cooper pushed more of the brown stuff around his plate and said nothing.

"It's a little salty. I can get some if you want."

"S'OK," said Cooper. "It int too much."

"It was kind of Dad to do this for us but it might be easier with a glass of water."

"I said I liked it, dint I?"

Cooper glanced up through his hair and went to say something, an apology even, but nothing came out and a moment later he disappeared behind his hair again and Peter was left watching the snow falling across the window behind.

"I started at the movie theatre today," he offered.

"Oh yeah?"

"Yeah."

"How's that?"

"It was good, Coop. Marge, she's the manager there, made me feel so welcome. Gave me the guided tour and everything. She showed me the auditorium, projection room. Her office. I'm working in the ticket booth for now but she told me that if I continued to show this much promise, she couldn't see why I wouldn't make promotion to assistant manager in no time. I got a brand-new T-shirt, factory pressed, with a dickie bow on it and everything."

The corner of Cooper's mouth creased into a half-smile, like there was genuine pride there. But he didn't take his eyes off the plate.

"That's really somethin', Pete."

"Yeah. I can't wait to go back tomorrow."

"And it don't get too busy?"

"No. Not at all. Just enough so I don't get bored."

"And this manager won't be gettin' on your tail or nothin'?"

"No. I don't think so. I think she likes and trusts me. She largely stays in her office, anyways."

Cooper nodded like that could only be a positive. "Great. Cos she's on to a good thing with you."

"You think?"

"Of course, I think. Reckon she should be grateful to have you. Any of these people should be. So, if she winds up giving you shit, you tell me, OK?"

A smile welled in Peter's chest. "I don't think you'll need to take her out to the back of the barn and shoot her, but OK."

"I'm bein' serious, Pete. Pa said he never quit on a good job, not never. Only ever bad managers."

"OK."

"They gave him all kinds of shit over the years. Making him suffer just cos his readin' weren't so good. Lettin' him go just cos he got fired up a couple of times. The Dead got rid of most things but there's probably plenty of bad managers left in the world ready to come back again."

"Yes," said Peter. "Probably."

"But I'm proud."

"Oh yeah?"

Cooper nodded. He kept his head low so the tips of his hair swished across the gravy, and continued to push his food around without saying anything else. But his chest started to rise and fall swiftly beneath his T-shirt like he was working up to something, and a little while later, he lowered his fork.

"So, it was worth it, then?" he said. "Comin' back?"

Peter sat back in his chair. "Yeah." Then, "It'll only be worth it if you're happy too."

Cooper shrugged. "Reckon I'll be happy if you're happy."

"That's not how this works."

"But—"

"But what?"

"But I can get on with things as long as I know you're OK."

"But I don't want you to just be getting on with things," said Peter. "You have to be happy, too."

"Well, I don't know 'bout that."

"Well, I do."

"Pa said that the most you could hope for back then was to just get by."

Peter smiled. He could only imagine how difficult Bud would've been to manage. But he didn't have the heart to say it. They continued eating and the snow continued to fall when the nick on Peter's neck began stinging.

"Anyway," he said. "How was *your* day?"

"Oh, you know," said Cooper.

"No. I don't. Tell me."

"It was good."

"Oh yeah?"

Cooper shovelled a forkful into his mouth. "Uh-huh."

"Why? What happened?"

"I stacked stuff."

"Right. And?"

"I stacked stuff, Pete. What more do you want me to say about it?"

"Well, I don't know."

"Well, there you go, then."

"What kind of things did you stack?"

"Tins."

"OK. And?"

"And I stacked tins."

Cooper mopped gravy up with the last of the brown

wedges and shoved it in like there was nothing more to say about the day.

"So, nothing's wrong, then?"

"Nope," said Cooper. "Although the supermarket don't got no ventilation, so I reckon I might smell a bit funky."

Peter glanced at Cooper's sweat stains. If they'd been on the lake he probably would've made him wash that T-shirt down at the water's edge a dozen times over by now. But in these moments, when they were together but not together, distant and outside of each other trying to find a way back in, Cooper's scent might be the only part of him he could get close to.

Cooper lifted his arm up and took a sniff. "Yup. I honk."

"Why don't you put my Dolly Parton one back on? It's as good as yours now, anyway."

Cooper tucked his hair back behind his ear and nodded.

"Where is she?" Peter asked.

"In my rucksack still, I guess."

"I'll get her for you."

"No."

"It's OK, I don't mind."

"I said no."

Peter winced, shocked by how abrupt that had sounded. And Cooper must've realized it too. He set his knife and fork down deliberately as if trying to compose another reaction, a better reaction.

"Why?" Peter asked looking back towards the bedroom. "Is there something in there you don't want me to find?"

"Don't be dumb. I just don't wanna ruin your favourite tee or offend poor Miss Dolly."

"You wouldn't ruin it. And I expect she can handle some no-good stinking man."

"Oh yeah? And what 'bout you? What can *you* handle?"

"Coop, don't avoid the—"

"And what can you handle?"

Cooper sat up, at once present and broad inside his chair, with the devil's twinkle in his eye now his mind was taken over by flirting.

"I dunno," said Peter. "But Dolly Parton was nobody's fool. Besides, she only married once."

"Sounds 'bout right."

Peter smiled. "Is that so?"

Cooper pretended to draw on a cigar and tipped his chair back so the front legs left the floor.

"I int got no prospects to speak of, Master Peter," he said, "And your pa will likely have to bail me out of jail on more than one occasion on account of me being a wrongen n'all. But I must confess I want a marry ye."

"Why, Cooper Donaghue, is that so?"

Cooper blew a trail of hair from his lips. "Reckon so." He placed both hands behind his head so the hair beneath his armpits poked out beneath the sleeve of his T-shirt, and eased back into the chair yawning. There was a brightness in the depth of his dark eyes that hadn't been there for what felt like the longest time, and Peter was so relieved to see that he could still inspire those feelings, that the other part of him that knew Cooper was using his wiles to distract him from what he was hiding in the rucksack had no power to take over.

Cooper slipped further down in the seat now, so his crotch thrust further forward. His jeans were so worn out from years spent riding the saddle that sweat and good luck were the only things holding them together. Silence fell between them and the hairs on the back of Peter's neck stood.

Cooper was looking directly at him now. But not like you look at someone when manners forbid you from straying too far from the face, but when the other person is looking the other way and your eyes are free to roam elsewhere with wonder. Except he was doing this knowing full well that he was being watched. Peter's hands fell to his side and Cooper's eyes journeyed across his body, his chest, his lips, his crotch and hair, finding beauty in those nowhere places another person would never have even noticed, and loving them, wanting them and longing to make them his all over again. Peter's throat tightened and Cooper's gaze fell into his.

"Peter?" he whispered.

"What?" Peter asked.

"Nothin'. I just wanted to hear your name is all."

The sounds of the apartment and movement of snow at the window vanished, and they were in that secret place only the two of them knew. And that place might've been home and the journey back from the boathouse that night they first kissed, when the night sky was reflected so perfectly in the lake's black mirror, that the canoe wasn't even travelling across water but through air, cast adrift among the shimmering stars. But wherever they were, they were outside the real world, in a world of their own making where only they existed.

Peter blinked once, softly, to deepen their gaze and Cooper blinked back. They'd be all right. Peter could feel the reassurance of that now, swelling deeply inside him. Cooper would shake the trance from his skin. Peter would make up with Becky. Maybe the pair of them would move in with Dad and Marge would fling the movie theatre doors aside ready to make him assistant manager and everything would be all right just as it was supposed to be.

Cooper pushed the chair away from the table and stood with his arms at his side in a way that told Peter they were about to kiss.

"Where do you go?" Peter asked.

"Huh?"

Peter's throat tightened. He'd spoken before he'd even decided to mention anything.

"Where did you go when you were standing in the middle of the aisle? I was there today. In the supermarket. I saw you. You were there, but you weren't there. Where were you?"

Cooper's whole body seemed to sink. The twinkle in his eyes faded, like the dazzle of sunlight on water when dulled by clouds. He shoved the chair under the table and Peter watched him stand there, chewing over whether to pick a fight for watching him when he had no right to. Cooper's chest heaved. It was coming any moment now. The argument. But it never did. He looked to the window where the snow was falling and shrugged.

"Don't you remember anything?" said Peter, aware once more of the sting on his neck.

But Cooper pretended to take more interest in the view than was likely and Peter felt his instruction to drop the matter.

The clock ticked.

The snow kept falling.

Peter pushed the dinner plate away from him and looked up. "Am I going to lose you?"

Cooper looked back with his dark eyes all wide and full of fear. And Peter felt his closeness reaching out across the dining table like it had done that very first day in the tunnel beneath the car. His eyes told him *I love you, Pete.* It felt urgent, as if they'd never told him properly before now. Cooper sighed and Peter's name whispered across his lips. *Peter. Peter.* Peter's heart pounded and there was his name again. Not as it really was, weak and unassuming, but as it existed only inside Cooper. Precious. So very precious.

"Come to bed?" said Peter.

"I'm tired," said Cooper.

"Then, tell me the story to *Star Wars* again?"

"I think I'm just gonna go to bed, Pete."

"Why don't we go take a walk to the edge of town?" Then, "OK. If you're tired."

"I'm tired."

"Then go to bed."

Cooper quietly made his way into the bedroom but briefly held back at the door. "I'm real glad the movie theatre's all you hoped it'd be, Pete."

Peter clasped both hands tightly across his lap and nodded. "Yeah. Me too."

The bedroom door closed behind him and Peter was

left alone with the clock and the walls and the sound of the neighbour clearing his throat on the other side. And when, some time later, he too went to sleep, Cooper didn't stir to wish him good night and the space between the beds became a canyon.

17

Peter realized he was dreaming when he heard the loons. They never sang at night. Not in reality at least. But in this moment of half-sleep, their ghostly cry was so clear to him that he was able to feel the rest of the lake when the islands were so still; only the tickle of snow at the window disturbed them. Logs on the burner were crackling. There was his dad's gentle snore. Peter rolled over, drawing the duvet even tighter across his body and waited for the wolves to come. But their lonely call never broke across the mountains and the illusion didn't last.

He came to. The apartment's windowless bedroom was so dark, he wasn't sure whether, if he got out of bed and walked forward, he'd even find a wall, or just more darkness to pass through. Here, inside this room inside another room, away from the snow's comforting glow, there was no midnight world, only hollow silence and the faintest tick of the clock through the wall.

Peter stared into the darkness between his bed and Cooper's. He considered calling out his name just to be sure of him but decided against it. There was no point in the two of them being kept awake, so he let Cooper's name break into a sigh across his lips and waited for his eyes to adjust so that he could at least watch him sleeping. But a few minutes passed and Peter couldn't even see the bed, let alone make out which silhouetted mounds were duvet and which might be Cooper. He flopped his arm out of the side of the bed, fingering the air for the edge of the other mattress. The gap between the beds was too wide. He reached a little further and his fingertips grazed material with a cool sheen to the touch. Peter found the zipper to Cooper's rucksack and a thought surged like dread through the pit of his stomach. It would be easy to take it into the living room, right now while Cooper was sleeping.

Peter sat upright and the word *Timberdark* stirred from its hiding place in the darkness. It knew Peter was there. It knew he was close now. He pushed the duvet aside, bringing both feet down to the floor and stood. He was going to do it. His body had already made the decision for him. His breathing became heavy. Uncontainable. He opened his mouth, but every exhalation seemed louder than the last and enough now to wake Cooper. Peter hooked his finger through the hoop, lifting the rucksack from the floor and waited. The springs of Cooper's mattress didn't creak. He didn't even stir. But there was something else, just at Peter's side near the foot of the bed where the bedroom door would be. The hairs on the back of his neck stood up, alerting him to the presence of danger and he turned. Inside the darkness of the doorway, came breathing.

18

Cooper was watching from the darkness. There was no silhouette to mark his body out from the door, or any source of light to spark a glint in his eyes, but Peter could feel them on him all the same. He lowered the rucksack to the floor as if preparing for the argument that would follow now Cooper had caught him with it. But he knew it wasn't *that* Cooper he was alone with right now. The Cooper watching him from the darkness wasn't going to express anger or disappointment in Pete for betraying his trust. This Cooper didn't know those things. But any relief Peter had felt that his actions had gone unnoticed didn't last. He was with Cooper but he wasn't with Cooper at all. Like in the supermarket, he was alone with something else entirely.

Peter inched back until the bedframe tapped his calves. He pictured himself scrambling underneath it for safety just like he used to do whenever the Dead would pass beneath the tree house when wandering from one part of the forest to the other. When he was growing up, his dad did everything he could to reassure him that they had no ability to climb ladders let alone open doors. But that didn't stop him from spending whole nights underneath the bed praying he wouldn't hear that familiar shuffle of their feet across the floor.

Peter dropped to his knees. He felt for the frilly valance covering the bed frame, patting the floor underneath just in case any boxes had been stored there to block his hiding place. There was nothing. He was about to crawl under when Peter was struck by a strange absence. He couldn't hear Cooper's breathing any more.

The bedroom door was ajar. Peter hadn't even heard the handle turn. It was just open. Bluish light at the doorway struck a path to Peter's knees, illuminating patches of bare weave in the carpet. But the front room was dim. The neon lights of Mainstreet were out for the night. Only the veil of snow falling past the bay window made silhouettes of the dining table and couch. There was silence. But there was no Cooper.

Peter stood at the bedroom door. His eyes travelled across the walls, taking in the rectangles of darker wood where the picture frames and television set used to be, almost expecting one of them to be shaped like a Cooper. But he wasn't one of those either. Peter crossed into the front room, noticing how the softness of the carpet changed to the tacky sheen of the floorboards against the soles of his feet. But his eyes remained forward.

The clock made its presence known, ticking quietly at his shoulder. The refrigerator purred. But Peter was almost glad of the company. Cooper wasn't in the kitchenette either. A draught brushed across his ankles and he turned. The front door was open. He hadn't heard the handle turn. It was just open.

Peter stood at the window, hands pressed to the glass, watching the street below. There was nothing but snowed-up cars and the night. And footprints. A deer's perhaps, or a wolf's. Maybe the animals had wandered into this world while Cooper had wandered into theirs. Peter looked again. One of the footprints was human. Not booted, but bare, with the pad of the foot and five little indents in the snow, one for each toe. He turned back towards the hallway and saw Cooper's boots still standing there. His toes would freeze then turn as black as charcoal if he stayed out there too long. If he was even out there. Perhaps the feet belonged to one of the Dead. Perhaps there was no difference now – the Dead and the Returned made one at night, free to stalk the streets, free to roam the Earth while the rest of the world slept. Peter's stomach swilled, guilty to have had another thought like Darlene's. He moved along the bay, following the footprints, watching them tail off inside the hurrying snow further up Mainstreet. It was almost as if Cooper had been right there but not there at all. Like the rectangles on the wall, the footprints were merely an echo of something that once was. An imprint. A memory. A ghost.

The canoe's red paint, now full of heat, blistered beneath the burn of the midday sun. Blue jays swooped down from the forest's gleaming pines to drink. Bull elks took to the shore. Peter waited in the middle of the lake and something slipped beneath the hull of the canoe.

Cooper's body rippled in broken prisms beneath the surface.

The blades of his back flexed.

His body twisted.

Thick hair beneath his armpits and navel ebbed inside the lake's dark waters and Peter stood. He heaved the paddle out of the water, propping it up against the thwart of the canoe and stripped down to his undershorts. Cooper swam on and Peter plunged into the depths after him.

Currents of surging water fizzed across the soles of Peter's feet, travelling up between his legs to his groin and buttocks. He thrust his legs downward, breaking through the surface of the lake and his body crested.

Cooper rose up out of the water, his birch-white skin luminous in the glow of the sun, and made strides towards the middle of a tiny island where a log cabin stood. He briefly turned back, making sure he was being followed, then slipped inside the island's wooded chamber. Peter smiled, taking giant stokes out across the water and swam on towards land.

19

The next day at the movie theatre passed pretty much like the one before. Marge's shadow hovered at the door to her office while Peter waited for the kettle to boil. He could practically feel her praying for him to go away, so he rinsed the one spoon with a soggy teabag and thought about seeing Dad that evening after work. But not yet. Not until everything was OK with Cooper. Not until he could be sure everything was perfect.

The kettle boiled and Peter took his mug back to the ticket booth. But nobody came for the matinee and his reflection kept staring at him like it had higher hopes for the pair of them, so he took an early lunch and paid a visit to the Old Western Outfitters store across town where bronze stirrups and cowboy boots with intricately decorated flowers scored into the leather stood proud in the window. He bought a neckerchief for Cooper ticketed at $90 from the nice old man with a gap in his teeth that whistled every time he said 'Stetson', and made his way up to the supermarket. But he didn't enter.

Peter crossed the parking lot, picking his way past the dead birds that'd turned into clumps of frozen carrion overnight, and stood some distance from the large front window. Rows of brown-paper packing bags half-filled with groceries stood deserted at the foot of the cash tills. The clerks had abandoned their stations. Some of the customers had already run for safety and gathered outside by the dumpsters. Others, trapped on the other side of aisle five from the door, huddled in small groups down the adjacent aisles, peering round occasionally on the off-chance that help was on its way.

In the middle of all this was Cooper. He wasn't moving. Like yesterday, he stood motionless in the middle of the same aisle with both arms limp at his sides, head lolled forward and inclined towards the shelves. Two yellow signs warning *Caution, wet floor* had been stationed down either end of the aisle to cordon it and Cooper off from the rest of the store, like the situation was just an accident waiting to be cleared up. But everything about that dormant state was dangerous.

Peter's dad had told him that once, when he was six, he'd rushed down to say hello to a stranger who'd appeared at the foot of the island looking out over the frozen lake. The man didn't take any notice of Peter jumping up and down up to say hello. Nor did he turn round when he was invited to make snow angels. It was only when Peter took him by the hand and that stone-cold thing bolted round with swivelling eyes to take him into his mouth that he realized how like the living the Dead could be. Peter thought back to what Essie had said about the Returned being able to mimic and shuddered. But she was wrong and she was dead and he wished so very badly that those thoughts would just die with her.

Peter stood on the lot shivering, barely noticing the snow flurrying into his face. After a while Sheriff O'Hurn came, looking first at Cooper through the large front window and then back across the lot directly at him with the same troubled expression and that word *Timberdark* blazing in his eyes. But Peter had nothing to offer the sheriff, so he hurriedly turned away and made his way back towards the movie theatre.

He was halfway down Mainstreet, passing the diner with the busted neon sign at the window that read *DI ER* whenever it flashed, when the door opened and Becky stepped out. She pulled her pink waist-apron off and locked eyes with Peter. He didn't even have a moment to decide if he wanted her to know he was standing there. But she didn't have a chance to compose her reaction either and before she could make the decision to look defiant, he saw her hurt. And in that moment, it would've been so easy for the pair of them to have rushed in and said sorry. Sorry for punishing her. Sorry for letting it go on so long. Sorry for not being there for her now. It would've been so easy to say all those things if the hurt in her eyes had stayed. But it didn't.

Becky stuffed the apron down the back of her jeans and there was her anger. Anger that Peter had done nothing to check on her this whole time. That he hadn't been to see her once since the night she killed Rider and took chances with her own life by saving his dad's. And seeing her anger made Peter's all the easier to find. She went to Cooper now. She was *his* friend, *his* confidante and the keeper of his secrets. Becky glanced in the direction of the movie theatre as if to acknowledge that she knew he was working there now. She might even have had something to say about it. But whatever it was, she decided against it. Then she walked away. Peter watched her make her way down the street, but before he could decide if he should wait to see if she came back, he spotted his dad.

He was sat hunched over the front step of the barber's shop where a red-and-white-striped signage pole was twizzling as madly as a candy cane in a hurricane. Snow had started to gather across the hood of his parka. He held a shovel in one hand. A soggy sandwich hung from the other. But he didn't seem too troubled by either. He just sat there staring at the mounds of snow he'd cleared off the sidewalk.

Peter looked at the area directly beneath the barber's window. It was so clear you could almost see the concrete now. He had no idea that his dad had taken a job shovelling snow. But then he hadn't seen him since they'd settled in.

Peter flexed his fingers ready to count the days that had passed since their arrival. But the count stopped abruptly at his index finger. It'd only been two days. He gazed down the length of Mainstreet watching snow-dust snake across the middle of the road like smoke on the wind and wondered how it was even possible that so much time could pass in so little time.

When Peter looked back towards the barber's, his dad's eyes were on him. He stood, brushing breadcrumbs from his beard and mouthing the words, *You OK?* Peter mustered a smile and nodded, which seemed to please him. His dad looked over his shoulder as if to check no one was watching then mimed hanging himself from a noose with his tongue lolling out. Peter pointed towards the movie theatre and pretend-shot himself in the head. His dad laughed then finished the mime off by doing the exploding exit wound thing with his hand bursting away from his temple. He mouthed the words, *Come over later?* Peter nodded. But he knew right then that he had no intention of visiting his dad. He'd only see right through him and know that he was struggling, when what he needed to show him was what a success story his son was turning out to be now he was living the life he was born for.

His dad didn't look away. It was as if he was waiting for something he hadn't got yet. And it took a moment or two for Peter to work out exactly what that was. He wanted reassurance of his boy's happiness. And Peter had never seen that look before now: not the need to know how he was really doing, but the request for reassurance regardless. Peter smiled. He wasn't convinced he'd remembered to tell his eyes, but strangely enough it didn't seem to matter. It was enough. His dad smiled back and his world was good again. Perhaps that was what being a grown-up meant, or being a grown-up son. Big-boy smiles. Noses to the grindstone. Regardless of how either of them were really doing. And it was easy. Easier this way, even. But it came at a cost. Peter felt the smile die inside him and waited for his dad to notice. But he didn't. And right there and then he learned something terrible. His dad would no longer be able to tell the difference if he didn't want him to. Peter's throat went tight. Suddenly he wasn't sure what he'd done by letting such a thing in.

Someone rapped the barber-shop window indicating that his dad had missed a patch of snow. His dad pooh-poohed any suggestion he hadn't done a thorough enough job but the fist knocked again, more insistent this time, so he shoved the rest of the sandwich in his pocket and indicated to Peter that it was time to crack on. He mouthed the words *Love you* and pulled the shovel from the snow.

Peter watched him for a little while. He wanted a hug, or to hug his dad, he wasn't entirely sure which. But something stopped him from acting on either impulse. He briefly turned back just in case Becky was making her way to the diner. But there was no sign of her, so he walked back to the movie theatre and entered the lobby.

Marge stood upright from the popcorn stand with her back to Peter. "You're back."

"Yes," said Peter. "I thought I'd cover the screening this evening, too."

"Great. I can't get enough of you."

"You're probably out here wondering when I'm going to tackle those holes in the carpet."

Marge released a fistful of popcorn back into the stand and sighed. "Sure."

"But I can vacuum the lobby for now, if you like, and fix the broken light bulb underneath the marquee."

"And make the birds perch on your finger when you whistle for 'em?"

Peter forced a smile. "Sorry. I don't know what that—"

"Forget about it."

231

Peter looked around the lobby waiting for the awkwardness to subside and Marge made for the office door.

"So," said Peter stepping forward.

"So, nothing. There's no one in tonight."

"But—"

"Go home, Philip."

"Peter. My name's Peter."

"Look—"

"The apartment gets quiet."

Marge drew in a deep sigh, seemingly irritated now by the sudden need for kindness. She held back at the door, strumming her fingers across the frame like Peter's existence was nothing but a nuisance to her. But after a moment or two, she let all the air out of her lungs and quietly turned round.

"That's why I keep the movie running even when no one's in," she said, her tone much softer than before. "I like the sound of people."

"You do?"

"Don't be so surprised. Just cos I don't like having you around."

"Sorry, it's just that—"

"It was never this quiet in Yellowstone. Always rumbling. Always grumbling."

"You were at Yellowstone?"

Marge picked a piece of popcorn from her breast. "You think I've just been standing here tolerating intolerable small talk for the last sixteen years? Yes, I was at Yellowstone."

"I just meant that—"

"What?"

"I just meant that you must've known Henry and Darlene, that's all."

Marge looked down, rolling the piece of popcorn between her thumb and forefinger, and the music coming from inside the auditorium where the movie was playing seemed to grow louder, like a party taking place in another room.

"I knew of them," she said after a while. "And I'm sorry they found the lake and caused so much destruction to the original community hiding there. But I can't say I'm sorry those poor people were stupid enough to give their whereabouts away in the first place."

Peter's stomach turned. "How can you say that?"

"Quite easily. That Darlene woman was bad news. It's only a blessing we didn't know about the Returned back then while the pair of them were still around. I dread to think of losing our friends like you did. It was no good what that ranger did to young Wyatt and Daisy."

"You knew them?"

"Yes, I knew them. We were friends."

Marge turned her back so Peter couldn't see her face. And it came as such a surprise to hear her call anyone a friend that when her chest started to heave, Peter wasn't entirely sure what to do about it.

"I didn't know you knew them," he offered. "Why didn't you say something?"

"Why do you *always* have to say something?"

"I don't know. It's just the way I am."

"Well, there you go, then."

Peter made his way back towards the entrance, positioning himself some distance from Marge so she didn't have to feel he was watching her, and looked out on to the street.

"I'm sorry for your loss," he said quietly.

"Tsk. Don't be giving me that bull. It's not my loss. And it's not yours neither, no matter how badly you feel about what you saw when you went poking about up there. It's theirs."

"I know, I was just trying to—"

"Well, don't. They were trying for a baby, last time I saw them. Asked if I'd be its godmother, too, like I'd have the first clue what to do with some bawling baby. It's only a blessing that poor wretch never made it into the world."

"Yes," said Peter under his breath. But he could feel that terrible silence hanging over the cot in the cabin even now. It wasn't the silence of an empty room, but the deafening kind that came from there being a hole in the world where something good used to be. Peter clenched his fist. He didn't have the heart to tell Marge that she had been a godmother.

A wind caught one of the cars outside, shaving a surface layer of snow off the hood. Peter watched it skitter and snake out across the road, aware that without even trying to, he'd stepped through a door into a more private room in the conversation.

"Jim reckons the government had their reasons for killing them both," Marge went on.

Peter shrugged. "They sent a marshal ranger out to all the parks to question any Returnees who've chosen to stay away, apparently. They're worried about something called *Timberdark*."

"That name means nothing to me."

"They think it's something the Returnees are mixed up in. Some code word for a plot against everyone else or something."

Marge caught Peter's reflection in the glass. "And what do *you* think?"

"I don't know. But my Cooper knows what it is. He just won't tell me and now I'm worried why."

A grim smile crept into the corners of Marge's thin lips. "Trouble in paradise, eh?"

"I guess."

"And now the Returned are falling into a trance all over town."

"Yes," said Peter quietly. "Cooper too."

"No wonder you don't want to go home."

"No."

"Well, don't be getting cosy here. You know I can't stand the sight of you."

"I can stay for this evening's screening."

"You can stay for five minutes."

Marge stood at the door to her office, so Peter zipped his parka up, feeling the inevitable pull of home, when something far deeper called out to him and he stopped. He pressed his nose to the glass, ridding it of his reflection, and gazed out into the flurrying snow.

"Did you hear that?" he whispered.

"Of course I heard it."

"The wolves, I mean."

"Yes. The wolves."

"They're out there."

"Go home, Peter."

"They're out there."

"Yes," said Marge. "They're out there. The Dead are out there. The whole world is out there and we're in here."

"But—"

"But nothing."

"But, Marge."

Marge stopped and for a moment Peter wasn't sure if she was going to snap at him for daring to use her name. But she didn't. Her head turned so her face was in profile across her shoulder as if she accepted the invitation of intimacy and Peter quietly stepped away from the lobby entrance.

"Do you think that when the Dead pass through someone, they leave part of themselves behind?"

Marge's eyes narrowed. But ridicule didn't cross them once. "Like a ghost, you mean?"

"I suppose," said Peter. Then, "Yes, like a ghost."

"No one gets through life without picking up unwanted ghosts. Not even Perfect Peter."

"I'm not perfect."

Marge grumbled. "How perfect of you to say so."

"But do you? Do you think it's possible?"

"Everyone lives with a ghost inside them. Sometimes many. Grief. Anger. Bereavement. The love you hold for someone who no longer loves you back."

Peter felt a sharp tug in his stomach. "Why wouldn't someone love you back?"

"Maybe they're dead. Maybe they're not. Maybe the love they felt for you has died but yours hasn't."

The wolf cried again. Distant this time. Further back inside the hills somewhere.

"And do you know what love does when it can't give

itself away to that person any more?" Marge went on.

Peter shook his head but no words came out.

"Well, do you?"

"No," said Peter. "No, I don't know."

"It turns on you. Love doesn't have a choice once it's trapped inside you. It's desperate to leave you and find the person it's meant for. It fights to get out. It struggles. But eventually love realizes it's never going to be back home with that person again, and it despises you for it. Trapped inside forever, love becomes a ghost. It haunts every thought. It ruins every happiness until eventually, it sits there inside you, rotting like a damned rose that somebody forgot to water."

Peter waited for the wolf to call out once more. But it was gone. Marge turned round. Stoic. Rebuffing any emotion. She held Peter's gaze and a tear broke across his cheek.

"But he still loves me."

"Then go to him."

"I've tried."

"Try harder."

"But I can't."

"Do it or don't do it. But I'm tired now."

"But what do I do?"

"I'm tired, I tell you."

"Marge, what do I do? He won't tell me anything."

"What does your gut tell you?"

"That he's disappearing."

"And?"

"And that something bad is about to happen."

"And who stops that, hmm? You or him?"

Peter had no answer. Marge nodded like that was too bad, but only as bad as everything else in this world of hers. She shuffled her weary feet towards the auditorium, sighing, like all her efforts were wasted on him somehow. Before she left, she briefly held back at the door.

"They never gave us any trouble in Yellowstone," she said. "The Returned."

"But—"

"Not once. And they weren't in no trance neither. Take it or leave it. Damned if I care."

"Then what made that change?"

"How do I know? But I tell you this, that ranger's barely spent two nights in his room above the diner this past year since he got here. According to Shelby, he's been all over the parks, from Glacier to Joshua. Until now, I'd presumed he was making sure no Returnees were left out there because we need all the numbers we can get to help hold back the Dead. But now Wyatt and Daisy are gone and he hasn't left town once since you got here. So, whatever this *Timberdark* is, it looks like his search ended when he found your Cooper."

"But Cooper was only bitten a month ago."

"Take it or leave it."

"He couldn't know anything or anyone."

"You sure about that?"

"Yes. I'm sure."

"What about that friend of yours? The one Darlene killed."

"Rider?"

"Yes. Could they have spoken?"

Peter shook his head. "No. When I found him, he'd been alone in the woods for years. All he wanted was to light a flare for his wife, telling her he was safe. And besides, he and Cooper barely spent a moment together."

Grim pleasure curled across the corners of Marge's lips. "Barely."

"No."

"Barely, Peter."

"I said no."

But the truth was, there had been a moment. While he and his dad were busy preparing to tell the lake about the Returned, Cooper and Rider had waited inside Henry's bedroom.

"Doesn't take a second for a rotten idea to seed," said Marge. "Maybe he put a plan in Cooper's head. Maybe he didn't. Maybe it was a good thing he did too, given what was about to happen to him. But what do you care? You couldn't care less if Cooper was planning on blowing the whole world up, only that he might want to do it without you."

Blood burned the base of Peter's skull like the fever. "That's not true!" And it wasn't. It just wasn't.

"Does Perfect Peter even know what he's fighting for?"

"We could be happy here."

Marge huffed. "Is that so?" She forced Peter's gaze and the grimace in her eyes deepened further. "Then I'm afraid I can't help you."

Peter shook his head. "But—"

"Go home."

"But what just happened?"

"Just go home. Go watch the pretty lights or TV, or come watch the damned movie. Because if it's a quiet life you're after, then you've come to the right place after all. All the world will ever want of you when you go back is for you to be quiet."

Marge opened the door to the auditorium and a shaft of light from the movie's projection broke across her back, forming a halo of thin hair across her head.

"Dreamland, dear boy," she said, her dark eyes glittering. "Keeping us quiet in our place in the dark."

The doors to the auditorium slipped back into place and she was gone.

A few minutes passed before Peter realized he was back

inside the ticket booth. He didn't remember crossing the lobby, or pushing the red curtain aside to take his seat. But the cold plastic of the stool beneath him told him he was there. So did his reflection. The Other Peter looked back at him again, faint, from inside the glass like a stranger. They were bound by the laws of nature to hold each other's gaze. But if he didn't know better, he could've sworn the Other Peter's eyes darted over his shoulder to Marge, as if it understood the things she spoke about more than he did. But two could play at that game. Peter looked right though his reflection to the street outside and the snow flurried across town.

A rectangle of yellow light struck the sidewalk and Becky left the diner. She squeezed between the hood of one car and the trunk of another, stuffing the work apron in her jacket pocket and made it to the corner of Mainstreet where Cooper was waiting. They spoke in hurried whispers. Briefly, Becky turned back, scanning the street as if her actions might look suspicious should anyone see her. She pointed in the direction of the hills on the edge of town and Cooper nodded. They seemed to come to some kind of agreement, then parted, quickly walking off in opposite directions. Agony gnawed at Peter's stomach. *Why won't you just be happy, Cooper? Why?* But the Other Peter reflected in the glass started to close his eyes, too bored or too tired to even care.

And somehow that option looked so peaceful that after a while, Peter sat there quietly watching the snow fall across the marquee and let himself do the same.

Insects swarmed the cabin doorway, rising up from the rushy grass and pines where sticky sap wept in golden globules. Heat broke through the trees at Peter's back. He'd stepped out of the lake on to the island to follow Cooper only moments before, but his shorts were already dry. The last bead of water coiled down the inside of his leg and he stepped up to the door.

The darkness within cooled Peter's skin, but his heart kept pumping. Inside, matching toothbrushes nuzzled each other in a tin cup on a shelf above the sink. His and Cooper's towels lay strewn across the floor, somewhere between the wash tub and the bed. Peter scooped the bedding up into his arms, cradling the scent of the night before. His body flexed beneath his undershorts. He and Cooper were everywhere. And yet Cooper was nowhere to be seen.

There was another door. Peter was sure the end wall had been decorated with moose antlers just a moment before. But in the exact moment he needed an explanation for Cooper's disappearance, a door appeared and was open.

Peter squinted. The light coming through was so blisteringly bright, the frame of the door dissolved inside the glare and was gone.

A desert stretched beyond the cabin, now. The scorched earth was cracked in hexagonal tiles, curled crisp at the edges. Above it, herds of white clouds roamed the doming sky. Somewhere between, but not quite at the point where the earth meets the sky, hovered another cabin. Peter set one bare foot down on to the clay and stepped out beneath the shimmering sky.

20

That night, the other Cooper appeared at the bedroom door again. They'd barely spoken at dinner. Cooper wouldn't even look him in the eye. Then they'd taken turns brushing their teeth in the bathroom alone so the silence they shared wasn't even louder in smaller spaces.

Breathing broke inside the darkness. Peter didn't dare reach out to touch in case something other than Cooper reached back and grabbed him. And yet, his being there almost became a comfort. At least Cooper was looking at him. And in the darkness of that blank space, where not even a silhouette or a glint of light in the eye marked him out from the door, Peter found that he could paint pictures of the Cooper he wanted. One with a freshly pressed tee and shoeshine on his boots ready for the movies. Or one with a smile in his eyes having made promotion at work. Any of those would do. It didn't really matter which. Just as long as Cooper's lips transformed his stupid name into wonder and his eyes brimmed with all his hopes and dreams again, ready to unpack everything he had inside him now he'd found a home in a little place called Peter.

Peter pulled one of Cooper's old T-shirts from beneath his pillow, inhaling the sweet tang of log smoke and sweat in the pits and stared into the darkness of the door. "Where are you?" he whispered. "Where did you go?" Finally. "Come back to me."

A dash of light struck the floor, illuminating tufts of weave in the carpet again as the door swung open. Peter stood, looking down the length of the front room. Once again, there had been no sound of the handle turning. The door was just open. There were no footsteps crossing the floorboards to the front door. Cooper was just gone. Peter rushed to the window looking down over Mainstreet. But Cooper wasn't down there either. Only footprints in the snow.

Enough. Peter threw his parka over the top of his pyjamas and ran out on to the sidewalk. The neon lights of Mainstreet were out. The shop windows were dark. Overhead, the little light bulbs clinked dully on their strings beneath the weight of the snow. Peter held back a moment, waiting to see if he could hear movement in the still of the night. But there was nothing.

He stepped out on to the road, his eye following the footprints all the way up towards the foothills at the edge of town. At the very end of Mainstreet, snow falling inside a shaft of light from the last of the streetlamps, fell back into place like something had just passed through it barely seconds before. Beyond it, the snowy pines of the foothills were blue. Peter inched forward, suddenly aware of the night and the cold and those things inside the trees he couldn't see. Wolves, perhaps. Restless Ones. Secrets. He was about to turn back, when a square of yellow light from one of the guest rooms above the diner struck the sidewalk below and he glanced up.

The skull of a deer, with its two branching antlers, was set on a table beside the window. The hollow eye sockets, that had once borne down over Cooper, gazed up at the ceiling. But without a face behind it, the mask was stripped of menace. There, surrounded by empty beer bottles and scrunched-up napkins, it was nothing but part of a uniform, no different from any other kind of helmet set aside after a hard day's work.

Peter looked back up the road towards the trees, unsure whether to follow Cooper any further, when the square of yellow light on the sidewalk went out. He looked back towards the window. The room was dark. The mask had gone.

Footsteps struck the staircase leading down to the front door. Steady. One by one. In no hurry, but deliberate, like they had every confidence the things they hunted would allow themselves to be caught.

The door opened and the Ghost Ranger stepped out from the darkness of the doorway, the skull's sockets at once alive with the hunt. The skull turned on a fluid neck without once moving the shoulders and looked out towards the foothills. But the Ranger didn't step forward. The skull turned back, holding Peter's gaze for the first time. The Ghost Ranger knew the things that brought him out here. He knew the things that kept him awake at night. The same things as kept him awake.

Peter glanced down. He was only wearing his pyjamas beneath his coat, but he had to get to Timberdark first. The deer's empty eye sockets held firm. Without skin or muscle to form eyelids, there was nothing but that singular cold glare. It watched. It waited. It held for the longest time, goading Peter into the chase. And it worked.

Peter ran. He made it to the last of the streetlamps at the top of Mainstreet where he stopped. He held back, watching the snow fall like gold dust within the circle of light at his feet, finding comfort in its perimeter and fear in the blue of the night outside of it. He turned his head towards his shoulder. But he didn't look back. He knew the Ghost Ranger was still standing there, so he stepped out of the light and, with nothing but the creak of snow beneath his feet, walked on.

The road took a twist, winding round a bend before stretching out as far as the eye could see among the towering pines like a river through a valley. Above the frosted spires, a full moon hung low inside a black sky, making the icy road gleam. But the footprints didn't follow it any further. Movement in among the trees pulled Peter's attention back towards the woods. Cooper appeared. Or at least, Peter thought it was Cooper. He didn't have time to take in the full form, just a dash, a smudge, passing among the trees. Emerging from behind one, disappearing behind another.

Peter's heartbeat quickened. He left the road, staggering down the bank, clutching at tufts of frozen grass to steady himself. He lost his footing and grabbed hold of a branch. But his hand slipped, skinning the snow from the bough. Sharp pine needles sprang up, pricking the palm of his hand. He let go and tumbled into the woods, carried forward by his own momentum, and before he knew it, the road disappeared behind him and the woods rushed in and he was running. And he ran. He ran, stumbling over bumps and hollows buried by snow. And he thought he saw Cooper or a dash of Cooper weaving in and out of the trees. And the forest got darker and the trees grew tighter until the canopy closed over, blocking all starlight out, when his foot snagged across a root and he fell.

Peter lay there for a moment, cheek to the ground,

watching blood trickle from his palm. It pooled like liquid night across the snow. He blinked to dislodge snowflakes that had started to bank across his eyelashes and became aware of a dull throb across both shins where bone had bashed root on his way down. But he was somehow untroubled by all this. There was a stronger sensation.

The night was dark, but snow-glow lit the forest from within, transforming the night into day. Peter pushed back on to his knees, watching the bluish snow falling gently across the drooping pines, and a pair of eyes turned towards him. A bobcat looked down from its perch in the snowy boughs. The black tips of its ears were alert to Peter being there. Its yellow eyes were wide. But it wasn't alarmed to find a stranger sharing its midnight world. It acknowledged his presence, then looked off deeper into the woods to the night and the things that stirred there. Peter pulled a pine needle from the heel of his hand and followed the bobcat's gaze, seeing its world now the snow had lent him night vision to do so. But neither of them were the strongest presence here.

The silence surrounded them, rising through the pines up into the star-strewn sky, and Peter's heartbeat stirred. Here, silence wasn't the absence of sound. It was a presence that had no sound. He pressed his hands to his knees to stand and the peace of the world arrived, settling among the trees like a living thing to greet him. And

250

out there, amid that silent wonder, something appeared beneath a tree. It was so white, it was brighter than the snow that dusted the jagged bark behind it.

All at once there was all of Cooper. His chest, buttocks, hips, hands, fingertips, nipples, earlobes and thighs. There were all the parts of him that Peter already knew. But Cooper's body was so luminous that the thick bed of black hair around his groin gave dark strength to those parts of him that Peter didn't know. Cooper's fingertips journeyed across the flat of his stomach, travelling over the navel into the hair below. He tipped his head back, eyes lost in moonlight, and took the weight of himself in his hand. His fingers played across his own body, stroking, holding, and it should've been so easy for Peter to imagine himself there instead. He could fall into those two dark pools so full of starlight right now and disappear inside Cooper's eyes to the boundless galaxies that existed inside him, and Cooper would do the same. Then there would be no separation. Then they'd be one. But there was nothing but cruelty here. Cooper's nakedness was triumphant. Peter's was nothing.

Peter looked away, his throat at once tight, suffocating. He would never be enough for Cooper. Never.

Further back inside the woods another figure, this one clothed, passed from one tree to another. It started to make its way uphill. Others broke out from inside the forest now, weaving, wandering, treading softly in the snow, moving one by one and then on together to higher ground. Cooper picked his clothes up to dress and followed. Peter hung back, watching the figures pass along the sharp ridge of the hill, spindly in the moonlight like the roughened hackles of a coyote's back.

He could hear them talking now. There was Becky's voice. Tokala's, too. Peter thought he heard their laughter. Then laughter he didn't recognize. More voices. Different voices. Those voices echoed, yowling and howling further back behind the ridge where the snow-capped pines glowed red. Red, even though dusk had passed several hours before. Peter closed his eyes and a wave of nausea crashed through his stomach. But soon they were gone. He braced his palms against the bark of the tree, willing the night to be over. Willing a great many things to be over. To be over. To be not here right now, or then, or ever. To not ever have existed. He felt the weight of someone watching. He opened his eyes, scanning the trees, and another pair of eyes looked back.

Teddy pulled a woollen bobble hat from his head, his face flushed and disturbed. Peter didn't know how long he'd been standing there or what he'd seen, but the violation of being watched without his knowledge disgusted him so greatly, that he suddenly despised Teddy for making him feel like he was no better than he was.

"Teddy, what are you doing here? It's the middle of the night."

"Looking out for you."

"Well, don't."

Teddy offered a smile and pointed at a tree. "Tree!"

"What?"

"That was a joke."

"Hardly."

"I made a joke, because of all the things that don't need pointing out to you, trees are probably one of them."

"Right."

"It was just a joke."

"Yeah," said Peter. "I got it."

"Oh. It's just that you're not laughing."

Peter glanced towards the tree Cooper had been standing beneath only a few moments before. The sight of him naked, holding himself, burned the back of his eyelids deeply, like staring into a blinding light then blinking.

"You don't laugh much, do you?" said Teddy.

"Do you find that you have to say that to a lot of people?"

"Actually, I do."

"What do you reckon that tells you?"

"I don't know."

Peter turned back. "Teddy, what do you want? It's late. What are you even doing out here?"

"I'm just checking that you're OK."

"Why wouldn't I be OK?"

Teddy shrugged like he didn't know but absolutely knew, which only irritated Peter further.

"It's good for me to take a walk anyways," Teddy went on. "The space between the buttons on one of my favourite shirts has started to gape open real wide when I sit down. It's like they're screaming, *No, Teddy! Stop eating, Teddy.*"

Peter wandered off, looking up towards the ridge where the red glow was coming from.

"I tend to put on a few pounds when I stress out," said Teddy.

"What do you have to stress about?"

"Oh, you know. Christmas and stuff."

"Does the town even celebrate Christmas?"

Teddy sighed. "No. And that really stresses me out."

The glow in the hills seemed to fade then get brighter, like the sun setting behind a cloud. But dusk was long gone and dawn was still some hours away. Peter scoured the ridge, trying to find a source for the light, cursing the day this boy decided to make a best friend of him.

"Now," said Teddy. "Guess what my business would be called if I opened a foot spa."

"You know you don't have to find something new to say all the time, don't you?"

"Guess."

"I'm OK with silences."

"Teddy-Cure!"

Peter wasn't entirely sure he got the joke. But once again, Teddy's face told him that he'd made one and he simply didn't have the heart or the patience to disappoint him, so Peter faked a smile and wandered over to the tree that Cooper had stood beneath.

He ran his fingertips down the length of the trunk, feeling the coarse hairs on the husk of the copper bark, rough but warm against the palm of his hand. He leaned into the tree, feeling the weight of it against his chest and watched the red glow over the hills, aware of the opportunity he had to go up there. Aware of the opportunity he had to empty Cooper's rucksack while he was away, too. Peter's hands fell away from the tree and he heard Teddy approach. He was about to make his excuses when he felt the mood in the air shift and Teddy's voice came in quietly behind him.

"They're out here most nights," he said.

Peter turned. There was a seriousness in Teddy's face that hadn't existed before, like all the pitiful energy he spent trying to please people had suddenly dropped away to reveal another Teddy beneath.

"Who's out here?" Peter asked.

Teddy held eye contact. But he didn't answer that

question, like he refused to pander to any stupid attempt at ignorance, so Peter changed it.

"Are they? Are they out here most nights?"

Teddy nodded.

"How do you even know that?"

"I've watched them. They leave town a little after midnight and go up on to the ridge where the red glow is coming from."

"It's probably just a campfire," said Peter, relieved that this sudden suggestion seemed to fit so nicely. "And they probably just have things in common to talk about."

"Yes," said Teddy. "A bit like us."

Peter winced. "Us?" There was no us. But he didn't have the heart to say it.

"I know you don't like me much, Peter, but I can go up there and find out what they're doing if you like."

"It's not that I don't like you, Teddy. It's just that—"

Peter didn't know how to finish that sentence. Then he got irritated at being made to feel worse than he already had.

"It's OK," said Teddy. "You don't have to think of something nice to say."

"But why would you go up there for me?"

"Because it won't hurt me."

"I wouldn't get hurt," said Peter. "Why does everyone always think I'll get hurt?"

"I only meant that going up there won't hurt my heart. It might hurt yours."

Peter clenched his jaw and said nothing.

"I'm here for you," said Teddy.

"Cooper's here for me. And my friend Becky too. It's just that they're—"

"It's just if you needed a friend."

"I've got friends."

"Oh, I know."

"And Cooper's more than my friend."

"I know that too."

"He's my boyfriend."

"Yes. I know."

Peter nodded. "Good."

Peter kicked the base of the tree with the heel of his boot and started to make his way back through the woods in search of the road.

"Haven't you looked forward to being here for so long?" said Teddy calling back. "People like you and me have longed to be part of a world where we know we'll make more sense. But now all everyone can talk about is what Cooper knows and what he might do and why the Returnees have started to fall into that trance, and it sometimes feels like they've forgotten all about *us*. Sometimes it doesn't even feel like it's our turn at all."

Peter stopped. He wasn't sure about anything any more. He tugged a frosted pine cone from its branch, crunching it inside his fist until the brittle scales bit. But the truth was, it did feel that way. He didn't know if he liked Teddy. What was taking place here was hardly friendship. Maybe it was nothing more than an understanding. But it felt good to be understood. And it felt good to be wanted. Peter turned back and held Teddy's gaze. Whether he liked it or not, Teddy had come out here looking for him when all Cooper had done was head into the woods to escape.

Peter offered a smile. "Pedicure."

"What?"

"The name of your nail spa. *Teddy-Cure.* It's a play on words for pedicure."

Teddy beamed like his whole life had been made and Peter drew that warmth right in, feeling better for gifting him with it.

"I don't think some of the people Cooper's spending time with are even from here," said Teddy.

"What do you mean?"

"They're not from town."

Peter sighed. The only good thing that could possibly come out of knowing that would be if this whole mess had something to do with them instead of Cooper.

"My Dad says Cooper's mixed up in something called Timberdark," said Teddy after a while.

"Yeah. Perhaps it's just the name of that group he's hanging out with."

Teddy started to fiddle with his woollen hat. "But didn't Cooper already know that word before you got here?"

Peter nodded. "Then, what?"

Teddy pulled on his pompom, teasing strands of flattened wool out with his fingertips until it was completely round again, but said nothing. Peter looked back up towards the ridge and the red glow throbbed beneath the boughs of the trees.

"But what if it's something else? What if they're planning something bad?"

Teddy stopped what he was doing. He took a step closer and the distance between them seemed to disappear altogether. "So, what do we do now?"

But Peter didn't know.

"If Cooper, Becky and Tokala don't attend the reintegration meeting tomorrow, I guess we'll know where they stand, won't we?"

"Why?"

Teddy merely shrugged. "Well, then we'll know that they're not interested in coming back to the real world, won't we? And we'll know they don't care about the rest of us, either. After all, Peter, what will we do about the Dead if the Returned aren't around to help us?"

Peter nodded. Teddy was right. And somehow, right there and then, a pact was made.

Peter reached the cabin in the desert. Inside was another way through. He crossed the front stoop, taking note of the same matching toothbrushes and towels inside as the cabin before, and left by the back door. He passed through a forest of dense fern, where tightly coiled fiddleheads unfurled into broad blades even though it was night, and made his way towards another cabin.

The third cabin interior was completely dark. Peter fumbled for the same toothbrushes and towels, but didn't find them. He reached out, searching for the timber walls. But there weren't any. It was as if the cabin was made of pure darkness. Only the scent of the bed and their bodies mingling marked the cabin out as the same one as before. And their scent was strongest here. A sliver of light on the floor highlighted the back door. Peter called Cooper's name inside his head and the door was open.

A carpet of stars stretched beyond the cabin now. There were no mountains on the horizon, or islands to break the perfect mirror. The black lake reflected the starry night completely. It was as if Peter occupied an empty ribbon in space where the Earth should be, somewhere between the galaxy above and the one below. Peter peered down into the inky water, but there was no reflection staring back at him, just more stars reaching further back into space. He set one foot down upon the lake. He didn't break through the surface. It held him, forming a rim of water around his heel and toes. It took his weight, so Peter set the other foot down. The stars quivered at the pressure of his body on the surface, making them dazzle more brightly. But they held their shape. Briefly, he turned back. There was no cabin behind him any more, just a door-shaped hole. It closed and the galaxy surrounded him infinitely. In the distance was a little red canoe. Peter set one foot down after the other and journeyed on towards the middle of the lake.

21

Peter bolted forward in his chair. He couldn't have nodded off for more than a moment or two, but by the time he came round, the circle of empty chairs they'd laid out for the meeting had begun to fill and the town hall echoed to the thrum of a dozen different conversations.

Everyone was due to attend. People his dad's age or older weren't expected to take part in the workshop on account of the fact they needed little reminder of what life was like before, let alone take a refresher for all those independent living skills you needed to make it through. But a series of stands strewn with red, white and blue bunting framed a sequence of white lines painted on the floor where the hall had been used for sports, offering advice on a range of topics such as budgeting, health insurance and CV building. And now several older community members were milling among them while Sheriff O'Hurn tried to coax many to the chairs with promise of a fresh donut, in the hope they'd stick around long enough to give the younger ones some advice.

It was good to see that the town was even full of people. On the lake, barely an hour went by before you'd spot somebody out on the islands or paddling by in their canoe. But not here. The streets were quiet for the most part. You'd never even know anyone was behind all those little doors and windows half the time. But here they all were, arriving in their droves. New faces. Old faces. Regulars and Returnees alike, all chattering among themselves. If there were any concerns about the Returnees' trance at all, then you'd never know it. Peter sat forward. His heart swelled. The integration from Yellowstone they'd been promised, and that he and Cooper had gone on to promise everyone they'd rescued this last month, was alive and it was here. He swung round, looking towards the front door, and now more than ever willed Cooper to arrive, just so he could see first-hand that those hopes were working.

Peter looked across the way, worried that an old-timer sitting opposite him in a Stetson and T-shirt with a moose on it that said *I Don't Find You Very Amoosing* was alone. Peter smiled, but the old man gave a gruff nod like he was already done with being here and looked down at an envelope he held clutched across his lap. Whatever was in it worried him. The gruffness slipped from his face, leaving him small and vulnerable. And he wasn't the only one. Three seats down, the girl who worked the cash till at the supermarket, the one who didn't smile back, had her envelope scrunched up in her fist while she chewed the skin around her fingernails. Peter looked for Teddy. Perhaps he'd know what the envelopes were for. But he was too busy budging between two women over at the trestle table for more donuts before they all went.

Peter peered round, but there was still no sign of Cooper or Becky. One girl, a Returnee, and broad as a bear with both ears poking through her fine hair, sat in the circle staring at the door. Peter hadn't seen her before now, but perhaps she was waiting for Cooper too. For all he knew, she'd been out in the woods last night with the rest of them. Peter glanced down at her boots, noticing the thick wedge of mud and dead pine needles crusted into the tread, and wrapped his fingers over the lip of the chair. If Cooper planned on coming, he didn't have much time left. He started to look around the hall for a clock, when he realized the girl was looking at him. Like Cooper, her eyes were two dark pools from her journey to death and back again. And she was looking at him strangely. He was sure of it. Peter shuffled round in his seat, troubled by some of the things Cooper might have been saying about him, and pretended to take interest in the stalls. But her gaze only followed him. He sat forward, willing Teddy to come back, when the girl sat upright, her eyes notably brighter now that someone she knew had arrived.

Tokala walked in. He mingled. He shook hands with the sheriff. He patted the back of the girl's chair as if to check in with her and stood watching the door. Peter sank down into his chair. Was Cooper coming or not? Or was something else about to happen? He supposed he should try talking to Tokala about it. But now he'd seen him in the woods with the others, he wasn't his to talk to any more.

Peter looked back towards the stands where a woman in pigtails with a smile wider than a canoe was standing, and wondered if now might be time to go talk to the nice people at the credit ratings stand, when Teddy came back.

"Don't let Dad catch you dozing off," he said, sneaking in at Peter's side. "There's an exam after."

"You're kidding."

Teddy dropped a donut on Peter's lap and pointed at it. "Donut!"

"Thanks."

"Course I'm kidding, and don't tell Dad I told you this because he bet me anything I wouldn't be able to keep my mouth shut, but you should stick around. They might have some giveaways at the end."

"Might?"

Teddy clutched Peter's knee and wiggled his eyebrows up and down to indicate that *might* meant most definitely.

"What kind of giveaways?" said Peter looking back towards the door. There was still no sign of Cooper.

"I can't say."

"OK."

"But televisions! Lots of them."

The sheriff checked the street one last time just in case someone else was on their way.

"That's tel-e-visions, Peter."

"Yes. I heard you."

"OK. Only it's just that you don't seem that excited about it."

But no one else arrived, so the sheriff removed the chair propping the door open, letting it swing shut, and nodded for them to make a start. Peter sat back in his chair, taking a bite of the donut. The pink fondant was so sweet, he thought his lips would peel back off his face.

Teddy leaned in. "Do you think that girl would like me?"

"What girl?"

"That girl with the ginger freckles like the stars coming down from heaven."

"What, like, *like* you, like you?"

"Yeah?"

"Oh," said Peter tucking the donut underneath his chair. "I don't know."

"You seem surprised."

"No, it's just that—"

"It's just that what? You think because I like to wear fun shirts that I'm just here to be your comedy sidekick or something?"

Peter stared at Teddy's short-sleeved shirt with the ice-skating reindeers on it. "No. No, it's not that."

"Or maybe you thought I fancied *you*."

Peter choked on a bit of donut.

"Because," said Teddy, "ew!"

"OK. You don't have to—"

"I mean – just ew!"

A woman with grey hair and a kind face stepped into the circle with a clipboard pressed to her breast and Peter leaned in.

"Teddy. What are credit ratings?"

"They assess how likely you are to pay back your debt."

"Oh. OK." Then, "Why would anyone have any debt?"

"Because of the loans they're going to give everyone to get started again."

"But what if you can't pay them back?"

Teddy nudged him in the side and offered him some of his donut. "Don't be silly."

"And why have some people got envelopes?"

"Because they haven't been able to make their rent. They've been given notice already so I guess they'll definitely need a loan."

Peter looked across the way at the old man in the Stetson. His hands were trembling fiercely now. The envelope was crunched up inside his fist.

"But I haven't paid our rent yet either," said Peter. "Why don't we have one of those?"

"Because my dad's covered it for you. You know, so you and Cooper don't have to worry."

Peter looked across the hall towards the sheriff. But he was already looking his way. He wiped beer foam from his moustache and, with a wink, raised a tin cup towards him like he was toasting his thanks for taking Teddy in as a friend. Or thanking him for something.

"But that's too much," said Peter.

"Ssh," said Teddy.

"But—"

"Forget about it."

"And what about everybody else?"

Teddy licked his fingers.

"What about everybody else, Teddy?"

But the woman tapped her ring across the side of the clipboard, calling attention for the meeting to start, dulling all chatter, so Peter sat forward watching the snow tumble across the tall window at the front of the hall and hoped a couple of figures would hurry past it on their way in.

He scanned the hall for a clock. *Go on*, he said. *You can come out now.* And it did. In this place, it didn't really matter if you could see a clock in a room or not. It could be hiding underneath a table or round the back of a radiator for all he knew. But there always was one. It only took a moment for the chatter to die down and the ticking made its presence known at the back of the hall, its only purpose on this occasion to make one thing perfectly clear to him. That Cooper wasn't coming.

The woman introduced herself as Terri, and it struck Peter as strange that this was the same person as had joined Tokala on the lake the night they'd responded to the flare. Barely a month had passed since then, yet that time felt like it belonged to another life now, or somebody else's life, perhaps. He'd forgotten all about her. And her voice was muffled, in the background somehow, like the meeting was taking place in another room and Peter was left alone to consider what would even happen to them both, now Cooper had made it clear that he was never going to join him back in the real world.

A draught whipped the back of Peter's chair and Terri's voice came in louder again. However, she was no longer addressing the group, but rather someone who stood at the front door where snow was now hurrying in.

"S'OK, hot stuff," said Terri, her eyes soft and warm. "Don't worry. I haven't even begun to bore these good people yet, so you haven't missed a thing."

Cooper stood at the door. Snow dusted his collar. He shook his head to see through the ribbons of his own hair a little better, then nodded in the direction of the group to make his apologies for being late. Peter sat forward in his seat, relief and anxiety swapping places without either emotion sticking around long enough for him to work out which one he felt more. But Cooper didn't look his way, or even attempt to find him. Becky appeared over his shoulder, whispering, like the pair of them had shared a secret just seconds before.

But none of that would have mattered had it not been for one thing. Becky was wearing his Dolly Parton T-shirt. Peter looked away. If he'd hoped for anything, it was that when he gave his T-shirt to Cooper, he might keep it close for those times they were apart, just like he did with Cooper's now his scent seemed to be the only part of him Peter had left. But it wasn't to be. Instead, Cooper had the woods now, and the woods had Cooper, and Becky had Peter's T-shirt and by wearing it, had stolen another part of them.

"Miss," said Cooper, digging both hands down the seat of his jeans. "I can just as well leave."

Terri shrugged. "You can just as well stay."

"Pa reckoned lateness is folks' way of sayin' somethin' dint matter much to them. Only, I don't want you thinkin' that."

"Don't be silly. It's easy to get lost in those damned supermarket aisles at the best of times. Look! I even kept your seats warm for you."

Peter looked around the circle. All the chairs were taken.

Terri pretend-cleared her throat. "Ned, you big hunk-a-love. Shift it."

A thickset man in a baseball cap glanced up with a *why me* look on his face, giving rise to a wave of chuckles around the room, and slowly made his way to the back of the group so Cooper had a place to sit.

"You too, Val."

A wiry old man with a gap between his front teeth wide enough to herd cattle through clapped both hands across his lap and did the same, then Cooper and Becky took their seats. The girl who'd been staring at Peter earlier followed the pair of them until she could establish eye contact. She didn't have to wait long. Becky sighed so her whole body seemed to melt into the seat and sat there with her arms folded. She looked in the direction of the girl. Cooper pretended to look around the hall then did the same with Tokala, and there it was, the group's connection to one another. Peter stared at Cooper. *Look at me*, he thought. *Just look at me. I'm sitting right here.* But he didn't. The only one paying any attention to him at all was the sheriff, and there was that damned word again. *Timberdark* broke across Peter's lips, as if the mere whisper of it would be enough to drive the hairs on Cooper's neck upward, forcing him to acknowledge him. But it didn't work. Cooper's eyes stayed with Tokala and the sheriff's stayed on Peter.

"So," said Terri. "For those of you who don't know, I'm Terri."

"Good evening, Terri," said the group in unison.

A wry smile broke across Terri's face. "Good evening, all. And aren't there so many of you this evening? If I didn't know any better I'd almost believe a certain someone had let slip about tonight's giveaway."

Teddy sank down in his seat like that would make him any less visible and the whole group pretended not to look at him.

"So," Terri went on. "Let's get housekeeping out of the way first. I'm going to pass the clipboard round for you to all sign in. And Val, that *will* require your full name and not just a love heart scribbled next to some old landline number you're still banking on getting back. And yes, the answer is still no. In the unlikely event of a fire, I remind you to all leave calmly and quietly and congregate in the parking lot at the top of town. They used to advise that you leave all your belongings behind during these kinds of situations but please don't. I'm not sure even one of Teddy's hugs will keep the cold off your kidneys, so please bring your coats with you. Finally, please feel free to help yourself to tea, coffee and a pee as and when you need to. There are no hall passes here, so no need to ask me. Restrooms are right at the back of the hall through that door, so none of us have to listen to Val's IBS wreak havoc with some poor cubicle. And no, Val, that's not the only reason I'm always gonna say no to you, sweetpea."

"Now," said Terri, passing the clipboard out, "tonight's a special one in that we welcome some of our friends from Lake Wranglestone to the group. So please can we all give them a warm West Wranglestone welcome?"

Everyone looked around to extend their greetings and Teddy pointed at Peter. "Peter!"

"Don't," said Peter slapping Teddy's thigh.

Teddy chuckled to himself, which was both intolerable and endearing, and Cooper glanced his way. Peter quickly withdrew his hand and for a moment at least, it crossed his mind that he really should be doing the opposite. Cooper was making it so obvious to him that he was finding replacements by turning up late with Becky and giving her his T-shirt, that he should be doing everything he could to show him how much his and Teddy's friendship was growing too. But he couldn't bring himself to. While any friendship with Teddy felt like a playdate, Cooper was up all night in the woods with the others. And before that, naked and with himself. Peter saw the mass of dark hair below Cooper's navel in his mind's eye, luminous against the glow of his skin. Lower still, and those parts of him that stayed secret. Tears began to well deep inside Peter's chest. If they broke out, they'd be unstoppable. He pretended to laugh at a joke Teddy didn't even make. But he needn't have bothered. Cooper's hair spilled back across his face and his attention was gone again.

"In previous weeks," said Terri, walking around the circle, "we've workshopped the practical things some of you have started to worry about now we're getting close to returning. Things that are either completely new to you or in need of a refresher, like how to change electrical fixtures and fittings, budgeting, how to open a bank account if you lost your documents during the exodus to the parks, setting up your bills and making sure that you prioritize paying them and so on and so forth. But tonight, I'd like to spend some time looking *at* time and how we get through it."

Whispers broke across the group and shoulders leaned into shoulders as people tried to figure out what Terri meant by that.

"Now, I don't need to tell you good people that a year out there in the parks passed like five minutes. If we weren't busy keeping the Dead from our doors, we had the boardwalks and cabins to maintain. And as you all know, the summers, especially in Yellowstone but also up in Glacier and Wranglestone too, were short, bringing winter round all the quicker. And well, then we were just flat-out carving blocks of snow the size of refrigerators from each other's roofs on a fortnightly basis. But some of you might begin to notice, or perhaps recall, that time can pass quite differently down here."

"Differently?" came a voice from the group. "Heck, it's as slow as Val's . . . Nope. I don't got nothin'. Hell, it's just as slow as Val."

Val's eyes peered out from beneath folds of saggy skin. "Was-he-say?"

"But he's right," mumbled a voice beside Peter. "Three days passed last week without me seeing a living soul."

"Me too," said another.

"Yes," said Terri, holding her hands up to placate the crowd. "Yes. And in some instances, time passes more slowly. When we relocate, our lives aren't always going to require that we spend as much time outdoors and for those of you seeking work, the vast majority of jobs will actively keep you indoors most of the time, which I know isn't what we've all grown accustomed to. So, one of the ways folks used to get through the working year was by looking forward to things. Can anyone give me an example of what that might be?"

Teddy jumped up from his seat quicker than a dog after a biscuit. "I know. I know!"

"Teddy, you don't have to raise your hand, sweetness," said Terri. "We're not in class. And as I said, you don't need a hall pass if it's the toilet you're after. I actually can't be too sure which it is right now."

The group shared a laugh and Teddy put his hand back down.

"But," said Terri looking around the room now. "I would be interested to hear from someone who hasn't spoken before."

Peter lowered his eyes so Terri couldn't engage with him. He knew that people used to save up for a whole year just so they could get away on vacation for two out of the fifty-two weeks they spent working. According to his dad, he used to work over Thanksgiving and Christmas just so he could take Mom away in the summer. His colleagues did the same. But Peter didn't want to be the one to say it.

"Anybody got anything for me?" said Terri. "Or am I just going to have to stand here dodging tumbleweed?"

Terri looked around at all the blank faces, desperately trying her best to ignore Teddy who no doubt already had twenty different answers lined up ready for her. But before she was left with no choice but to defer to him, a voice broke across the other side of the circle.

"Fall," came a voice, low beneath the silence of the room. "I always look forward to fall."

Terri turned towards Cooper, her face lit with gratitude for saving her. "And what is it about fall that you like so much, Cooper?"

Cooper shrugged. "The colours, I guess."

"But what is it about the colours? Can you tell us more?"

"What more is there to say?"

"You tell me. You seem to feel strongly about it."

Cooper tucked a strand of hair back behind his ear, self-conscious about the group looking at him now that he'd dared to speak. "The way the leaves are dyin' but they still show up with all them colours. They know it's the end for them, but it's not the end they're celebratin'. All them reds, miss. All them golds and yellas. It's like, look at the life we just lived out here beneath the sky. Look how lucky we had it."

Peter watched the ridge of Cooper's Adam's apple. The way it breached the surface of his throat sharply like a dorsal fin in water now he was desperate to swallow his nerves. But he had no reason to be nervous. His words had power to stir. They always did. Cooper had no faith in them, but there would never be anyone else who knew how to take those two weakling syllables *Pe-ter* and transform them into something of power and beauty.

Never. And in this moment, it was barely even possible to remember all the different reasons they'd fallen out, let alone conjure up the pain they were causing. There was the boy on the white horse with the mountains in his eyes. And everyone could see him. The group seemed to lean into Cooper like flowers towards the sun and for a moment at least, snow at the window was the only movement, and the silence he brought was the peaceful kind. And Peter felt proud to call him *his*. But it wasn't the answer Terri was looking for.

"Good, Cooper," she said. "Now, can you be more specific?"

Cooper shrugged. "There ain't nothin' more specific than the seasons."

"I know. But can you think of anything during fall that people might have to look forward to?"

"But people can look forward to that. I reckon there ain't nothin' more beautiful."

"And I'm sure they do. We all do. But can you think of anything else?"

"Else?"

"Yes, something more than just the colours we can all look forward to."

Cooper slumped back in his chair. "Hell. If you got all your own answers, why bother askin'?"

Terri recoiled. She tried to cover her shock by bluffing

a smile. But it was no use. Everyone looked away to spare her embarrassment and an awkward silence gripped the hall. She exchanged uneasy glances with the sheriff who quickly set his cup down on the trestle as if he was readying himself to intervene. But Becky placed her hand across Cooper's knee to pacify him and a moment later, Teddy took his cue.

"Thanksgiving!" he offered.

"Birthdays," came another voice behind them. "Christmas!"

Yes!" said Terri, relief flooding her face. "Yes." Then, "Absolutely. And can anyone think of some of the ways we might celebrate those?"

Teddy raised his hand. "Turkey and cake."

"And?"

"And corn and cranberry sauce and pumpkin pie."

"Yes," said Terri. "And someone else with anything other than food?"

Ned stayed low beneath his baseball cap and cautiously raised a hand. "You might like to buy your sweetheart some pretty flowers for her birthday."

"And she'd be a lucky girl, Ned," said Terri. "But if it was Christmas and you really loved her, what do you think you might buy her then?"

Ned shrugged. "Some fancy dishwasher?"

A woman in the group cleared her throat. "It would

have to be real fancy if you planned on gettin' lucky, Ned."

"OK," said Terri. "And moving on. But a dishwasher is going in the right direction. Anyone else at all? Anyone? Just keep them coming."

Terri continued pacing the circle looking for more suggestions. But Peter could only see Cooper, who just sat there, hair spilled across his face, chest heaving. He never answered back to people. Never. But it would've taken more courage for him to talk in public than a rabbit scurrying beneath an eagle sky and now he'd been made to feel stupid. Becky's hand stayed on his knee and Peter leaned forward. It should be him doing that.

"What about you, Peter?"

This should *all* be him.

"Peter?"

"What?"

Terri smiled as if to absorb how rude that had sounded. "Do you have an answer for us?"

"No. I'm OK."

"Now, come on," she said.

"I can't think of anything."

"From what I hear you were a real little shopper back on the lake with all those river traders."

Peter shook his head and willed Cooper to look at him. "I guess."

"So, hazard a guess."

"I couldn't."

"Try."

"I—"

"Try, Peter."

"A damned car. I guess you could buy your loved one a car."

Peter sank back into his chair, too scared to look Cooper's way now in case he was disappointed in him. But Terri was jubilant.

"And he's gone big, folks," she said slapping her thigh. "Huge! So, you see, these are just some of the ways we can get through a year, looking forward to things and celebrating them. And our friends from the credit rating department are here today to help you achieve those goals with a range of available loans so you and your loved ones don't have to miss out on a single celebration together."

Terri held her hand out towards the stand where the woman with the smile wider than a canoe was standing, indicating for the group to applaud. And they did.

"They're coming now," said Teddy leaning in. "It's the televisions."

"But before all that," said Terri. "We have a special surprise to help get you all back on your feet."

"Told you."

The hall rustled with expectant whispers. Terri clasped her clipboard to her breast and Peter watched her for a while. Despite her methods, she took genuine pleasure in the joy she was about to offer. And somehow, it felt wrong choosing not to see the hope she so desperately wanted to gift her people. What a joy it was that the world her generation had only ever been able to describe to their children in bedtime stories had finally become real. So, when she briefly looked his way, Peter found that he was powerless to deny her. He smiled. Terri held his gaze a moment and smiled back. The last fifteen years were finally coming to an end. She looked to the double doors at the back of the hall just as they flung open.

Everyone took to their feet. Chairs scraped violently across the floor. Whispers erupted into excitable chatter and before Peter knew it, the circle had emptied as everyone moved to gather around a trolley stacked tall with giant rectangular boxes. There was a television for every household, Terri told them all. And soon, the boxes were unloaded and passed out and hands were shaken and backs were patted and Teddy set the last of his donut down on the chair and turned back to Peter, both his cheeks flushed and burning.

"Don't let Cooper make you feel bad about wanting to be here, Peter," he said, moving through the crowd. "This is your time now."

Peter nodded, suddenly unsure how to take that, but not wanting to spoil Teddy's fun any more than he wanted to spoil Terri's. So he urged Teddy to go bag himself a television like he was right behind him.

After a while, the sheriff slowly started to guide people to the stand so that they could begin conversations about the loans they were being offered. Terri noticed that the old man in the Stetson was still in his chair. She quietly squeezed through the crowd, making her apologies as she went, and crouched down before him with one hand soft across his knee. The old man's eyes retreated beneath the heavy folds of his eyelids. Then the rest of him disappeared beneath the brim of his hat. But Terri stroked his knee to calm him and gently prized the envelope from his fist.

She took a moment to read its contents then started to say things like how this was only the beginning and that things would take time to sort out and for him not to worry. And the old man wiped his eyes on the back of his hand and Terri continued to stroke him and offer her reassurances that the government were all set up to help anyone in financial difficulty upon their return. She continued in this way, trying her very best to put the poor man's mind at ease until quite suddenly, and without any warning, he looked up. *That life*, he told her, his eyes at once harsh and appalled. *That fucking life*.

Peter looked away, ashamed to have been eavesdropping. He made his way towards Teddy. The group hadn't even noticed the outburst. They were too busy ripping the boxes open like it was Christmas morning, which only increased the chatter further. But the old man had Terri by the wrists. His eyes raved, madness and misery changing places inside him like neither one of them was stronger than the other. And he shook her. And he shook. And the sheriff dashed back through the crowd ready to yank him off her when a chair scraped violently across the floor. It screamed, running across the shiny surface like a fork down a plate, and everyone stopped. And Cooper looked so calm standing there in the middle of the circle with his dark eyes burning behind his hair, that when he finally spoke, his ability to silence the room and hold it silent was all the more alarming.

"Reckon we won't be able to say the same as the leaves," he said. "Not when the time comes. I mean, what colour do you seriously think you'll be when you all die down here? Cos it sure as hell won't be gold."

The snow at the window seemed to hurry across the glass at a bullying pace, but inside the hall was so still. The old man's hands fell away from Terri's wrists. The group set their boxes down across the floor and stood silenced. But nothing was stiller than Cooper. He spoke of everyone's death, yet not a single part of him was troubled by his own words.

"Son," said the sheriff quietly. "What did you mean by that?"

"You heard me," said Cooper.

The sheriff stopped at the perimeter of the circle looking in at Cooper like a rancher might at a bronco that hadn't been broken in yet. And the rancher always knew better than to enter the ring.

"Mr Donaghue, I'm beggin' you. I'm beggin' you real hard right now to just think. What, exactly, did you mean when you said that everyone would die?"

"But everyone will die. Eventually."

"Sure. But that's not what you were implyin'."

Cooper chewed down on his jaw and said nothing.

"Cooper, why would everyone die down here?"

But it was Becky who spoke next. She entered the circle to stand at Cooper's side, her attention entirely on the sheriff but her eyes roaming the room.

"You're only giving those televisions away because you don't know how else to fill these people's lives."

"Miss, we're not talking about—"

"I mean," Becky went on. "You don't have the first clue what else you can possibly do to compensate for the emptiness that's about to be handed back to them, so you're just filling it up with stuff and the same old shit they've always been sold, hoping nobody will even notice."

The sheriff looked to Terri for help. But it was all Terri could do to stand by and listen.

"Becky," the sheriff went on. "It's Becky, isn't it?

Becky held his gaze and said nothing, which the sheriff took to mean yes. "Well, Becky, we're not talking about no goddamn televisions right now. We're talking about why you think everyone will die."

"Yeah," said Becky. "We are."

"And you're scaring people with it."

Cooper nodded. "They should be scared."

"Now, son, I'm begging you to tread so carefully right now."

But the sheriff was running clean out of options. He needed to appeal to some part of Cooper that wasn't even in the room right now, so Peter stepped between two of the chairs to enter the circle, his heart so tired of aching, and stood there until Cooper had no choice but to look his way.

"You haven't even given this a go."

"I've given it plenty."

"You promised me you'd try."

"But—"

"You promised me."

"Peter," said Becky, like she still had every right to his friendship. "Don't you ever sit in that ticket booth and quietly wonder if that's all there is to it?"

Peter cleared his throat. "Marge reckons I'll make assistant manager inside a year if I keep it up."

Becky laughed but forgot to tell her eyes. "Keep what up?"

"What?"

"Keep what up, Pete?"

"I don't know. Look, why are you trying to trip me?"

"Nobody's trying to trip you."

"This is our home now."

Dark amusement filled Becky's eyes. "Is it?"

"Well," said Peter, "whichever state we're resettled in will be, yes."

"And then what will happen?"

"Whatever we want. College. A job."

"And then what?"

"And then we go get a nice home."

"And then what?"

"And get nice things to put it in."

Becky shrugged. "And then what?"

"And then what, what?"

"And then *what*, Peter? Think."

"Stop trying to trip me! Why are you trying to trip me?"

"We're here and then we're gone, Peter," she said. "And all people do in this place is bide their time until their time is over. You just won't see it."

Peter shook his head. Every emotion strangled so tightly in his throat. "Why are you even being like this? Both of you. I've dreamed about this my whole life."

"Yeah," said Cooper. "When all I ever dreamed about was you."

And there it was. The sum of all their time together. Peter's chest shuddered. That wasn't fair. They weren't being fair. But before he even had a chance to say anything that could pull all this back, they were done.

Cooper looked across the hall towards Tokala who'd been silent until now. He nodded, as if an agreement had been reached. Becky looked to the girl broad like a bear and another boy Peter hadn't even noticed before. In a matter of moments, they all made for the door and Peter was left standing.

"What are you even doing up there in the woods?" he called out. "I've seen you. Don't think I haven't seen you."

Cooper briefly held back at the door, his dark eyes turning towards his shoulder. But he didn't turn round. His hair spilled across his face, like any chance Peter had left to sweep it to one side and see himself and all the love Cooper had for him, had finally been lost. Then he was gone.

Teddy took Peter by the arm. "Leave them."

"Get off me!"

"Come back to mine for dinner."

"I said get off me."

Peter grabbed his coat off the back of the chair and ran outside. And the snow hurried over Mainstreet so thickly now that the neon signs were nothing but smudges of bright colour behind the grey. The others started to gather at the door behind him, all thick with whispers. He held back until he was completely sure Cooper and the others had cleared the Lone Star. Then he ran. But he'd barely passed the town hall when a voice shouted after him. Peter turned back and the sheriff staggered out on to the street, his eyes burning with worry for the town and a single word that would topple them all.

"I know," said Peter. "Don't you think I don't know?"

He ran back to the apartment up into the bedroom, tipping the contents of Cooper's rucksack out across the floor. Undershorts and tees. Tin cups and penknives. Bits of old wood ready for whittling. Nothing. Nothing. Nothing but junk and nothing of use until, finally, there it was.

Peter couldn't remember the last time he'd seen Rider's silver snowflake. He supposed he must've been wearing it the night he died. But as hard as he tried to picture it nestled across the breast of his poncho, he could only recall how empty a person's eyes became the moment their life left them. Perhaps the pendant wasn't even there at all. Perhaps Cooper already had it in his possession when he and Rider spoke privately in Henry's bedroom just minutes before. That symbol of frozen life was the way Returnees could share their allegiance to one another in secret. Maybe Rider had given it to him as a gift of solidarity now that Cooper had taken the same journey into death and back as he had. Perhaps it was more than a gift. Perhaps it was an invitation to take up the cause, whatever that might mean. Peter picked the snowflake up. It glinted as it turned in his hand.

"You were *my* friend," he whispered. "What have you asked him to do? Why did you have to ask him anything?"

Peter put the snowflake in his pocket and made his way outside. He barely remembered hurrying back to the woods, but by the time he'd left the cover of the pines to follow a trail left by the others and taken the steep walk up the ridge, it'd stopped snowing and a round moon made the snow bright underfoot.

The ridge gave way to a rocky bluff that fell away sharply into the forest on the other side of the hill from town. Briefly, Peter looked back, noticing how the neon strip of Mainstreet formed a dome of smudgy light over the town. High above it was the dome of the actual world. The star-strewn sky. He hadn't even seen them once since beneath the haze of lights since they'd arrived. And for a moment, from this higher vantage up in the stars, it almost seemed strange that people's worries, their lives, their cities and towns were ever allowed to take up so much of the world.

Peter heard voices. Laughing. Chatter. The babble of many conversations. Beneath him, down off the bluff where the bald rock met with pines to mark the forests on the other side, came smoke. Peter scrambled down closer, ducking in among the first of the trees some distance away to make sure he wasn't seen, and watched.

The flickering flames of a campfire lit a clearing in the pines, making the shadows of Cooper and the others see-saw woozily across the snowy boughs. At first, it was hard to make out what was silhouette and what was shadow, but every now and then, someone turned towards the fire and the bright burn of its flame made masks of all their faces.

There were more people up here than had left town with Cooper. Easily a dozen or so. Peter didn't know where they'd come from, but the girl from the town hall was sitting on a log with the boy and talking to a woman who hadn't been at the meeting earlier. There was a man too, sat across the way with Tokala. And perched with his back to Peter, the silhouette of his Stetson bold against the light of the fire, was Cooper. Becky was at his side, busy talking to someone next to her. Peter couldn't make out a face, but every now and then she'd touch Cooper's shoulder or knee as if the conversation she was having with the other person constantly referred back to him. A joke. A memory. New friendships shared. She took a swig from a bottle she was holding and tried to pass it to her neighbour, but they dropped it. Becky apologised, as if the fault had been her own, and rushed in to pick it up before the remaining liquid bled out, offering the rest to Cooper. Becky continued her conversation with the man so Cooper removed his Stetson and jacket, setting the latter across the snow for a blanket, and sat back against the log, legs splayed out, watching.

A few moments passed while he raked both hands through his golden hair to ease out a stretch. He was relaxed, happy even, gazing into the fire with the hubbub of chatter going on all around him, but without having to be the centre of any one person's attention. And yet, he was at the centre of it all. Every now and then, the girl looked away from the woman she was chatting to, to check in with him. Cooper nodded as if giving his approval somehow and she returned to her conversation. The boy did the same. Throughout all this, Cooper maintained a constant connection with Tokala, whose dark gaze held his from across the other side of the campfire. They were apart but together at all times. Peter's throat became tight and sore. Cooper was more than a friend to these people. He was their leader, present but removed, quietly taking in a world of his own making.

The woman the girl from the town hall had been talking to suddenly stood up and walked off. For some reason this seemed to worry the girl. She started to scratch at her collarbone like she might have said something to offend the woman and looked through the flames to Cooper for support. But he wasn't troubled. He calmly shook his head to reassure her, and let the woman leave the clearing. She was coming this way.

Peter ducked back behind the tree. He looked up towards the rocky bluff knowing that his best chance of not being seen was to head down the other side of the hill towards town. But the route was too exposed for him to make it there without being seen now. He flattened his back against the tree trunk and hoped the woman wouldn't glance round.

He watched.

He waited.

He heard the woman coming up through the woods towards him.

A twig snapped, followed by the sound of footfall creaking through the snow, and the woman passed him. She stopped, with tangles of grey hair falling about her shoulders, and looked up into the night. The cardigan she wore hung long to the back of her knees. The knitted belt had slipped from its hoop and dragged across the ground behind her, weighed down by clumps of frozen earth. Pine needles riddled her hair too. But none of this seemed to bother her. Yet it didn't even cross Peter's mind that she would be fatally cold in only a cardigan and jeans until he saw her bare feet.

The remains of her toes were as black as charcoal. Her rotting fingers were no thicker than twigs with bulbous knuckles like the knots of a tree. The woman's head twisted round into profile as if conjured by some strange calling. It hung low on her neck but alert, watching, with cloudy eyeballs wide as moons. Hunting.

The hairs on the back of Peter's neck stood. The Restless One's jaw ground and sagged and ground and sagged, its mouth having greater power to scour the woods than its eyeballs. And he was up here without a staff or Cooper's scent to protect him. All it took was for one of the group to call out and that thing would turn back in his direction and see him.

Peter dropped to his knees, burrowing his nails into the frozen earth. Perhaps the smell of soil would mask his own scent. But the earth was too hard to break up. Someone in the group laughed. The fire crackled. The Restless One's eyes swivelled round and Peter took a stone. He threw it. The snow softened its landing and for a moment, he thought it hadn't been enough to call the Restless One's attention away. But like an owl to a mouse, it was. The thing's head twisted round. She blinked.

She stumbled on deeper into the woods, jaw wide and clacking.

Peter closed his eyes, feeling the sigh of relief crash across his chest, and looked back towards the campfire. The man Becky had been talking with was no more likely to take hold of a bottle or talk back than that poor wretch. None of them were. One by the one, the Dead left the clearing and wandered out into the light, their ashen skin lit by the moon as if its ghostly light had made them. Made of moon. Made of dust. Made of rot and pale luminescence.

"When are we going to take them down there?" Becky asked.

"Soon," said Cooper.

"But when?"

"Soon."

Cooper kicked snow over the campfire, killing the flame. It was only now Peter noticed that the red glow he'd seen over the ridge the night before hadn't come from the fire at all, but something else much further down off the bluff inside the forest below them. But there was no time left to wonder what that might be. They were coming.

The Dead dispersed into the night. Peter waited until Cooper had led the others back down the ridge towards town. Then he ran.

22

Peter pounded the door with his fist. "Hello?" he called. "Sheriff O'Hurn? Teddy?"

He knocked again, more urgently this time, causing the bunch of bricks the old trailer was balanced on to shift. There was no answer. He stood on tiptoe, peering through a set of tie-back curtains left half-hanging off their hooks at the window. The glass was misted, but still no one came. Peter turned round, looking back into the night where rows of drunken telegraph poles hung over the snowbound road, their shadows striking out tall across the land in the light of the moon. In among them, old billboards at the roadside creaked and groaned beneath the weight of the snow like bison worn ragged by winter. Ahead, beads of light marked the town out from the vast, white land.

The trailer was only half a mile south out of West Wranglestone, kicked back off the road like a used tin can, but the town already looked so far away. Everything felt so far away.

The billboards moaned like their time on this land was nearly done. Peter stood listening to them while he caught his breath, when a rectangle of yellow light struck his feet.

"I take it Teddy pointed at the billboard and said *billboard*?"

Peter turned round and the sheriff leaned into the doorframe, a cigarette hanging loosely on his lips. He smiled. "In order for you to find us, I mean."

"Oh," said Peter clearing his throat. "No, I saw your Jeep tracks and followed them here."

The cigarette stub left the sheriff's mouth, dropping to sizzle in the snow below. "I was on the john just now and Teddy's busy making dinner. I dint mean to frighten you by making you think we weren't in."

"You didn't."

"Well, I'm sure I did, son, you look fried, but it's kind of you to let me think so."

Peter offered a smile and an awkward silence passed between them.

"You OK?" said the sheriff after a while.

"No. I mean—"

"It's OK if you're not. It's been quite the day."

Peter nodded. "I'm OK. Teddy invited me for dinner."

"He did?"

"Yes."

"He did," said the sheriff, taking the correction. "That's right and you took pity on us poor bastards and came."

"No, it's not like that. I wanted to."

The sheriff brought a soft chuckle into his chest. "Your tracker skills are better than your lying ones, Peter, but I'll take your being here as a win. Now get your hide inside. He'll be thrilled to see you here."

The sheriff propped the door open with his heel for Peter to follow and made his way in. Peter stepped up, stubbing loose snow from his boots on the set of bricks that'd been fashioned into the side of the trailer for front steps and closed the door behind him.

Inside was a squeeze. Wallpaper decorated with cherry trees over a white picket fence for that home-away-from-home feel during long trips on the road, curled off the walls into dog ears, giving the appearance that the whole trailer was about to peel away. But seating, built into the curve of the trailer around a table down one end, was cosy and dressed with a candle for dinner.

Teddy shook a match and turned. "Banquette!"

"Hi, Teddy."

"That's what the seating's called. Not a chair, but banquette seats."

"OK."

"But you say it like bonk-et."

"Right."

Teddy laughed. "Banquette."

"Yes."

"The more you say it the more—"

"OK, son." The sheriff swiped his moustache. "We had a talk about this."

Teddy shrugged. "I know."

"Even the snowman you built outside decided to leave town on account of you telling him what his nose was made out of, so I think it's best you dial the verbal guidebook down, don't you?"

Teddy squeezed past them to the kitchenette where something was busy twirling around inside a microwave.

"What are we going to talk about, then?" Teddy asked. "I saved up the banquette conversation especially."

Peter noticed the sheriff glance at his boots which were still muddy from the hike up the ridge. "I'm sure Peter's got bigger things to be worrying about."

"Oh," said Peter. "I should take these off."

"It's OK."

"No. No, it's not."

Peter struggled out of his boots, setting them down on the front step outside, and the sheriff poured himself a whisky. "So, how are you finding Marge?"

"Inside her office with the door closed, mostly."

"Sounds about right. I think she's enjoyed having the

place to herself this last year before pesky Pete showed up."

"Wasn't she always a loner even at Yellowstone?" Peter asked.

"Perhaps."

"Well, don't you know?"

"Not really," said the sheriff, taking a sip. "She lived in another part of the park to Teddy and me. Although I hear she was a first responder to the twin towers that morning, so I suppose that must have something to do with her solitary nature."

Peter caught the door before it had a chance to clack shut behind him. He gently pulled it to and the sheriff swilled his glass round and round. And even though the microwave didn't stop whirring, silence fell over the trailer and suddenly Peter wondered if he'd done enough to make Marge realize he was just trying to be her friend. Either way, the thought of befriending her had become easier to tackle than the subject of Cooper.

"She was there that day?" he asked after a while.

The sheriff nodded. "She was a firefighter. She lost her partner Barbra, in the North Tower that day, too."

"But—"

"I know. Hard to imagine who any of us were before all this, right?"

Peter nodded. "Right."

"Those of us who are old enough have led two lives.

And I have no doubt that going back will be harder on some than on others."

"What about the old man in the workshop earlier?"

"Oh, don't you worry about ol' Walt."

"But the envelope."

"But Cooper?" said the sheriff holding Peter's gaze. "More importantly."

"Yes. Yes, I know. I—"

Peter glanced at Teddy, hoping for more conversation. But he was too busy staring at the microwave making waiting look busy. And it went so quiet that Peter even considered asking him why the seating was called a banquette even though he already knew the answer, just to get things going again. Anything but tackling Cooper's intentions.

The sheriff shoved his arms into the sleeves of a cardigan and squeezed in behind the table, gesturing for Peter to do the same and soon the microwave pinged and Teddy proceeded to slop the brown contents of a Tupperware box across all three plates. They sat down to eat.

"So, do we need to talk about Cooper?" said the sheriff after a while.

"I don't know."

"Because I'm pretty sure I don't need to point out to you how worried the government would be if news of that behaviour got back to them."

Peter set his knife down and carried on pushing brown stuff around the plate with his fork. "He's finding it hard, that's all. It was my dream to come back to the world that was before, not his. And now it's all happening so fast. I think he's just angry and frustrated."

"There's no *just* about it."

"He needs time."

"And none of this even factors in what's happening at the supermarket," said the sheriff. "From what I hear, he's gone into that trance in the same darned aisle every day since he's been here."

"But it's not just him, is it?" said Peter. "It's happening all over town."

"But your boy and his friends are the only ones who ain't reached out for help about it."

Peter let go of the fork and sat there feeling the steam rising up off the plate, all sticky and warm across his face compared to the coolness of the trailer.

"I'm sorry."

"Son, you don't have to apologise."

"But—"

"We're all under a lot of pressure here and we only have ourselves to figure this whole mess out. Now, if you don't mind, I might just have another cigarette. And you don't mind, do you?"

Peter looked up. "Well—"

"I mean," said the sheriff striking a match against the table, "it is terrible table manners while you two boys are still eating, but I really thought those TV sets were going to brighten up everyone's days and—"

"And Cooper pissed all over it."

The sheriff offered Peter a smile. "That he did. I mean, God only knows what folks are expected to watch on them. Just a bunch of *Lucille Ball* and *Friends* reruns sandwiched between five hours of infomercials, most likely. But we did get them for free. We all did. From what I hear, dozens of companies reached out to all the communities across the whole of the Escape Programme, offering to be our official sponsor. Everyone just wants to get back to how it used to be."

Peter set his fork down and listened to the billboard just outside the trailer moaning softly. "They did?"

"They sure did," said the sheriff, drawing deeply on his cigarette. "They didn't take much persuading at all. Half of the world's population is gone, but God bless Uncle Sam, everybody's back in business."

Peter stayed with the sound of the billboards creaking for a while and eventually the clatter of busy knives and forks picked up again. Every now and then he felt the sheriff's eyes on him. But he couldn't tell if he was trying to find more small talk or push past all that in the hope Peter would explain the real reason for his being here. A short while later, Teddy cleared his throat.

"Did I tell you that banquette seating is called that from olden days when castles used to have banquets. 'Medieval Times, Dinner and a Show' restaurants used to have loads of it, apparently."

Peter held Teddy's eye. "*Banc* is French for bench."

Teddy's face dropped and the conversation dried up. And it turned out that the best time to catch some peace with him was while he was eating. He barely came up for breath after that and a good ten minutes passed in silence. Every now and then, the sheriff glanced across the table at Peter and smiled as if to make sure he was having a nice time. Peter smiled back and continued to push food around his plate. But he wasn't hungry. And after a while, the silence became the void in which to see Cooper and Becky sitting there, side by side around the campfire surrounded by all their new friends. Surrounded by the ones nobody should be making friends with.

Peter stared into the candle's softly flickering flame. It curled then tapered back into a point and the trailer, along with all his thoughts, dissolved into the darkness behind its golden halo.

It would have been easier if Cooper had died. If Cooper had died back there at the falls and never returned, Peter's life would have been over, but at least he would never have gone on to suffer this. The rest of his life would have been empty, but it would have been full of imagined memories. Like love letters left unwritten, those memories would never come to be, but he'd have imagined their lives being perfect. They would've been filled with that time yet to come when he and Cooper took Snowball out across the plains just to watch stardust and glitter hurtle silently over the mountains as a meteor shower passed by. Or that time yet to come when Cooper, much older now, rose from their bed in the middle of the day to stand at the open door where blue jays played. Blond hairs between his legs would be all downy in the sunlight; both his beard and hair now tied back with an old bootlace, as golden as their matching wedding bands. Cooper would run down to the water's edge naked, calling Peter's name as he went. Peter would go to answer but knowing full well that Cooper was only ever saying his name just so he could hear it. And all those imagined memories would have filled so many unwritten love letters that it'd be all he could do just to stuff them inside every pillowcase and cupboard for safekeeping. And inside the emptiness of his life without Cooper, those memories would have been everything, everything and anything but this, the pain of being around long enough to see the moment someone doesn't love you any more.

Peter hated them for all of this. He hated them so much. Becky. Tokala. Those friends. All of them and for everything, whatever everything was about to be.

Whatever it was Cooper was about to do that he now had no choice but to tell on. And as that betrayal of love started to swell, snow tumbled across the trailer windows. Peter glanced up, and while the other two were busy eating, very quietly wished that he were dead.

"There's no need to be frightened."

The sheriff's voice quietly pulled Peter's focus back into the room.

"I'm not," he whispered. "I'm having a nice time."

The sheriff smiled, but he understood the situation all too well. "I mean, don't be frightened if you have somethin' difficult you need to share. Isn't that right, Teddy?"

"That's right," said Teddy. "You're with friends now."

"Yeah," said the sheriff. "You're with friends and there's nothing you can say here that will lose you that position."

The sheriff set his cutlery down, wiping some brown sauce from his moustache, and eased back into the seat, watching him. The candle's flickering flame danced across the darkness of his pupils. But there was no malice hiding there waiting to step out of the shadows, just a kind of worn-in warmth that reassured Peter the truth was safe.

"Cooper's leading a gang of Returnees," he said. "They're up in the woods right now. And they're planning to lead the Dead into town."

23

The sheriff exchanged glances with Teddy. But surprise didn't enter his face once.

"Good lad," he said. "Now take a deep breath. I know it won't have come easy on you sayin' that, but it could be the only thing that stands to save your boy and the others right now."

Teddy leaned forward. "Dad's right. We know they've been sneaking out of town every night since they came here. We just didn't know what they were doing."

"And I don't know what they're doing now either," said Peter, "but—"

"But your gut's tellin' you somethin' ain't right."

Peter pushed his plate away, watching the snow fall across the windows. But there was no escaping it. He nodded and the sheriff dropped his cigarette into the whisky glass to douse it.

"Tell us what you saw."

"Cooper's taken Becky, Tokala and two others from town up on the ridge where they've built a camp. There were others there too, people I didn't recognize. For a moment I thought they must've made friends with a group of wanderers or people from another town. But they hadn't. They were sitting there talking to the Dead."

"And what were the Dead doin' in return?"

"Nothing. They were just sitting there."

"They weren't agitated?"

"No," said Peter. "But then, they wouldn't be. Not when they're—"

"With *them*. I guess not. They'd be quite the opposite in fact. You could almost say they'd be under their spell."

Peter shook his head. "Spell?"

"Control, then."

"I guess. But they weren't making them do anything bad when I was up there."

The sheriff's eyes narrowed. "And yet you're here, Peter."

"Yes. Yes, I know that."

"And it'll hurt as all hell because you love him but—"

"But what?"

The sheriff eased back into his seat and maintained eye contact with Peter, as if he was waiting for him to make another connection.

"But I know that something's wrong."

"Yes," said the sheriff. "And that?"

"And that something's wrong with *him*."

Peter clutched at his stomach and the sheriff leaned forward. "There. Feel that sting now? Right there in the pit of your guts?"

Peter nodded.

"Yeah. Well, I reckon that sting's the worst. Hurts like all hell, don't it?"

"Yes. But why? What is it?"

"While a weaker part of you is busy keeping you in the dark, trying to convince you that your doubts are all wrong because he's your Cooper so it can't be true, that's the sting that tells you your instincts are right."

The candle's flame curled over and snow started to pummel the windows, making the billboards outside groan like they'd give up the fight any moment now.

"Teddy," said the sheriff. "Go fetch the whisky from the stoop, there's a good boy. I reckon we could all do with one now."

Teddy did as he was told. He quietly got up from the table, stacking the dinner plates, and dumped them in the sink. He left them alone and the sheriff sat there, fingers toying with the rim of his whisky glass, looking across the way at Peter. But he didn't speak. He gave him time to be alone with his thoughts and soon Teddy stepped back inside, dusting snow from the base of an old whisky bottle. He cracked a tray of ice cubes across three tumblers, dousing each glass with a neat shot and passed them round.

"Here," said Teddy, "take this."

"No, thank you," said Peter. "I'm fine."

"Go on. It'll help."

Peter did as he was told, trying not to wince every time a sip burned the back of his throat, and Teddy sat back down. The sheriff rotated the tumbler in his hand, watching the way the golden liquid coiled its way down through the ice. Snow skittered across the windowpane, heavier than before. The net curtains stirred, making the candle's flame bend and quiver. But they were in the pocket of the conversation now. Peter could feel it. The sheriff had made a good fist of small talk and given him ample time to settle in, but there was no disguising that this was the real reason they'd all gathered here. And as the sheriff downed his whisky in one shot, Peter felt Teddy looking at him. He smiled warmly, but more intently this time, as if all his little ways, pointing at things and naming them, were nothing but a preamble leading up to the moment the three of them would find themselves here.

"Perhaps they were just rounding up the Dead in order to destroy them, Peter," Teddy offered.

"Perhaps," said Peter. "Perhaps." Then, "Thanks Teddy."
Teddy shrugged. "That's OK."

"When I was young," said the sheriff, "my old man's
neighbour, Duke, owned a dog. Now, Buckle was the
sweetest lil thing. You could throw her rag doll a hundred
times over and she'd bring it back with her tail still a
wagglin'. But one day when I tried to pass Duke a cigar,
she jumped up, clean out of the blue and took a bite out
of me. The puncture hole in the crook of my arm didn't
even bleed. The dog's tooth pierced it so neatly that it
went straight through the skin to that thick layer of white
fat and the cavity below. As clean as a bullet through a
mattress, it was. And I just sat there in shock, staring
down inside this big ol' black hole in my arm. But when
I looked up, that dog was fraught with panic. Now, there
isn't anything like a dog's shame. Buckle knew she'd done
wrong. But I'd never seen a dog left so utterly confused
by its own actions. There she was with her tail between
her legs, whimperin' for Duke not to take a belt to her. All
she knew was that her master had been in danger. All she
wanted was to protect him. She really didn't like the wolf
that leaped out of her with its teeth all drooling ready to
take care of him. She didn't like it one bit. But it didn't
matter a jot whether she liked that part of herself or not.
Out came the wild animal she really was, just the same.

"So, the thing is," said the sheriff. "It doesn't really

matter whether they plan to use the Dead to harm us or not. Perhaps it doesn't matter at all whether they mean to do anything. The question is, do you think it's possible that they could, no matter how inadvertently, become dangerous back in society should that trance ever escalate to violence?"

Ice at the bottom of the glass burned the skin in Peter's palm. He could sit here all night waiting for that question to go away, or the ice to melt, whichever came first. But like all questions with dark and troubling answers, the only thing that would ever make it go away was the hardest thing of all: accepting the truth. Peter looked up with his stomach all in twists at how it ever came to this.

"It's possible," he whispered. Then, "Yes. I think that's possible."

The sheriff blinked deeply to mark his respect for Peter's bravery. "But we still don't know what Timberdark is."

Peter pulled the silver snowflake from his pocket and held it over the table where it spun in the candlelight, glinting.

The sheriff shifted forward in his seat. "What is that, son?"

"It's the Returnees'. When the Dead first came, and Returnees began to realize that people would hunt them down just because they were scared they'd turn out to be just as bad, one woman, Selma, led a band of survivors to freedom. The snowflake was used to communicate not only their allegiance to one another but to every Returnee left out in the world who needed their help. Each founding member of the original community who took refuge at Lake Wranglestone wore a silver snowflake and this one belonged to my friend Rider before he died. But I found it in Cooper's rucksack. At the time, when you first asked me about Timberdark, I couldn't see how Cooper could even have heard of that word, let alone know what it was. But there was a way. Just one."

The sheriff shook his head. "How?"

"While you were living peacefully alongside the Returnees at Yellowstone, the leader of my community, Henry, kept their existence from us by killing them out by the falls or trading them in for weapons and medicines. When Rider helped me rescue Cooper from a cowboy he'd been sold to, we planned to go back to the lake, not just to tell the rest of the community the truth about the Returned, but to flush out the one remaining member who'd helped Henry."

"This is Darlene," said the sheriff taking a swig from Teddy's tumbler.

Peter looked away and nodded. "That night, we held a party at Henry's place. I can't remember which one of us suggested that now, but while everyone was arriving, Rider and Cooper waited inside Henry's bedroom. Even my dad wondered what they might be talking about given time alone. I was annoyed with him for being suspicious, but now I look back, that's when it could've happened. That was the only time Rider had Cooper on his own. That's when he had his chance to say something or show Cooper something."

The sheriff reached out, placing his hand flat across the table as if holding it to Peter's heart somehow, and thanked him for his candour. And the three of them sat in silence with nothing but the wind and the snow all about them.

"But what could that something be?" the sheriff asked after a while.

"I don't know. There was nothing in there. It was just Henry's bedroom."

"But it wasn't always Henry's bedroom."

"What do you mean?"

"You said that a community of Returnees had lived on the lake before Henry and Darlene took it over."

"Yes," said Peter. "But what difference does that make?"

The sheriff held Peter's gaze and once again waited for him to make the connection.

"Selma," said Peter bolting forward. "That room and

cabin were built and lived in by the Returnees' leader, Selma."

The door flew open, clattering back on broken hinges into the side of the trailer. The candle's flame lassoed once in the wind and was gone. The sheriff jumped up, pulling the door to, and looked back across the darkness of the trailer, his eyes heavy with the burden of things yet to come.

"We have to notify the marshal ranger of this."

Peter pushed his chair back and stood. "No."

"Son, my hands are tied. And I can only keep the government at bay for so long."

"But—"

"But nothin'. Now come on. We need to leave now and find whatever it is this Selma left behind before Cooper has a chance to."

"But what could she have left behind that wouldn't already have been taken?" Peter asked. "Henry lived there for years before Rider got a chance to get back into the room."

The sheriff nodded. "And that might turn out to be the case. But the Returnees managed to hide there for some time without being discovered. What if the thing they were hiding was much smaller?"

"How small?"

The sheriff clenched his jaw and said nothing.

"How small?"

"Like a device, Peter. Like a damned bomb."

The sheriff took his parka from the back of the door and Teddy did the same. Peter held back, watching smoke coil from the candlewick. But no amount of stalling would ever make such a threat go away. None.

The trailer was left rattling in the wind. Within the hour, the four of them made the return to Wranglestone.

24

Stars grazed the snowy peaks above Wranglestone, mountains made spears by ice on the tip ready for skewering comets with. Streaming stars that darted now like scores of silver minnow out across the galaxy's inky waters, if only those peaks didn't catch them. And the islands of Wranglestone were so small beneath them, it barely seemed possible that a secret as heavy as Timberdark could find a hiding place here. But it was out there somewhere, waiting inside the stilly darkness of a frosted tree house or cabin, and those watchful mountains knew exactly where, if only they had a heart to share it.

They left the Jeep outside Wranglestone's border, entering the park via the secret tunnel behind the waterfall. Peter had led the group down through the woods to the boathouse, taking care to show them the combination of stepping stones used to cross the river and then, when the watchtower finally came into view, where the lake was. But it was when Peter saw the mountains from the boathouse again that he asked for a moment to be alone. He wandered in among the jumble of canoes left frozen into the ice and, with no sound but the clink of metal weaponry swaying gently on its hooks behind him, stood gazing up at those mountains. And he wondered how very small all life down here must seem to them. His worries no bigger than a pine cone. All of humankind's troubles nothing but a blip against the vast reach of those eternal peaks. If only his troubles felt that way to him.

Peter took his staff in hand and pointed towards the island of Cabins Creak. "This way."

"Son," said the sheriff, jumping down off the boards to join him, "are you sure that's where we should be looking?"

"I'm not sure of anything."

"But—"

"But if Selma left something behind for the others to find, then yes, it would be there."

The sheriff turned round, stretching both arms out ready to catch Teddy the way you might a toddler. Teddy made it on to the ice, pulling the bottom of his jacket back down to straighten it, and slip-slided out on to the lake. But to Peter's relief, the Ghost Ranger was to wait here. The deer skull appeared to hover above the ground unsupported by a body. The black robe was indistinguishable from the darkness of the boathouse interior. And the Ranger didn't move. He stationed himself by the back door, tall and immoveable with those two hollow eye sockets watching. He may just as well have been mounted on the wall.

Peter leaned into the sheriff. "Does he really need to be here?"

"I don't like it any more than you do, son. But he's a state marshal. If we find anything here today we'll have to report it back."

Peter glanced over his shoulder, looking for the single handcuff beside the bench he'd found Cooper shackled to that night. If only he hadn't been in the woods that day. If only a great many things.

"And what about Cooper?"

"We're not here just because we're worried about him, Peter," said the sheriff. "But *for* him. Try and keep that in mind, OK?"

"OK."

"I know it's hard. And there ain't a single soul out there who'd think otherwise, ain't that right, Teddy?"

Teddy nodded more times than was necessary. "That's right. It's very pretty here, Peter."

Another shooting star passed over the mountains and Peter held a sigh in his chest. "Yes."

"It must feel like coming home," said the sheriff.

Home, Peter thought. But he didn't answer. "It's that island. The one with the steps leading off the jetty up through the pines. Henry's cabin's on top of the hill. That was Selma's home before him and that's where Rider spoke with Cooper."

The sheriff pulled down his trapper hat by the ears, clapping both hands together to warm them. "Then let's go. The sooner we get this over and done with, the sooner we can get back home."

They travelled out across the ice. Peter kept his eyes on the forest borders as they went just in case one of the Dead should follow, but nothing shook the snow from the branches at the lake's edge or broke out from behind one of the islands to tail them like a shadow. And soon they made it to the jetty of Cabins Creak, taking the steep flight of steps up through the pines to the crest of the hill where Henry's cabin cowered beneath an open sky, frosted with spears of ice hanging from every window.

The front door resisted them, as if the wood had started to grow back like skin over a wound now the cabin no longer had any inhabitants to disturb it. But it was just iced over. The sheriff leaned into the door, jostling the handle about and with a loud crack, it opened. He stepped to one side and Peter felt his invitation to enter first.

Peter braced both hands against the doorframe and

held back a moment. It wasn't just that this was the first time he'd set foot in Henry's place since that night. Just like the cabin at Yellowstone, stepping into a home when you hadn't been invited automatically held danger. Peter scanned the darkness, desperate to find comfort in such familiar surroundings. He'd spent so much time at Henry's during his childhood, he knew the layout well enough to walk through blindfolded. To his right, running the full length of the long window at the side of the cabin, was the dining table. Left of the door, the fireplace and two armchairs, both sunken from those long winter days snowed-in playing Scrabble. But here in the darkness and without invitation, the cabin and its contents seemed eerie and unfamiliar. The armchair's broad back with loose stitching in the arms that once hid the Q tile for Peter when he didn't know how to make a word from it, was now an ominous black mass in the room, like it'd transformed into something unwelcoming the moment it was left alone.

"It's like this place never knew me," he said.

"All places become ghosts once we leave 'em," said the sheriff. "Don't pay it no heed."

"I guess."

"Not just places neither."

Peter's white breath broke across the darkness and his thoughts returned to Cooper. He crossed the room, lighting the candle above the fireplace with the box of matches Henry kept tucked in the log basket, and listened to the wind whistle through the boards covering the window he'd broken to make their escape that night.

"I suppose we start looking, then," said the sheriff, his face shifting in and out of light and shadow as the candle's flame flickered.

"I guess. But I've spent so much time here over the years, it's hard to believe that something like a bomb could've been hiding all this time."

"But Henry was hidden from you that whole time and you were looking right at him."

Peter turned away, feeling the sting of that truth in his belly, and made his way towards the bedroom. "I still can't see how anything like that can be hidden, though. It's not as if we're going to turn a painting over and find one there, is it?"

"Not all of it, son, no."

"What do you mean?"

"It might be made of many separate parts hidden throughout the cabin, Peter. There might even be something written down giving instructions on how to assemble it, hidden in another part of the lake entirely."

Peter turned back and the sheriff's gaze held his, all dark in the half-light. "But Rider didn't have enough time to go through that much."

"Then just enough time to tell Cooper where to start."

"I guess."

"It might be that we find random things in a random order," said the sheriff. "And, of course, it might be that we find something else we hadn't planned for. It might not be a bomb at all."

The candle's flame flickered and Peter's imagination started to wander. "But what?"

"We won't know until we start searching now, will we?"

Peter looked back towards the front window where Teddy was standing and gazed through the snowy pines to the lake below. "The tree houses were built after."

"After the original community of Returnees, you mean?"

"Yes. My dad helped build those when we arrived."

"I see, son. So, we need only concern ourselves with the rest."

Peter nodded. "I guess I'll make a start in the bedroom."

"I'll get a fire going. Then if Teddy takes the kitchen, I'll make a start in here."

"OK."

"And," said the sheriff, removing his trapper hat and waggling it in Peter's direction, "if you find anything, call me."

"I will."

"Don't touch it."

"I won't."

"In case it's dangerous, I mean."

"I understand."

The sheriff smiled. "Course you do. Sorry, I'm just bein'. . ."

Peter presumed the sheriff meant to finish off by saying *protective*. But his sentence tailed off. Instead, he held back a moment as if to communicate his concern for Peter and how difficult this was going to be for him. Peter felt tears well from deep inside him. They were close to finding out the truth now. He could feel it. But he didn't want the sheriff's sympathy. He didn't want anybody's sympathy.

The three of them split off into their separate searches. And as the clatter of drawers opening and closing again was followed by the screech of chairs scraping back across the floorboards, Peter entered the bedroom and closed the door behind him.

"Rider," he whispered. "What have you done?"

That day out in the woods, Rider had saved his life. He'd watched the Bearskin leave Peter at the foot of the falls to die at the hands of the Dead and Rider had rescued him. Until now, Peter had always been so sure that the reason he'd helped him rescue Cooper was because he'd witnessed the possibility of love again, in them, when his

324

wife had rejected him the moment he'd turned. But what if it was never that at all? What if Cooper was only ever the Returnee Rider could finally share his plans with?

Snow came tumbling out of the darkness to strike the windowpane. Peter crossed to the middle of the room and imagined himself in Cooper's place that night. He looked back at the bedroom door. While he was in the front room with his dad preparing for everyone's arrival, Rider was already in here busying himself with the task at hand, so that in the event of his own death, his knowledge and his secrets wouldn't die with him.

Peter tossed the quilted blanket aside and stripped the bed. There was nothing under the sheets. He flipped the mattress, heaving it over on to its belly before it buckled back on top of him. But there was nothing on the underside either. He scrambled under the bed, reaching up to finger each of the wooden slats in turn in case something had been placed there. Again, nothing. His attention turned to the painting on the far wall. He unhooked it. He turned it over. He pulled the sticking paper away to remove the backing board and turned the canvas over in his hand. But there was nothing. Nothing but the rug and the curtains and the rocking chair in the corner of the room beside the wooden drawers Peter had already tipped out. And as he fell back against the bed, the door opened.

"Anythin'?" said the sheriff leaning into the frame all a huff.

"Nothing."

"And you've checked underneath the drawers?"

"I've checked them all."

The sheriff swiped his hand down the length of his moustache and nodded like that was a job well done but frustrating all the same. "Teddy's got plenty of jars and whatnot left to rummage through in the kitchen, but it's pretty damned near raided in here."

"Why don't we take a break and look again?"

The sheriff nodded. But it was clear he was in no mood for waiting. "You said everything except the tree houses were here from the beginning, right, son?"

"Yes."

"The watchtower, too?"

"Yes," said Peter. "I think so."

The sheriff nodded again. "Both of you keep looking. I won't be long."

Peter went to tell the sheriff how you had to pull the bottom step down on to the ice to make your way up the tower. But his advice went unnoticed. The sheriff swiped his trapper hat up off the dining table and in a flurry of snow, the front door slammed behind him.

Peter wandered over to the front window, looking down through the pines to the lake below, and a few minutes later the sheriff appeared, small, like a fleck out on the ice.

Something made of glass smashed, followed by Teddy's voice calling back from the kitchen reassuring everyone that nothing was broken. The sound of bits of glass being furiously swept away was replaced by cussing and Peter smiled to himself.

The sheriff made it to the foot of the watchtower safely so Peter turned back, looking down the length of the dining table to the far end. Someone had done their best to wipe Rider's blood away, but it had seeped into the grain of the wood, forming lines like a fingerprint. And now he thought about it, he realized that you could probably find fingerprints or other kinds of marks left by the Returnees before their home was stolen from them, across the whole lake if you looked hard enough for them. The trace of a life. An imprint of their being here. A ghost.

The candle's flame curled over then fluttered, making the shadows splutter. Peter looked back towards the bedroom. From the darkness of that room, only the snow was visible, gentle at the window, but persistent. The flame flickered again, even though there wasn't so much as a breeze beneath the door tonight. Only now did he notice the pattern on the rug in the bedroom. Something in the middle caught his eye. It was luminous, even from here, against the darker weave around it. Peter took the candle, making his way back to the bedroom, and the central pattern seemed to respond to the light approaching it. It wasn't just that it was woven with white thread. It contained flecks of silver that glittered, giving the illusion that it floated above the rest somehow. Peter stood over the rug, holding the candle away from his body, and the embroidered snowflake woven into its core glimmered in the half-light. He knelt. He ran his fingers over the four points like the quills of an arrow and saw how they formed an X.

"X," he whispered. "X marks the spot."

He got up, pulling the rug to one side, and a trapdoor was revealed.

25

The trapdoor had a brass ring. Peter set the candle down on the floor, lifted the hoop with his finger and pulled. He assumed that the density of the wood would make the trapdoor so much heavier than it was. But there was no resistance. It lifted as lightly as a lid on a box.

The darkness below was unfathomable. And freezing. Peter peered over the lip of the hole and his breath unfurled into the space beneath him. He counted the first four rungs of a metal ladder, but the rest of it disappeared into the darkness below. He cleared his throat, forming a gob of saliva in the front of his mouth, and spat. The glistening bauble caught the light before vanishing. He waited and all expectations of there being a room directly beneath the cabin vanished. Five seconds passed before Peter heard the distant splat of the spit hitting the ground below. And it echoed. It was no room down there, but a cave.

Peter looked back towards the bedroom door. He could still hear Teddy tidying up after himself. He should call for him, or wait for Sheriff O'Hurn to return. He didn't know what was down there. He didn't know if he could cope once he did. But if Cooper had been taken down there, he should go too. And alone. Peter swung both feet round into the hole. He took the candle in one hand and the ladder in the other and slowly made his way down.

26

The trapdoor became a rectangle of dark light above. The cave was so vast that candlelight couldn't reach the ceiling to make out its features. It was almost as if Peter had dropped through a hole in the night sky. He lost count after the thirtieth rung, but it became clear that the ladder extended the full height of the island. Every now and then, he held the candle away from him, hoping to see the ground below. But he couldn't see past the flare of the flame, so he continued his way down and another rung appeared from the darkness to take him even deeper.

Peter's foot reached for another rung. It lunged, like he'd missed a step and was about to fall to his death. But instead his toecap touched rock. He lowered his bodyweight on to his foot and with a sigh, let go of the ladder.

It was as if the night had walls. Peter couldn't see the cave, but he could tell he stood in a vast enclosed space by the sound his breath made. When he sighed, the sigh would only travel so far away from him before circling back. He took a step and the thud of his boot on the rock ricocheted all around him. The island was an overturned bowl. And the cave was connected to the lake. Peter took a few steps forward and the rock beneath him dissolved into ice. He set the candle down and inched on to the frozen pool. The darkness directly in front of him was broken. It wasn't bright, but it was as if part of the cavern wall was transparent somehow. And it was coldest here. Peter braced both arms, rubbing them for warmth, and walked a little closer.

A shallow arch just above the line of the water formed an entrance to the lake. But it was completely frozen over by spears of drooling icicles. Henry had never mentioned there being a cave, but now Peter thought on it, perhaps he hadn't known about it. Nobody did.

In the middle of the pool, a little red canoe lay gripped by ice. Its paintwork had blistered like a log on the flame. Peter looked up towards the arch, noticing now that it was only high enough for a canoe to pass beneath in the summer months. The cave was a boathouse, perhaps. A hiding place. A secret escape. He made his way off the ice, stooping to take the candle back in hand. It was only now he noticed the boots. There was a bunch of them lying there, all tipped on to their sides, soles facing out, in a row together. And the boots were attached to legs. Peter stumbled back, desperately cupping the flickering flame before it went out. It steadied. He steadied. His heartbeat settled back into a resting pattern and he stepped closer.

Fifty skulls looked up at him. Fifty lost souls looking back from across time. A time Peter had come to know all too well. Their huddle told him they were cold and scared. The silver snowflakes hanging from many of their necks told him the corpses were Returnees. Peter looked back across the pool to the frozen mouth of the cave. Like the cabin he and Cooper first encountered in the woods the day they herded the Dead from the lake, the community had many hiding places ready for when Henry and Darlene came to kill them. But winter had played a cruel hand in this group's death and the ice at the cave's mouth had locked them in. Peter gazed up at the little rectangle of light coming from the trapdoor and wondered how long it had taken for them to die down here. Were they still alive, praying for the thaw of spring when Henry moved his belongings in and slept soundly in the bed above them? He hoped not. He hoped that they'd died long before that. If you can hope for such a thing. And as that guilty little thought wormed its way into Peter's heart, another presented itself. As terrible as this discovery was, it brought him no closer to Timberdark.

Peter wiped his eyes on the heel of his hand, saying

sorry to the people buried here. Sorry for everything that had taken place at the lake back then. But he already knew about that day. He held back a moment, feeling shame at the thought that this wasn't the answer he'd come looking for. But it was no use. It didn't matter how long he stood here, this was all there was or would ever be. Death and misery and guilt that he'd ever got to call this place home.

Peter started to make the climb back up the ladder, watching the hole in the darkness above him get bigger with every step, when the word *Timberdark* came to him in another guise and he stopped.

"Timberdark," he whispered. "*Timbered Ark.*"

He looked down, seeing only the silhouette of the canoe against the light of the ice like a fish swimming in the depths below, and wondered how such a little thing could hide so big a secret. He clambered back down, rushing back across the frozen pool, and set the candle on the seat of the canoe. He lifted his leg, stepping over the lip of gunwale, and reached for the seat. But his back foot slipped. Peter fell forward. His stomach smashed into the thwart. He screamed into his mouth, taking the surge of pain to his ribs inside him. But no echo cracked out across the cave, and he was OK. He was OK, he kept telling himself, as he scrambled to his feet and slowly began his search.

There was nothing in the ribs of the canoe. The undersides of the bow and stern seats were empty too. He searched the underside of the gunwale, running his hand across the lip down the length of the canoe on both sides. Still nothing. He stopped. He waited. He took the candle in his hand, watching how the changing shadows highlighted inconsistencies in the panelling as the light travelled across it. To the stern of the canoe, just beside the tip of the deck, was a gap where a piece of wood had been prized away from the frame. It wasn't wide enough to hide much in there, but Peter brought the light closer and saw that something had been wedged inside. Paper. A papered file, even. For a moment he thought it must be the assembly plans Sheriff O'Hurn had told him about. But when he tugged on the folder to release it, he saw that it was no such thing.

The dossier came from the U.S. government. A sticker as red as a branding iron, declaring *Top Secret*, had been stamped above the document's title, Operation Code Name: TIMBERDARK. Peter stuffed it inside his jacket and made the climb back up to Henry's bedroom. When he hoisted himself back out on to the floor, Teddy was still clattering about in the kitchen and there were no signs that the sheriff had come back yet. He placed the dossier on the floor and quietly opened it.

Operation Code Name:
TIMBERDARK

Joint Resolution
To authorise the use of United
States armed forces to destroy
all persons hereby defined as
being direct descendants of the
Dead: 'Returnees'

Purpose
To deter any future acts of
terrorism. And to pre-empt
any existential threat posed
to humankind by the Returnees
either through their violence or
evolutionary replacement.

Whereby such acts render it both
necessary and appropriate that
the United States exercise its
rights to self-defense and to
protect its citizens from grave
acts of violence and their future
extinction.

Warnings Overruled

- Returnees' known abilities to protect the living from the Dead, as highlighted by the minority representative.

- Returnees' explanation for humankind's extinction.

- Any other (as yet undetermined) anthropological opportunity to learn lessons from the Returnees that could later be used to help stop the Dead, as highlighted by the minority representative.

Outcome of the Resolution

The Nationwide Destruction of all Returnees

Resolved by the Remaining Senate and House of Representatives of the United States of America in Congress by the Following Signatory:

Senator James O'Hurn

The senator's name stared at Peter like it wore a smile. O'Hurn was a name he knew. A name he'd come to trust, but that was in reality as trustworthy as that sheriff badge. And in that reassuring image, the sheriff had taken a seat in front of Peter that very first day in his office and planted a seed inside him: the seed of the idea that his own monster, Timberdark, was Cooper's. All he had to do was plant it deep enough, then sit back and watch it grow. Peter clenched his jaw. He'd trusted Henry and Darlene, but no one had twisted his trust in them more cruelly than Sheriff O'Hurn. He'd achieved what no one before him had been able to. He'd turned love into hate and his Cooper into a monster just so that he'd lead him straight here.

A tear fell across the page and Peter wondered if he might just be left alone to die. Why did anything further even need to happen? He could fall, or he could sit. Soon something would simply come along and take him away and then he'd never have to see Cooper's face the moment he walked back into his life with an apology that could never be enough. Peter stared into the never-ending darkness of that abyss, when a draught caught the back of his neck making the candle's flame curl.

"Well, I reckon I did my twenty thousand steps just taking that watchtower alone," called the sheriff from the other end of the cabin. "But I can't say I achieved much else."

Dread surged down Peter's body into his fingertips like a living thing had burrowed its way right through him. He stuffed the dossier inside his jacket.

"You boys had any luck?"

Quickly, Peter shoved the lid of the trapdoor underneath the bed. "No!" he called back. "Not yet."

Then he dragged the rug back over the hole and stood facing the window. He checked his reflection for tears, then tried to compose his face back into a Peter. A Peter he could recognize. A Peter he could stand to recognize. And it crossed his mind that if he was able to watch himself standing at the foot of his island that day the river trader had travelled to the lake seeking help, he might not even see the same boy standing there. But it was no use having those thoughts. None at all. What was gone was gone. Time and choices saw to all that.

"No joy?" said the sheriff, much quieter now that he was standing directly behind him. "But you've been in here longer than a couple on their wedding night."

Peter stood with his back to the bedroom door, watching the sheriff's reflection in the window. The sheriff leaned into the doorframe, toying with his trapper hat. Snow on the flappy ears began to thaw, making the tips of both straps drip, drip. And he was calm, unsuspecting perhaps, but his expression was indiscernible behind the constant movement of the snow outside.

"It took a while getting the back off the painting," said Peter quietly. "Unfortunately, when I did, there was nothing there."

"That's too bad, son."

"Yes," said Peter. "It is. But I'll double check everything in a minute."

Snow skittered across the windowpane.

A log on the fire in the front room popped.

"It's really picked up out there," said the sheriff after a while.

Peter nodded. "And now the wolves have come."

"Yeah, I could hear them from the top of the watchtower. It's quite the place."

"Yes," said Peter. "Quite the place."

"But at least you've found sanctuary from Teddy's infernal pointing and naming. I don't suppose even he would dare tell you what's what, up here."

Peter said nothing and the snow continued to tumble across the sheriff's reflection. And the pair of them stood there for a while in the pocket of each other's silence with nothing but the persistent drip of water falling from the hat, when Peter made the decision and turned to take in the sheriff with his own eyes. And it wasn't hard at all to see how that kind worn-in face, with a moustache as endearing on a man as any he'd known, could've inspired millions of people to vote for him as their senator. Even now, it wasn't hard to see how he'd achieved the kind of power that could consign a whole race of people to their deaths. Not at all.

"Why did you offer to pay my rent?" Peter asked.

"I think you know why."

Peter nodded, the sheriff stood away from the doorframe, and an understanding that they'd moved past each other's pretences stepped into the room with them where it waited, still unspoken.

"And that offer still stands," he continued. "Not just for you and your boy, but for your dad too. From what I understand, he's been keeping his financial struggles from you."

Peter's throat tightened and the sheriff stepped into the bedroom.

"You just need to hand it back to me, son, and walk away from all this."

"But you were the reason the Returnees had to flee in the first place. You wanted to kill all those people. You authorized their genocide. The new government know nothing about you or the Ghost Ranger, do they? Now you know you're on the wrong side of history, all you were ever doing with him was looking to retrieve something you knew would incriminate you."

"Son, I don't expect you to understand."

"No. I don't suppose you do."

"The Dead were wiping out whole cities. The president was already dead. Congress had days left to make a decision about these so-called Returnees. Then, when the world finally went dark and I was the only senator left standing, hours. Minutes, even."

"You had no grounds."

"The world was on fire. And the world was homeless. Once it became a war with the Dead, it became a war against anything that scared us. Now, what would you have me do?"

"Then politicians are not us."

"No, Peter. That's exactly what we are. We are whatever people elect."

"But you already knew the Returned could shield people from the Dead by this point and you ignored that."

"That's right," said the sheriff. "We knew that they could, not whether they would."

Peter clenched his fist and a wave of heat burned across his skin. "But that's—"

"But that's what? Not fair?"

"Don't patronize me."

"Peter, you should know better than most after what you and Cooper suffered here that night, that the one thing people are not when they're scared, is fair."

"But didn't people choose you because they hoped

you'd do better than they would in your position? Wasn't that what you were for?"

The sheriff raised both eyebrows. "What, the government? I suppose. Except, all any of us are is people, Peter, all alone on this damned planet trying our best to govern ourselves."

"But that's not good enough."

"No. I don't suppose it is. And you'll find no further argument here with that statement. But when you get older, I'm afraid you'll only realize the same is true for you also. If your being here instead of at Cooper's side hasn't taught you that already."

Peter bit into his bottom lip. "Don't say that."

"I mean, you're living proof that if people are isolated and scared enough, they can be turned against anyone."

"That's not true. I was just—"

"You were just what? Scared?"

"Yes."

"Terrified? Hell. All any of us is, is terrified, Peter. Terrified of each other. Terrified we'll never get it right. Terrified of getting it wrong if people aren't what we think they might be."

"But you put the idea into my head."

"No!" The sheriff stepped forward. "No, no, no, son. You don't get to put that one on me. You got there all by yourself. Weren't you the one who assumed Timberdark was something terrible between the Returnees just because Cooper kept it secret from you? Weren't you the one who saw terrible things in the woods without knowing what any of those things actually were? So, you see, I don't know how it is that you have me so different from you."

Peter glanced at the embroidered snowflake in the middle of the rug and cleared his throat. "Because—"

"Because what? Tell me how we are not alike?"

"Because of what I'm going to do with those things now I know better."

"Oh?"

"On the dossier it says that you ignored explanations made by the Returnees about why humankind had been threatened with extinction. What did they mean by that?"

The sheriff's eyes glinted in the candlelight. "It was nothin'. Nothin' that could be trusted at any rate. Mutterin's. Hate talk. The ramblings of a people already consumed by death."

"But what did the Returnees mean? At the town hall, Cooper said that leaves turn wonderful colours just before they die because they're celebrating the life they've lived, not death. But he wasn't so sure about us. He wasn't so sure about what we'd have to look back on. Why did he say that? Why did he say those things?"

The sheriff held Peter's gaze. But he was interested in only one thing. "Where is it?"

"Answer me," said Peter.

"Tell me where the dossier is, and I'll help you."

"And where's Teddy?" Peter looked past the sheriff to the front of the cabin now. "Teddy!"

The front room glimmered dully in the half-light of the fire, making snow at the window burn red like embers. The only sound came from the crackling kindling. In the past that sound had been the song of home in winter and meant nothing but comfort. But it seemed eerie now, giving weight to the silence that existed outside it. And it suddenly occurred to Peter that he hadn't heard Teddy's movements in the kitchen since the sheriff's return.

"Teddy!" he called. Then once more, but barely above a dying whisper, "Teddy."

"It's no use. He won't hear you."

The cabin walls swam with firelight and silences. "Why won't he?"

"Because he's not here any more. At least, not in any meaningful way. And I regret that, I do, but having brought you to me, he's fulfilled his purpose."

The hat slipped through the sheriff's fingers. He started to rub his palms to soothe them now that trying to hide what he'd just done, and the pain such exertion had caused his hands, was no longer a concern.

"He was never even my son. I found him as a baby in those early days after the Dead came, and the thing is,

Peter, you'd be amazed just how far a man can get when he has a child to make people trust him. Now I think about it, I can't think of a single darned politician who hasn't made that work."

The sheriff sighed deeply as if all that could be done had been done, and all that could be said, had been said. He nodded once as if to draw matters to a close and all kindness and patience abandoned his face. "Give it to me."

"I'm not taking another step in your direction."

"I said, give it to me."

Peter pulled the dossier from his jacket. "You thought you'd written a death warrant. Instead you've signed your own. Here. Come take it."

The sheriff crossed the room in a single stride. Peter didn't even see the decision to do so flicker across his eyes, it all happened so fast. But Peter had anticipated the move.

The rug gave way beneath the sheriff. The corners slipped across the floor, gathering quickly about his waist to hold him in place, and drew him down into the hole. The sheriff's eyes rolled back, wild and raving like an animal which didn't have the wherewithal to ponder its own existence but knew all too well that death was upon it. His hands flailed, clawing, clutching, scratching at the floorboards to get purchase enough to pull himself back up. But it was no use. The weight of his feet in the pocket of the rug drew him further down through the trapdoor as if he was sinking in quicksand. He sank even deeper.

"Peter," he whimpered. "Peter."

But Peter was quite unmoved. "Senator."

The sheriff struck the ladder on his way down. His body buckled, legs folding backwards in unnatural ways to lie flat against his back. There came a clack. And then a thud. Then the darkness of the cave took him and made silence of his screams.

Peter collapsed over the foot of the bed, shivering. He fumbled in his jacket pocket, squeezing Rider's silver snowflake tightly in his fist, and looked to the door. "Teddy."

Peter closed first Teddy's eyes and then, after a while, the front door quietly behind him and made his way downhill back on to the lake. And he ran, turning only once to see the flames. He'd held the candle to the curtains in every room. The fire quickly took hold, and as it breached the walls, erupting into broiling flames above the island, the cabin became a pyre for all that were lost there. And soon those glittering embers were one with the stars and Peter said his goodbyes to Rider and then to those friends he'd lost to the caves, and quietly stepped up into the boathouse.

The white deer skull broke from the darkness before the rest of the Ghost Ranger became visible against the back door. The antlers tilted forward, acknowledging Peter's presence, but the blank stare made it impossible to know if he was also searching for the sheriff behind him. But he didn't advance. He stood guard, just as he'd been instructed to, beneath the hanging weaponry which came clinking in the wind all about them.

Peter pulled the dossier from inside his jacket and held it flat in his palms, first looking at the senate insignia with the bald eagle crowning the flag, then into the Ghost Ranger's hollow gaze.

"Did you even know what you were fighting for?" he said. "Did you?"

The Ghost Ranger drew himself up to his full height so the points of his antlers were sharp above him, and said nothing.

"Because I don't think you did. I don't suppose you even knew why they sent you out there. And now people are dead who didn't even know anything about this. A baby who didn't know anything about this. But I don't suppose it's your job to even ask."

The boathouse creaked beneath the hurrying snow and the Ghost Ranger stepped forward.

"But you see," said Peter. "I need to get past you. I need to get back to the town because I think we're in trouble down there. Only I don't know why because I've been too stupid to ask my Cooper the reason why he's been going into a trance and what's troubling him about the Dead in the woods."

The Ghost Ranger took another step closer.

"So one of us has to get out of the way."

"Peter," came that reedy voice beneath the mask.

"One of us has to step aside."

"Peter!"

Peter recoiled, aghast to hear his own name break from behind the mask. It sounded as raggedy as razors but somehow so warm, reassuring even, like a loved one calling him back from a terrible nightmare.

The Ghost Ranger's gloved hands travelled the length of his gown like shadows up a wall. They stopped at the deer skull, the fingertips branching out in an echo of the antlers, and took hold of them. The skull shifted, then lifted, up and over the ranger's head. The skull dropped, fracturing into splintered pieces across the floor and Peter's dad looked back at him.

Peter's throat tightened. But his dad recognized the horror in his eyes and looked back towards the bench. Seated there with one hand cuffed to the wall, head hanging low and quite unconscious, was a young man in a white T-shirt and military fatigues. He couldn't have been much older than twenty. He couldn't have had a chance to be much of anything yet: just this solider on a mission with a purpose he probably knew nothing about.

"I followed you all out of town on horseback, Pete," said his dad. "You haven't come visit me once since we got here, and when I saw you out the other day I could see in your eyes that something wasn't right. I was worried you might be in trouble."

The word *trouble* sounded less like a judgement than it should have. Peter nodded and finally gave up the struggle to hold back his tears.

"I've messed everything up."

"No," said his dad. "We love you and whatever it is, it can be fixed."

"I'm sorry I haven't spent any time with you."

"It's OK," said his dad, pulling him into his chest for a hug. "It's OK."

"He'll never forgive me."

"Course he will."

"The sheriff was the senator who authorized all the Returnees to be killed in the first place. He's why they had to come here."

His dad gently pulled away, wiping a lock of hair from Peter's forehead. "And where is he now?"

"Dead," said Peter. Then, much quieter. "Teddy too."

His dad ran his hand down the length of his beard like too much had passed without his being there. "And now you think Cooper and the others sense that something's wrong in town?"

"Yes," said Peter. "But I don't know what. I need to find him."

His dad nodded. "Then we should go. If we leave now we'll be back by first light."

Peter took his dad's hand and held it for a moment just to be sure of him. But it was only now he noticed how pale he was.

"Pete?" said his dad. "What is it? You look like you've just seen a ghost?"

"Stay here, Dad."

"I should come with you."

"No. No, I think you should stay. You've probably exhausted yourself getting here. But just to be sure."

His dad brought a big sigh up into his chest like he wasn't too sure he liked this plan much. But there was more than tiredness inside him. There was something in his eyes that hadn't been there before; or something was gone from them, Peter wasn't too sure which. But they carried a sudden dullness that could no longer be hidden.

Peter brought his dad in for a hug, telling him to go back to the tree house to stay warm beside the fire until someone came back for him. And he desperately hoped that would be enough. He hoped, as he set off back inside the snow on horseback with those mountains watching over him, that the lake would be enough for all of them.

III

27

Sunlight was only beginning to break across town when Peter found Cooper back at the supermarket. The sun hung low over the parking lot, splintering into shafts down the length of the aisles, painting strands of Cooper's hair golden. A woman shouted across the lot, warning Peter not to go in. That he could get hurt. But he ignored her and instead paid attention to the hurt he'd caused by leaving Cooper alone in there, and quietly made his way in.

The supermarket was empty. Only the abandoned shopping baskets lay strewn across the floor, marking the spot where shoppers had been only moments before. But they were alone now. Peter removed the wet-floor sign at the foot of Cooper's aisle, collapsing the two panels to lean it against the shelves, and stepped in. And in his trance-like state, Cooper was almost perfect, standing there in all his untouchable beauty with his soul half in this world and half in another. There was the boy who could pop tin cans off a post simply by smiling at them. There was the boy with the horse and two back pockets worn down by the ride. There was the boy he loved from afar without any of the pain that came with actually loving someone. And it crossed Peter's mind that if all he ever wanted to do was look at Cooper and see him exactly as he used to be from across the other side of the lake before he went on to ruin everything by actually loving him, then he should've left him exactly where he was and never once set foot off the island. But watching someone like a photograph so they never get to change or change you, wasn't love. And wishing things could go back to how they used to be without doing his best to make things right again wasn't love either.

Peter edged a little closer. He should've spoken to him in the ravine regardless of the outcome. He should've spoken to him back in the police station or over dinner or any number of other times regardless of what Timberdark was. Because to love someone was to live with the possibility that things might not work out and do them anyway.

Peter took another step forward and Cooper's fingertips twitched. It was as if some part of him, the part keeping watch while the rest of him slept, was alert to the intrusion. Cooper's shoulders expanded with a sudden inhalation of breath, scoping the proximity of another, then contracted again. Peter stepped closer and Cooper unclenched his jaw, releasing threads of drool across his chin. He leered, his head heavy on his neck like a sunflower unable to support its own weight any more, and sweat broke out on the spine of his T-shirt. Peter's throat tightened. He couldn't touch him. Cooper wasn't his to touch any more, in this state or any other state. His breathing accelerated. Then came the panting. Panting, panting, panting, panting and his head lolled deeper towards his chest in Peter's direction. And yet his gaze never once left the same set of shelves where he always stood.

The shelves were lined with cans of tinned salmon. The label was brightly painted with rapids of white water toppling over rocks where leaping salmon flew. Most of the salmon had been caught and were already bundled up at the bottom of the label in a little red canoe. But not all. One salmon breached the product's name: *Big Red River's All Fresh Salmon*. Its silver body crested the mountains made pink by dusk. And it crossed Peter's mind now that this picture did so much more than give Cooper a window back to the mountains in a town without that view to look upon. That one little salmon was free.

Peter leaned in, careful not to make a sound, and slowly started to turn the tin cans around so the back of the labels faced out, until all that was left on view were the barcodes and ingredients. Then he waited. He waited for what seemed like an age, standing just far enough away from Cooper to give him room, but close enough that the sweet tang of log smoke and musk on his skin could cross the distance between them where it hovered like a kiss not yet taken.

Cooper's fingertips brushed Peter's. It was just a graze, faint like tall summer grasses across the back of the hand, but it was so electric, his heart leaped like it hadn't been alive before now. Peter held his breath, watching Cooper's drowsy eyes search first his body and then his face, finding thrill and excitement in the act of being seen again after so long without it. Their hands gripped on to each other's tightly and Cooper looked up, his dark eyes still full of dreams but bright. So bright.

"Your hair's gotten real curly," he said.

Peter's throat went tight. "Oh yeah?"

"Yeah."

"I'll get Dad to cut it some time, then."

Cooper shrugged. "Only if you don't like it."

"I don't."

"Best get it cut, then."

"Yeah. Maybe."

"Mine smells funny," said Cooper after a while.

"That's because it's clean."

"Like I said. Funny."

Peter smiled. "We can soon fix that."

"Will we, though?"

"Yes. We'll fix everything, I promise."

"But I thought you dint like it when I honk."

"No," said Peter. "I like it. It's you. It just hasn't been *us* for the longest time."

Cooper's dark eyes journeyed across Peter's face like he was travelling over vast mountains and lakes and finding great wonder in them. "I get real scared if I can't smell you, Pete."

"I know. Me too."

Cooper nodded, as if he took comfort from knowing that Peter didn't want to lose that part of them either. Peter smiled. Few things in life were more painful than the distance two people can place between them when they choose to close themselves away. Whole worlds could exist between one soul and another. And yet it was somehow a greater wonder how quickly all distance could be removed when two people decided to banish it.

"I don't know how to snap out of the trance by myself, Pete."

"Ssh."

"I can't seem to shake it off no matter how hard I try."

"It's OK now. You won't have to try any more."

"It's like I died but my body stayed here. That's what

being here feels like. And I don't even know where I'm gone to."

"But I do."

Cooper looked up, his dark eyes wide and full of wonder that he might have all the answers and for a moment something struck Peter. No matter how old they'd grow to be together, and no matter how old the world would turn them, the two of them would always be boys, to each other at least, each in need of the other's safety. Peter swivelled one of the tin cans round to show Cooper the salmon flying above the mountains and gently wiped a strand of hair from his lips.

"Coop, you went home."

"It's the mountains," said Cooper. "A canoe, too."

"I know. I think you've just been daydreaming this whole time."

Cooper's dark eyes widened to the hope of such an explanation. "You do?"

"I do."

"So not a trance?"

"Just daydreams," said Peter. "Getting away when the rest of you is stuck here."

"But ain't they been aggressive?"

Peter recalled the nick on his neck where Cooper had accidentally struck him, but thought better of mentioning it now. "Who isn't mad as hell when they're pulled away from their dreams?"

Cooper smiled. "I guess."

"And I've seen a canoe in my dreams too."

"You did?"

"I did."

"You was away, too?"

"Yes," said Peter realising it only now, in the moment of saying. "I was away."

"But how come?"

"I don't know. Perhaps it came to get us."

But Peter didn't know. All he knew was that, like Cooper's, his dreams didn't come at night either.

"And I could see it," said Cooper. "I could see the mountains so clearly in my head it was like I was back there, Pete."

"I know. Me too."

"I tried to stay put, right here where my two feet was standin'. But it dint make no difference. No matter how hard I tried, my mind wouldn't keep me away."

"It's OK. You're back now."

Cooper nodded, like being back was good, like being back meant not being a monster, and sunlight struck the orbs of his dark eyes, flooding them with gold.

Peter squeezed Cooper's hand. "But why didn't you tell me what Timberdark was? That it was the government's plan against the Returnees?"

Peter pulled the dossier from inside his jacket and Cooper stood there staring at it for a little while.

"I dint want to say nothin' because I know you was trying to make a fist of it here. You want this world so much, Pete. I knew if you thought there was any chance another government might make the same decisions about us again, that you'd never leave the lake. And I dint want that for you. I dint want to hold you back. But I swear, I never saw this till now. Rider just told me that the document was underneath Henry's cabin so I understood everythin'. So I knew the risks his people had taken finding safety on the lake for the rest of us. But how did you get hold of it?"

"I'll explain later."

"But I did good keepin' it from you, dint I?"

"Cooper, I'm never going to be happy unless you are. That's not how it works."

"But you are happy here. And I thought you was making promotion and everything."

"No," said Peter. "I've been struggling too. And now I've said it out loud I don't know why I ever lied about it."

"I think people do that all the time."

"People?"

"Grown-ups," said Cooper "People our folks' age."

"But why do they pretend?"

"Cos everybody else is."

A sigh nestled into the pit of Peter's stomach and the

sadness of that thought sat there for a while.

"So, you're telling me you int happy, Pete?"

"Yes," said Peter. "I suppose I am."

And the weight of admitting to not being happy, of having failed at happiness, was almost unbearable. After all, he'd tried so hard to be. But that pressure had been so much heavier than Peter expected, that when his body finally let go of it, he felt ashamed for letting Cooper down. Shame that he was the main reason both of them were even here in the first place.

"S'OK," said Cooper. "We'll fix it."

"But how? You're never going to be happy here."

"No. Not here. It can't never be here. I think our daydreamin' is more than just because we int happy, Pete. It's somethin' else."

"What do you mean, something else?"

"There's somethin' you need to know about the Dead. There's somethin' I've gotta show you."

"Up in the hills above town."

Cooper looked up, seeming at once alarmed by what Peter already knew and somehow at peace that another part of him could finally be open.

"I saw you in the woods," said Peter. "I saw *all* of you."

Cooper squeezed Peter's hand, as if he knew that might be unsettling when they hadn't even shown all of themselves to each other yet.

"I was just marking the trees with my scent, Pete. To keep the Dead from town."

"But I thought—"

"What did you think?"

Peter shook his head. "It doesn't matter now."

"You sure?"

"Yes. I'm sure." Then, once his nerves had a chance to settle. "I don't think I was afraid of you changing into a monster. I think I was just afraid of you changing into someone who didn't need to love me any more."

"Pete, there's no part o' me that don't belong to you. But we ain't gonna be together all the time. And we ain't always gonna see eye to eye."

"I know that."

"It don't mean I don't love you."

"I know."

"Do you, though?"

"Yes."

"But do you?"

"Yes," said Peter. Then, "I think so."

Cooper held the back of Peter's head, lowering his forehead until it touched his. "Sometimes this is all too big for me too, Pete."

"What?"

"Love," said Cooper. "It needs both of us to look after it."

"I know."

"And you and me is gonna have to do so much better than this if we're ever gonna make it to the end."

Peter looked up. "Make it to the end of what?"

"Our lives together."

And there it was. Cooper's certainty about him, that their lives were forever forged into one, left unbroken, no matter what. And the mystery of having someone love you, of having someone in your life that loved you so completely that your life together only ever had obstacles, never a reason to end things, was so profound that Peter realized something for the first time, that the word love and saying *I love you* had their limits. What love actually was, was unfathomable and it struck him as a wonder that while humankind had set about defining and labelling every little bit of the universe, until even the other side of a black hole and the smallest creature in the depths of the ocean had a name, there was one thing it was helpless to pin down. And that thing lived inside two people.

"I saw the red light in the sky on the other side of the hills," said Peter.

Cooper looked up, his dark eyes at once alert and exploring. "I'll show you."

28

Tokala was the first to acknowledge Peter's arrival in camp. He was crouched in front of a cooking pot that'd been suspended above the fire by a tripod made out of three branches like a tipi. Whatever was cooking bubbled away so busily it made the lid rattle, causing steam to snake up through the centre of the clearing. The steam leaked across rays of sunlight that came pointing through the frosty pines behind the rocky bluff, and Tokala stood. He was upright with his back to Peter, alert to his presence as a deer might be to a hunter in the woods, and slowly turned round. Cooper let go of Peter's hand to make his way down off the ridge, but Peter held back a moment, unsure if he would even be welcome. But Tokala looked back, his hair unbound across the hood of his ski jacket and smiled as if he found peace in the return of a friend after so long away.

"We have some rabbit stew left over from last night, Peter," he said. "If you're hungry."

He stood there for a moment, holding Peter's gaze with all the things left unsaid hovering in the space between them. But somehow, none of those things seemed to threaten the truce that was taking place here. And soon, the others took his lead and followed. The girl as broad as a bear from the town meeting set her tin cup and spoon down on the log where she was sitting and made her way towards him.

"I'm Earle," she said, extending her hand, her voice husky and low. Both eyes dark and unblinking.

Peter shook it. Or rather it shook his. Her hand was huge, like a rubber glove that'd been blown up. "Hi, Err—"

"Earle. My dad got so carried away thinking I was a boy on account of what a thickset baby I was, that by the time he saw I don't got no pecker between my legs, the name had already stuck. So, I'm Earle, even though I'm a girl."

Peter smiled. "Which at least rhymes."

"Right. I mean what does boy even rhyme with?"

"Roy?"

"Yeah. I mean, the misery of that."

Earle patted Peter squarely on the shoulder and a small red-haired boy, with dark freckles on his pale skin like a mottled egg, peered round the side of her waiting for his turn to say hello.

Earle sighed. "I'm not a tree. Just say hello."

The boy didn't move out from behind her, so Earle took a sidestep and presented him with both hands like a bored magician might do his assistant.

"Peter, meet Emmett. Emmett, Peter."

The boy creased the corners of his mouth into an awkward smile and waved. "Earle likes to think that because she's built like a refrigerator she can dominate me."

Earle rolled her eyes. "A microwave could dominate you."

"She does that a lot too. Puts people down. But she's just an Eeyore."

Peter shook his head. "Eeyore?"

"Yes," said Emmett. "A sad donkey in existential crises."

"I'm sorry, I don't—"

"Never mind."

"Well," said Peter. "I wouldn't worry about being small. I'm sixteen now but people have always told me I look a lot younger than I am, too."

Emmett narrowed his eyes. "Yeah, but I'm only eleven."

Peter sighed and Earle held his gaze without blinking. "So, that's awkward for you."

"Yup," said Peter. "Anyway, I'm sorry I haven't met you both properly before now."

Emmett shrugged. "Cooper said you were awkward and liked to overcomplicate things."

Cooper hooked his Stetson on a branch beside the fire and proceeded to warm his hands with a *don't look at me* expression on his face.

"Oh," said Peter after a while. "Did he?"

"He did," said Emmett. "And I can see what he's talking about."

"Yeah," said Earle. "Me too."

Peter sighed. "Great."

"But," Earle went on, "I can see what he likes about you, too."

Emmett nodded. "I concur. You've probably made a lot of mistakes, like a lot, which is hard for you to cope with because generally you're probably quite nice. So don't beat yourself up about them too much."

"No," said Earle. "Don't. Even though the mistakes you've made are probably huge."

Emmett nodded. "Like, huge."

Earle just stood there looking at Peter, and he'd never felt someone communicate so much warmth and good humour with their eyes while the rest of them seemed to do the opposite. He liked her. He liked them both, then cussed himself for being surprised. And the fact Cooper had even told them anything about him at all, let alone things that helped them to make allowances for his absence up until now, suddenly overpowered him.

"I don't know why you're being so nice," he said.

"Don't cry," said Earle. "That won't look good on you."

Emmett nodded in agreement. "Yes. Please don't. Earle can't handle emotional outbursts. She has too much inner turmoil of her own to deal with."

Earle held Peter's gaze and said nothing to contradict that statement. "So. You comin' to see the ghost town with us, then?"

The hairs on the back of Peter's neck froze, but the expression on Earle's face remained calm like there had been no deliberate attempt to shock him. Cooper looked back, first making sure that Peter was with him, then away to direct his attention down off the bluff into the forest below.

At first, Peter couldn't see what it was Cooper was trying to show him. Sunlight on the bark of the snowbound pines was sharp now, making the wilderness beyond the hillside glitter. It wasn't until he made his way around the campfire, and stood on the edge of the bluff overlooking the forest, that he saw it.

The red light was only faint in among the treetops. And infrequent. Seconds passed before the white tips of the pines were singed with red again. But when they were, the light didn't glimmer like fire, but spluttered.

"You can see it much better from over here," came a voice at Peter's side.

Perched on a rocky outcrop, a little further along the bluff from where Peter was standing, was Becky. She didn't look his way, like the act of speaking to him first when he'd done so little as her friend, was more than enough to be getting on with. Her gaze stayed on the forest below them and on the red light, her legs swaying to and fro, to and fro. But just when Peter had gone through a thousand different ways to open an apology, she seemed to recognize his struggle and gently patted the rock for him to come join her.

"Becky, I—"

"Remember that time you were dumb enough to ask me how you can tell when someone likes you?"

Peter cleared his throat and said nothing.

"And remember when you were so clueless about how much Cooper liked you that you didn't even get that he only taxied people around the lake so he had an excuse to canoe by your place?"

"Yes," said Peter. "I remember."

"Yeah. You needed a good friend to spell that stuff out to you."

"Yes. Yes, I know I did."

Becky nodded. "Well, you need a good friend right now to tell you what a dick you've been for not knowing how much like a brother you are to me. That's why it hurts so bad."

"Becky, I'm so—"

"And do you know how I know that?"

"No," said Peter quietly. "No, I don't."

"Because I love you as much as I hate you."

And it was true. In a way, what they shared was even stronger than if they'd just been brother and sister. They had each other because they had chosen each other.

Peter got down next to her, swinging his legs over the edge of the rock. "It's just that you'll be able to understand parts of Cooper now that I never will," he said. "And share things with him that I'll never know."

Becky shrugged. "And you share something far deeper with him that will never match any of that."

Peter drew a deep sigh into his chest and watched a bird take flight over the forest, the beat of its grey wings fleeting across the forest's snowy spires. And he wondered if Becky might yearn for someone of her own.

The two of them sat for a while without either one of them feeling the need to say much, when sunlight dipped behind the clouds, dulling the snow of its glitter. Becky stood, and the red light spluttered, much brighter now. The sky grew darker and the light burned, hot and fizzing, like a branding iron over the treetops. It was only now that Peter noticed the neon sign.

Coca-Cola ™
Proudly Sponsors Your Welcome Home

For a moment, he thought he must've lost his bearings or that the hills had somehow double backed on themselves so he was looking back down over West Wranglestone. The sign was exactly the same. Peter stood, walking further along the bluff to clear some trees blocking the view below. There was another Mainstreet. It stretched out beneath rows of crisscrossing fairy lights with the same little red-brick houses down either side. Towards the middle of the street, a neon cowboy above the Old Western Outfitters store stood frozen mid-pose, caught in the act of doffing his Stetson and waving it. There was the movie theatre, too. It was the exact same town, but not the same at all. This town was dark.

The red *Coca-Cola* sign spluttered again, but some of the letters had broken away and swung dully from the hoarding on frosted cables. The town was mostly buried beneath a thick crust of snow. It had been abandoned so long ago that it had the appearance of being dusty, like a shoebox full of special things left forgotten beneath the bed.

"I don't understand," said Peter. "What is that place?"

But Becky didn't answer. She ducked back off the bluff. A moment later she reappeared with the others, heading out across the ridge in single file, then in and out among the pines beneath him. The gang called out Peter's name, whistling and hollering for him to follow. And soon the snow came, sprinkling its silence first over the forest as they went, and then the little grey town beneath the little grey lights where silence had already paid a visit and decided to stay.

29

The fairy lights above Mainstreet clinked dully in the drifting snow. But it was the only movement. Every shop window was dark. Every one of those little light bulbs that once ran around the *Wranglestone Roxy* sign had long given up their chase. Most were as broken as eggshells. And every one of the little red-brick houses stood frozen in snow. Put to sleep by winter. Put to sleep by time. Put to sleep by the absence of anyone living here. The neon *Coca-Cola* sign spluttered and fizzed above them, casting a pool of red light in the snow at their feet, and Peter gazed up, listening first to the giant *O* creak wearily from its cable, then the wet crunch of Cooper's boots as he broke away from the others. He took a few steps forward, pulling his Stetson down over his eyes to shield them, and raised a hand for the group to observe silence.

"We don't got much time if we want to make it back

before sundown," he said. "Tokala, if you stand watch I'll take the town hall. Emmett and Earle, you go check the diner and Becky, see if you can find one of 'em in the drug store."

Becky shoved her hair back inside her bandana and nodded.

"But take Pete with you."

"OK," she said.

"And make sure he don't leave your sight."

"I get it."

"I mean it. There could be any amount of 'em down here."

Becky rolled her eyes. "Yes, already. But only if Pete promises to stop apologizing."

"I think I should be the one to go with Peter," said Earle, clearing her throat. "He can go on about how sorry he is to me if he likes. Emmett can vouch for the fact that I won't be listening."

Emmett nodded. "I told her my entire tragic backstory once and when I'd finished, she looked at me and, with no hint of irony whatsoever, asked, *When did sheep happen?*"

Earle shrugged. "It's a good question. I mean, do any of us know if they were knocking around with the dinosaurs? Or did they just pop up with the Bible?"

"Conquistadors introduced them to my people in the

fifteen hundreds," said Tokala. "That and syphilis. But before that, I really couldn't say."

Earle nodded. "See?"

Cooper looked back, the dark of his eyes glinting beneath the brim of his Stetson. Briefly he held Peter's gaze. But his eyes didn't tell him he loved him. Not this time. They were saying something else. Peter cocked his head to one side to ask him what it was, but Cooper just flicked his collar up around his neck to shield it from the snow and stood there smiling at him for what felt like the longest time, or maybe just for the first time in a long time. Whatever they were about to do, whatever they were about to discover, it was the reason Cooper had come. This was what all the Returnees were meant for. Peter could feel it so clearly now, and the glint in Cooper's eyes was brighter than a cowboy's spurs after rain, brimming with pride that Peter was by his side in life to bear witness to it.

Cooper doffed his Stetson. "We meet back here in twenty minutes," he said. "And remember, if they don't got no uniform on, we won't be able to make the others see."

Peter didn't know what Cooper meant by that. But before there was any time to ask, he, Emmett and Earle ran off inside the snow and Becky started to make her own way up Mainstreet, beckoning for him to follow. Peter hesitated, listening to the broken lights of Mainstreet jostle and clink in the flurrying snow above him.

"It's their time," said Tokala, standing at his side. "But they want so very much for you to be a part of it."

Peter nodded, even though he still didn't feel he had a right to be a part of anything, let alone understand what he was being invited to be a part of.

"I found a document," he said. "It said that when the Dead first attacked, the Returnees were trying to warn everyone of humankind's extinction. The government at the time thought they meant to cause that harm themselves. But they didn't. I think they suspected that people were going to do something to hurt themselves. I still don't know what, but I reckon you all think that too."

"Then follow that feeling," said Tokala. "And follow the others now and see where it takes you."

Becky turned back, urging Peter to stay close, so he walked on. And soon Tokala was so small standing at the foot of Mainstreet beneath the hills that he very nearly wasn't there at all. Just a red smudge of his ski jacket inside the veiling snow. But it was a comfort knowing he was. And his friendship was a comfort, one that somewhere along the line Peter had simply stopped seeking. He walked on and his thoughts turned to the sheriff and then to Teddy. Always back to Teddy.

He came to the drug store with the neon medicine

bottle at the window exactly like the one back in West Wranglestone and stepped up to the door. Shards of wood surrounding the lock had exploded outward at force. Bits of broken glass beneath the window crunched underfoot. They formed a trail leading away from the store out across the sidewalk.

"Becky?" he whispered. "Becky."

"Gimme a minute," she said, stepping inside. "Wait there."

Peter clapped his hands together to warm them and looked back down the length of Mainstreet. Tokala raised his hand in a motionless wave. Peter did the same. He turned round, crossing the sidewalk and followed the bits of broken glass out on to the middle of the street where another trail of glass met him. Peter looked up. On the other side of the road from the drug store, the double doors to the movie theatre were locked, but something had clearly burst violently through their glass panels. And where the thrust of the theatre's marquee shielded the sidewalk from much of the snowfall, was blood. Perhaps the town hadn't protected itself from the Dead in the same way as West Wranglestone. But the doors hadn't been broken in by an outside attack. They'd exploded outwards. Peter swung round. Eyes wide. Heart alert. Something else had happened here. It was only now he noticed all the windows and doors across town. Every last one of them had burst out from the inside.

Overhead, the giant *O* of the *Coca-Cola* sign creaked on its cable.

The broken fairy lights swayed.

Snow drifted across each of the black letters in *It's a Wonderful Life* and Peter gazed up. The same movie, playing in the same town that wasn't the same town. His attention turned to the ticket booth. The glass frontage was mostly iced over, making it difficult to see in. And you could easily have passed by, believing the booth to be empty, if it weren't for one thing. Poking through the slot in the glass used to issue tickets, was a hand.

The skin was ashen, drained of any life by death. And yet, this hand wasn't like any Peter had seen before, where snagged nails poked up from rotting stumps. These fingers were clean of any decay with sheen still left on the nails.

Peter swung back round towards the drug store, looking for Becky, but she was still rummaging around inside. He knew better than to call out for her. He looked towards the foot of Mainstreet, noting that Tokala was still standing guard, and turned back towards the ticket booth.

The hand had gone. Peter's heart pounded, driving his fist towards the blade in his pocket. He focused on the theatre's broken doors, waiting for the familiar thump and scrape of footfall as the thing made its way out of the booth, followed by the dull crunch of glass into bare feet as it cleared the entrance on its way out to get him. But it didn't come.

The hand appeared through the slot again. Its fingertips searched like worms hungry for the light. A moment later, the hand retracted through the slot only to reappear again, repeating the action. Peter relaxed his fist, letting go of the blade. Instead, he took the ten-dollar bill given to him as change when he bought Cooper's neckerchief, and slowly made his way up to the booth. He set the note down inside the shallow trough beneath the slot and waited. He didn't have to wait long. The pale hand emerged, fingering the corner of the note like an animal making sure the food it found was suitable. Apparently it was. The fingertips clutched, scrunching the note up with it, and the hand quietly withdrew. But just when Peter thought it was done, the hand returned, only this time it wasn't seeking payment. Those pale fingers and thumb came clasped. It was holding an invisible ticket.

Peter stepped back into the street. Inside the ticket booth was a boy. Or something that had only just stopped being a boy. His floppy hair was much fairer than Peter's, but the white T-shirt with a black dickie bow printed across the neckline was identical to his own. The boy's milky eyes didn't widen in hunger on seeing Peter standing there. He just sat looking out across the road, his hand doing one thing, that dull gaze doing another. Vacant. Blank. Believing Peter to be his own reflection, even. And in the strange calm of that pale face, it was all too easy for Peter to believe he wasn't looking at another boy either, only himself. But this reflection wasn't the kind where you've composed the version of yourself you already know in front of the mirror, but when you haven't and you catch yourself completely unaware in the glass. Peter saw himself not as he believed himself to be, but as he really was to the rest of the world. Lost inside his own unhappiness.

He stepped away from the boy, the sharp crunch of glass beneath his feet barely registering. He must've been bitten, but something other than the Dead had taken hold of him.

An unwelcome visitor had made a home here inside this town just as it had made a home inside every town that ever was. It hid inside the walls. It hid inside the drip of a tap. The tick of a clock. Peter was so sure of it now. And that clock was waiting for him back in the apartment, or in the equivalent of their apartment in this equivalent town, and he could find out what that thing was if only he would go there. And before he knew it, Peter followed the sidewalk back down the road until he came to the door beneath the Lone Star. He took the door key from his jacket pocket and found that it fit. This town was the same. Every part of it was just the same. Every brick and every window. The same. The same. And he took the stairs up to the front door and entered, and the wood panelling on the walls with the darker patches that gave the illusion of the apartment having history like pictures that had once hung there, was exactly the same. And so was the kitchen diner and couch with the same sunken spot on the seat where another person had spent their hours. Another person. Another Peter. Finally, from nowhere, came the clock. Just as it did back in West Wranglestone, it didn't let on at first that it was already there. It wasn't a dog waiting at the front door for you with a wag in its tail. The clock held its presence in the room secret for a while, keeping close to the walls before its little sound crept its way inside you. But it was always there waiting for you, ready to catch you the moment you were alone.

Peter sat on the couch, feeling the springs give way beneath the seat to draw him down deeper, and the clock ticked. And the tap behind him dripped. And he saw it now. The silence of a mountain or forest brought peace. But clocks marked the kind of silence that only ever existed between walls, that of dead time passing. It was the sound of your own life ticking away. But this apartment had something his and Cooper's didn't. A television.

The shiny black rectangle in the corner of the room didn't even look like a solid object. Everything else in the apartment had weight and age to it. The table lamp at Peter's side, with the dented plaid shade and dust across its base, seemed to belong to the ring-stained coffee coaster it stood over. It was like the pair of them had grown old together and had stories to tell. But the black rectangle was none of those things. It was a weightless thing hovering in space, like a piece of the world had been cut out. Inside the black void was Peter's reflection. But the glass was so opaque, he was featureless. Just a shadow against the shadow of the couch against the shadow of the apartment behind it. The clock ticked and Peter picked the remote up off the arm rest. It had too many buttons, but only one of them was red. He pressed it and the black void vanished like the final piece of a jigsaw puzzle of the apartment had been put back.

A woman appeared. She was standing behind a counter with glossy red lipstick, bright across a wide smile. Her voice was comforting. So were her eyes, which looked directly at Peter like the pair of them were in the same room together. She was telling him all about the wonderful things the object she was standing over could do. How it could blend food and cook food and cook two types of food all at once. But it didn't really matter what she was saying. The fact she was even there at all made something very comforting happen. She made the ticking go away.

Peter eased back into the chair and the springs sank even lower to accommodate him. The woman in the black rectangle smiled and Peter smiled back. And the clock was gone and with it, the silence.

The little red canoe sat upon the carpet of stars. A paddle, set down across the width of it, dripped steady beads of water. But they never made it to the lake. The droplets fell upwards, falling across the star-strewn sky. Peter gazed up, watching the stars quiver then re-form as the ripple passed among them. He looked down at his feet. They were no longer being held by water. There was nothing beneath them now but the stars. What was above was now below and Peter was no longer standing or floating, but somewhere between. He set one foot down, neither held by solid space nor passing through it, and quietly approached the canoe.

Cooper was lying naked across the hull of the canoe. Peter's eyes grazed the darkness of the hair beneath his arms and groin. Blades of blond hair spilled back from his face across the rib of the canoe and those two dark eyes looked back.

"Where have you been?" Peter asked.

"Here," said Cooper.

"Where?"

"Right here, Pete."

"But where? You've been gone."

"No. Reckon you're the one who's been gone. I been here the whole time."

"But I've been looking for you."

"And I've been waitin'."

"You have?"

"Yeah. Waitin' for you to come back."

Peter shook his head. "Come back?"

"Yeah."

"Back to where?"

"Back to here."

A shooting star passed beneath Peter's feet, journeying further out into space.

"Why, where's here?"

"Us," said Cooper.

"Us?" said Peter.

"Yeah. Here is us."

"But how?"

Cooper smiled. "Quit overthinkin'."

"But how is here, us?"

"The lake, Pete. And the plains and the forest and the cabin and the stars. They're us, all of 'em. But you're slippin' away again."

Peter shook his head. "No. I'm back now."

"Not you ain't. You're slippin'."

"Slipping?"

"Yeah. Going further away. Back to that place. Don't go."

"I won't. I'm here."

"Don't leave me."

"I'm right here."

Cooper gazed up and a star passed beneath the hull of the canoe. "Peter?"

"What?"

"Nothin'," he said. "I just wanted to hear your name is all."

Peter's heart beat wildly into his chest. He longed to be inside the canoe with him and no sooner had that thought occurred to him, he was. He tucked his feet beneath the bow seat and looked down into Cooper's dark eyes. Cooper looked back, but not to observe him, or to be with him, even, but to be part of him. Peter wiped a strand of hair from his cheek and the feeling of being an *us* again, returned to him.

He lay there for some time while Cooper's eyes searched his body. Eventually the wet glint on the surface of those two dark pools shifted and Cooper's gaze settled upon Peter's lips.

"You still feel too far away," said Cooper.

"But I'm here."

"Come closer."

"I should get back to the ticket booth."

"Why?"

"I don't know. I just should."

"No. Stay here."

"Where's here?"

"Us, Pete."

"Us?"

"Yeah. Us. Come back to us."

Peter lay down on top of Cooper, feeling his body pulse in tandem with his own, and cradled his face in wonder. "Your eyes," he told him. "They're full of stars."

Cooper blinked deeply, clasping both hands and legs behind Peter's back to draw him closer. They kissed and Peter gasped.

"I love you, Pete," said Cooper. "I love you so damn much. But wake up. Wake up!"

30

"Wake up!"

Someone called again. Louder this time. "Wake up, Peter. Wake up."

The woman with the soothing voice had gone. The black rectangle was dark and in her place was another face, belonging to a person who had crouched down before him.

"What are you doing in here all by yourself?" came the voice.

Peter's eyelids drooped.

Heavy.

Unwakeable.

"Peter," came the voice. "Peter?"

"Dad?"

"No. No, it's Tokala."

"Where am I?"

"Peter, we need to go."

"Where's the nice woman?"

"We need to get you out of here."

Peter became aware of movement at his side. He turned, watching the snow fall gently across the window and for the briefest moment thought he was back at the lake. But there was no cry of wolves to accompany the snow. No chattering blue jays darting in bright blue flashes past the tree-house window. Here, in *this* life, there would only ever be the tick of the clock and the sound of time yawning as it slowly slipped by.

"Tokala, what is this place?"

Tokala turned towards the window, as if looking over the whole town somehow, and sighed.

"We think it's the town where they experimented with people's return to civilization before us."

"Experimented?" said Peter.

"Or trialled, yes. To see if the same thing happens to people as happened before."

"Before?"

Peter sat upright, so very awake now, and Tokala's dark eyes held his.

"Peter, the national parks were never just a refuge from the Dead. They were also a release back to nature, a release from a modern world we made but were utterly incapable of freeing ourselves from. A world of money and things and never-ending routine and rituals to pay for those things. Back then it was impossible for people to even comprehend the depth of their own misery because the world they were born into already had them tricked. First, it tricked us into believing that all we needed was stuff, then it trapped us into maintaining what we'd gained and encouraged us to reach for more. More things. More everything. And it tricked us early on. Children's toy collections that needed completing became the burn to have the latest gadget. We took jobs to pay for them. Then, as we got older, bigger jobs to pay for bigger things. Homes. Apartments. Houses. Houses that needed filling. Buy a vase and you'd need a table to set it on. Toilet paper needed a holder. There were cars, curtains, furniture and clothes. Except, you could never keep up. Fashion went out of fashion and needed replacing. Technology needed to be constantly updated. Phones. Smaller versions, then larger. Larger versions to store more stuff. Music, photos, videos and apps. When we ran out of stuff to fill them with, we filled them with each other. Social media. It was empty at first. It needed filling. So, we filled it up with family and friends. People who weren't even friends. It didn't matter, just as long as we had them and kept hold of them. So, we added more photos. More videos. More stuff. Dogs. Cats. Funny ones were best. Anything to keep up and keep people in our stuff until we were just stuff too. And we just kept going until we'd filled our virtual world with as much stuff as our real worlds. More things. More everything.

"It didn't make us happy, Peter," Tokala went on. "None of it did. But having all that stuff did something very clever: it stopped us from ever noticing. It kept us busy and, in turn, compliant, as others busied to make more money out of us. We never questioned it. We were too busy. Busy behind our bright screens, busy behind our followers, our likes, our filters, our work, our chores, our box sets, our things. Even movie theatres and televisions, filling our head with other people's dreams. Keeping us quiet. Keeping us in the dark. We just kept filling in the hole, filling in the empty space, filling in our empty lives with stuff so we never even noticed that something else, something better, should always have been there in its place. Life. Life and the natural world around us."

Tokala stood, making his way over to the window. "The Dead were the brutal revolution to set us free. They freed us from a materialist world we had created but were utterly incapable of changing. The planet tried to save us many times. Fires ripped through whole continents. Floods. Plagues took over the whole world. But we never learned. We just went back to how things were before. Buying things. Owning things. Owing on what we owned and letting that system continue to stuff us. But the Dead finally managed it. Or should I say that the people finally managed it? Don't be mistaken, Peter. *We* were the ones half asleep. *We* were the ones in a torpor. *We* were the zombies."

The darkness of Tokala's words danced across the surface of his eyes and Peter leaned closer.

"That boy you saw in the ticket booth wasn't bitten, Peter. There was no virus. There was never any virus. And we were never driven from our lives by monsters, only ever by ourselves. The Dead are us, Peter. They were only ever us, or what was left of us, once humankind finally gave up. And they'll give up again. That boy back there and the rest of this town already did. Despite the government's best-laid plans for our return to the modern world, it's doomed to fail and the people are doomed to fall, only to rise back up again just so that the rest of us are free to live. Yes, to live, Peter. To live. But not here. Never in here inside these glass coffins. But out there."

Peter's heart stirred as if the lake itself was calling and looked to the window. "Cooper's trance and my daydreaming are one and the same thing."

"Yes," said Tokala. "And not just the pair of you, either. I have often found myself standing in a room with no knowledge of how I got there or why. Or found myself stirring a spoon with no knowledge of how long I had stood there stirring it for. Kettles stand whistling longer than they should. And dogs bark. The whole town is full of people dreaming if only you look close enough to see them. But none of us are really dreaming, Peter, are we?"

Tokala maintained eye contact so that Peter could find some comfort there while he made the connection for himself.

"No," Peter whispered. "We're dying."

Tokala nodded.

"And it'll happen again if we go back to how things were before?"

"We think so, yes."

The snow hurried in drifts across the bay window now, darkening the apartment, and Peter stood.

"It's just that I always thought I was born in the wrong time. That I didn't belong out there in the wild."

"The world will always be harsh, Peter, but always in great need of gentleness too."

"But—"

"Never be told your gentleness is a weakness, Peter."

Peter looked above the shadow of his own reflection in the television and saw the clock on the kitchen wall mirrored behind him.

"Why did you let us come?" he asked after a while. "When you told me back on the lake that we already had everything we ever needed, you meant the natural world. You knew all this and you still let us come."

"Let?" said Tokala. "You're suggesting I had any say."

"But why don't you?"

"Because the pull back to civilization was unavoidable."

"No."

"Yes, Peter. There are forces greater than us that will determine it."

"What forces?"

"The government. Consumerism. Capitalism. They won't let us stay away."

"But why didn't you fight it?"

"Because my people know better than most what trying to keep our relationship to the land cost us. Early settlers to this country saw to that. Your country's founding fathers saw to it, and then they saw to us."

"But if you thought you never stood a chance of staying away, what changed your mind?"

Tokala smiled, like they might share the answer to that question, and invited Peter to join him at the window. Outside, Cooper looked up through the tumbling snow from the street below. He doffed his Stetson, indicating that their little sojourn was drawing to a close, and soon Becky and the others joined him. But they weren't alone. Snow hurried across the cables, making the broken fairy lights jump and jangle. Peter pressed his face to the glass. As if by some strange calling, their dull knell brought ghosts.

The Dead wandered out beneath the broken lights, weightless as ash and snow. They didn't lurch or lumber, but instead drifted among the snowed-up cars as if waking from sleep to become brighter beings. Emmett took the hand of a waitress in a blue checked shirt-dress, steadying her over the banking snow. Every now and then she patted the pocket of her apron down or reached for her ear, little knowing that she was still holding the pencil and pad in her hand. But then the snow kissed her face. She paused for a moment, gazing up like the world had reminded her of its being there. And then they all did. Snow flurried over ash and bone and those lost souls stood spellbound watching the sky.

"Remove us from the land," said Tokala, "and we return to dust."

Peter leaned into the glass, watching the boy from the ticket booth gazing up at the snow. "It was easier growing up on the lake all this time believing we only ever lived among monsters."

"But it's only ever been people, Peter. They're alive in death just so the rest of us realize how much we're meant to live."

Tokala made his way towards the front door, but Peter held back a moment. He dragged a dining chair over to the work counter, clambering up to take the clock down off the wall, and removed the batteries. *Be gone*, he told the silence. *Be gone.* He got off the chair, setting the clock face down on top of the counter. As he did, he caught his reflection in the glass. He looked tired. Drawn. But more than that, just like his dad back at the boathouse, there was something in his eyes that hadn't been there before, or rather something had vanished. A spark. He hadn't understood what that had been before. Now he did, he was glad to have left his dad back at the lake as far away from the town as possible. For a moment he wished he'd stayed too.

Peter pulled down on his lashes to inspect his eye. "Tokala. My eyes."

"I know," said Tokala. "It will pass."

"But—"

"It will pass, Peter. But we must leave now and go warn the others."

They left town, following the trail they'd made back uphill through the forest. They summited the ridge at sundown with a small troop of the Dead in tow, and with the little lights of West Wranglestone peeking through the snowy pines beneath them, started to make their descent down the other side. They came to a snow-strewn bluff when Cooper removed his Stetson, holding it low across both shins, and called back.

"Pa always said if you stand on a hill and look down over a town, that it begins to look like a cemetery. All those little houses lined up neat in a row are just coffins. Reckon he was right, Pete. Just look at how small our lives are down there, all stuffed up inside those little brick boxes. Life before the Restless Ones was a kind of livin' death. Their workplaces and houses were nothin' but tombstones. Don't you see it now?"

"Yes," said Peter taking his hand.

"Tell me you see it."

"I see it, Coop. I see it all now."

Cooper turned round, squeezing Peter's hand once to tell him he loved him. Then, with the ropes of his hair roiling in the spiralling snow, called back. "Reckon we round everyone up and take 'em to the town hall. Becky and Tokala, you take the apartments on the west side of the street. Earle and I will take the east. And Emmett, if it int too much to ask of you . . ."

Emmett let go of the waitress's hand.. "You're a good leader so you're worried about putting too much pressure on me because I'm young."

"I int your leader," said Cooper. "I'm just your friend."

Emmett shrugged. "We don't have time for semantics. But it's OK. You'll need Earle's big hands for knocking down doors. I'll lead the Dead to the hall and wait for you all there."

"You sure?"

"I'm sure."

Earle stepped forward, patting Emmett squarely on the back. "Are you sure these big hands can't give you a big hug first?"

"Only if you promise not to crush my vital organs."

"I promise no such thing."

Earle took Emmett in a bear hug, scrubbing the top of his head with her fist and everyone took a moment for their own handshakes and well wishes before splitting off. They started to make their way down when Peter cleared his throat.

Cooper turned back. "Pete, you's coming with me."

"No."

"Pete, that int no question."

Peter tucked a ribbon of Cooper's hair back behind his ear and kissed him. "And I'm really praying that any future marriage proposal will be a little bit more romantic than that, but there was a whole thing with a trapdoor and the sheriff I haven't even told you about yet, so I think I'll be OK without you for five minutes. And besides, there's someone I need to find. Someone who won't be home."

Cooper looked down so his hair covered his face, telling Peter he didn't much like the sound of that idea. But before they'd come to this town, during that month on the saddle, Peter realized that they'd become so much more than boyfriends. They'd become a team. And in this exact moment, Peter felt that return. They were partners, not only in daily life, but in adventures.

Cooper stepped forward. "Don't—"

"I won't take any risks," said Peter.

"I mean it, Pete."

"And I mean it too."

Cooper looked up, holding Peter's gaze, and Peter smiled back. "I love you too."

And soon the forest rushed in, followed by the road leading back into town, and the golden lights of the Wranglestone Roxy rippled, calling Peter from inside the veiling snow. He pushed the double doors aside, shaking the snow from his hood and entered the foyer.

Inside was quiet. The lights to the popcorn kiosk were out. Across the way, both lamps either side of the auditorium doors still glowed from inside their scallop shells, illuminating the green walls. And the movie was playing. Silver light from the projector shivered beneath the door. Inside, a man in the movie was shouting. *Hello, Bedford Falls*, he cried. Then, *Merry Christmas, movie house! Merry Christmas* something. Peter couldn't make out the rest. But he sounded happy. So very happy. Peter crossed the foyer, looking back towards the kitchenette. The kettle was silent and devoid of steam, but one of the mugs lay broken in pieces across the floor. Spilt coffee splattered the walls.

"Marge?" he whispered. "Marge?"

But he didn't dare say it any louder. He stared at the broken mug. What if he had already come too late? Peter's heart pounded. He called her name one more time and a shadow passed beneath the office door. He took a few steps backwards, feeling round for the relative safety of a solid wall behind him, and the shadow stepped back into place, striking out tall across the foyer carpet.

The shadow held. It waited. Marge's name broke across Peter's lips one more time, but he barely managed a whisper. He walked forward, crossing the length of the foyer up to the office. He quietly took hold of the handle. The other hand reached for his knife. Behind him, music was playing now. A Christmas carol, perhaps. But it wasn't one Peter knew. The music stopped and the projector lights went out. Peter turned round and quietly opened the door.

31

Marge stood perched on the lip of her desk facing the door. She was barely recognizable as the woman Peter had first encountered with popcorn shelving her white shirt the day of his interview. But this wasn't because death had taken her. She was snug inside a red cable-knit sweater. The floppy ears of a trapper hat framed the apples of her ruddy cheeks. At her waist, she wore a leather toolbelt kitted out with knives, hammers and screwdrivers all weighed down at the hip by bundles of suede pouches for nails. On the floor to the side of Marge's desk, her work shirt, pants and dickie bow lay strewn next to a sleeping bag and pillow. The sleeping bag had been slept in. A frying pan on a camping stove had been used recently and the smell of bacon hung inside the office, fusing with the familiar scent of log smoke Peter knew from home, coming from Marge's clothes.

Marge sighed. "That's one way to go about getting promotion."

"Sorry?" said Peter. Then he remembered he was holding a knife. "Oh, this? No, it's just that I . . ."

Marge took a sip from the tin cup she was holding and Peter noticed an old Yellowstone patch sewn into the shoulder of her sweater.

"You're wearing your park clothes," he said.

"You should leave."

"And you've been sleeping in here."

"Your powers of observation astound me."

Peter stooped to pick the dickie bow up off the floor and held it in the flat of his palm.

"When I first came here, you told me that survival didn't just look like a bloodied knife in the hand. You meant it looked like this, didn't you?"

"What does that matter now?"

"You meant it looked like getting by."

Marge gazed down into the contents of her tin cup and a moment passed in silence. For the first time since they'd met, this didn't seem to create a chasm for all their differences to tumble into, but relief now that the things they were saying to each other didn't only exist to hide the pain of the truth, that they both missed home.

"I used to spend my days in Yellowstone mending the boards," said Marge after a while. "Acid in the pools and geysers corrodes the nails. They'll dissolve right in front of you if you don't keep your beady eye on 'em. But you know what? I could spend whole afternoons just walking the western rim around the cabins and never once see the same burst of bright water. No two days are alike with the geysers."

"I was there with Cooper not so long ago. Just before we came here."

Marge looked up, her eyes suddenly bright. "Yes. Then you already know."

"I do."

"The geysers. Surprise you, don't they?"

"Yes. They do."

"Like a sudden whoop straight to the heart. They just come clean outta nowhere to steal your breath away and we're just powerless to do anything other than stand there gawping."

Peter stepped closer. "Marge. Come with me to the town hall. There's something you've got to see."

"Forget about it."

"But everything you've just said."

"I said, forget it."

"And everything you're wearing."

"What does it matter now?"

"But it matters a great deal. We're getting out of here. Back home on the lake, there's a cabin perched on a boulder right next to my island. If you lived there we could be neighbours. If you let me, we could be friends."

"Pah," said Marge, setting her tin cup down on the desk. "Friends."

"You can watch every season from the islands. The mountains too. And besides, my dad can't cope with mending the tree houses all by himself."

Marge's chest rose deep beneath her sweater as if the promise of all those hopes and dreams returning to her was so close she could almost reach out and feel the scale of a pine cone beneath her fingertips. But it didn't last. The tips of her doughy fingers clenched the tin cup until they turned red, and the thought left her.

"You're too late."

"No," said Peter. "No, we're not. We're rounding everyone up to leave right now. And you have to come. It isn't just the getting by. We've discovered something worse will happen to everyone if we stay."

Marge narrowed her eyes, scouring inside him for the things he knew. For the things she already suspected. But she didn't give in to those feelings. She stood up, withdrawing first her excitement and then eye contact, and quietly put the lid back on top of all that could've been.

"The bus is already here."

The hairs on the back of Peter's neck stood up. "What bus?"

"The military one come to take everyone over the park borders. They're taking us into the city. Everyone's already on board."

"What do you mean, everyone?"

"What part of *everyone* don't you understand?"

"But you're wearing your park clothes."

Marge glanced at her sleeping bag. And it was only now that Peter saw the bottle of pills beneath her pillow.

"No, Marge. That's not the way."

"Well, it's my way."

"But we're here now."

"And you're too late."

"We've come to take you back."

"And so have they."

"But they can't have you," said Peter. "They can't have any of us. Everyone will die."

Marge looked at Peter from the other side of the desk and smiled a sad smile. "There you are, dear boy," she said. "The fight, come at last. What a crying shame you've come too late."

Panic ripped through Peter's body like wildfire. He dashed back through the foyer, flinging the double doors to the movie theatre aside, and ran out into the middle of the road.

At the bottom of Mainstreet, just before the road spilled past the last of the red-brick houses out into the night, slashes of red light struck the snow. The vehicle was stationed just around the corner out of sight, but even from this distance, Peter saw how the rear lights were so much bigger than those of the sheriff's Jeep had been. He staggered forward, wiping snowflakes from his lashes, and watched the shadows of the people standing there crisscross the ground. Someone was talking loudly. Shouting followed. Then came gunshots. Becky ran out from beneath the shadow of a doorway next to the Old Western Outfitters store. Tokala too. They kept low behind the cars lining the sidewalk. But they were alone. High above them, the hot light of the neon cowboy burned through the tumbling snow. But the apartment window above the store was dark. All the windows across Mainstreet were. The houses had already been vacated.

Another gunshot sounded and Cooper spilled out from an open doorway. Earle followed. But they'd managed to find someone. Earle turned back, raising a finger to her mouth for the person behind them to stay hidden. Val, one of the men from the town hall, ducked back inside the door, pulling a jacket across his shoulders and another gunshot fired. Cooper walked out into the middle of the road. He was still some distance from the stationary vehicle, but he made no attempt to conceal his whereabouts. He just stood there, legs wide, heel of his hand on the belt, waiting. He looked back. His dark eyes peered out from beneath the brim of his Stetson, and he seemed to find comfort in seeing Peter standing there. He was scared.

Peter had never seen Cooper this way before. The boy that leaped into his canoe with a machete and an easy smile and never once rocked the water, had gone. It was only now Peter realized that Emmett was unaccounted for. Peter ran up to Cooper and took his hand. But everyone else was to stay hidden. Cooper looked behind him, instructing the others to hang back. Becky and Tokala nodded, ducking back down behind a car. Earle and Val did the same. With everyone in position, Cooper squeezed Peter's hand and they ran down to the corner of the street.

Two soldiers were stationed outside the army bus. One held his rifle low and stood guarding the passenger door to prevent the people inside from leaving their seats. The other stood beneath the red glare of the rear lights, rifle up, eye to the aim, pointing it straight at Emmett. Emmett was on his knees as if praying. Behind him, the Dead lay strewn in bloody piles across the snow. And they looked so harmless in their little array of uniforms, and Emmett so small, that somehow the soldier's fear of them seemed monstrous. But it was only now Peter saw that Emmett wasn't begging for the soldier's mercy. He was already dead. A black hole, no bigger than a penny really, disturbed the back of his head, making the hair gummy. Peter cupped the back of Cooper's head, quickly pulling him to his chest so he couldn't see, and Emmett fell face forward into the snow.

Cooper bucked, punching at Peter's chest like an animal desperate to get away. But Peter clasped his face with both hands, kissing first his cheek and then his nose, silently begging him not to give up their whereabouts, and shoved them into a doorway.

The bus revved twice, indicating that it was time to leave. One set of footsteps disappeared inside the bus. The other grew louder. Snow creaked underfoot like leather belts flexing and the soldier turned into Mainstreet.

"Who goes there?" he said, his voice dull and blank.

Peter pulled Cooper closer into the shadow of the doorway. Their noses touched. The quick exhalation of Cooper's breath across Peter's face seemed too loud, so he kissed him, holding his lips to his, and the soldier came closer.

"I said who goes there? Come out."

Cooper's hand found Peter's, just as it had done many times over these few short months they'd spent together. And it struck Peter as a wonder that he should ever have been so lucky as to live a life where someone would want to take him by the hand and by doing so, lift him from the world. The world beyond the doorway may have belonged to the soldier. But here, inside its shadow beneath the veiling snow, if only for one more moment, it was just *us*.

A man stepped out from between two cars. For a second, Peter thought that Val had created a diversion to stop the solider from noticing him and Cooper standing there. But it wasn't him. The fleeced hood of the man's parka jacket shielded his face, but he raised both hands to reassure the soldier that he wasn't a threat and stopped in the middle of the road across the way from where Peter and Cooper were hiding.

"I didn't mean to alarm you," the man told the soldier. "Forgive me. I left my ID in the apartment just now and had to go back for it."

Peter's legs gave way beneath him. "Dad."

Cooper pulled him closer to muffle his cry and Dad drew back the hood of his parka. The soldier took the documents, wiping snow from the plastic slip, and the bus revved. The soldier took a moment, checking first the ID then Peter's dad to be sure they were one and the same. But the bus revved a second time and backed on to the street. It was time to go. The red lights flashed across the snow and the back doors swung open. The soldier glanced down the length of Mainstreet one last time. But he was done here. He rapped the side of the bus with his fist for the driver to go on and bundled Peter's dad into the back. The doors pulled shut behind him and Dad took his seat. It was only then, just as the bus pulled away, that he finally turned round to look back.

And he stayed there watching for as long as was possible. The bus tumbled over the roughened snow and the rear lights swerved, catching in their red glare first a mailbox and then an elk, which stood looking on with nostrils flared, its white breath rumbling across the darkness. Peter's dad smiled sadly, as if taking sudden solace that his departure should occur at the same time as the animal's arrival. Then his eyes finally found Peter. Peter pulled free of Cooper's arms, then squeezing between two cars, dashed out into the middle of the road.

"Dad!"

His dad pressed both hands to the glass. *I love you*, his eyes told him. *I love you so very much*. But then they said, *No*. His dad shook his head and Peter knew he was asking him not to give up his and Cooper's whereabouts. *Go*, his dad told him. *Go be happy and never look back*. He blinked once deeply as if to hold Peter in his arms one last time. Then his dad's eyes told him no more. The bus turned a corner. The rear lights faded across the elk's hooves. Then both they and his dad were gone.

5 YEARS LATER

Drooping pines, too parched this late in the summer to hold up their boughs, ringed the perimeter of the lake. A family of deer made their way down to the water's edge to drink. Bull elks, too. Further up towards the boathouse, a pair of giant antlers breached the water, cutting through a haze of flies and gossamer, travelling on towards land. The antlers hit shingle, rising up sharply from the lake, and a moose hoisted its weary limbs off into the woods.

Peter rested the paddle across the width of the canoe, watching the lake dazzle like starlight in the late-September sun. He squinted, holding his hand to his brow and looked out towards the watchtower. Fishing lines, cast off from the stairwell, made a web of silver threads. But they didn't stop Becky from diving off the top, no matter how many times he'd warned her.

Peter sighed. "You're gonna die."

And this only encouraged Cooper. Soon that body, like

an arrow in white undershorts, darted into the water and made its way back towards the canoe. Peter supposed he should join him. They wouldn't have many days like this left this year. It wouldn't be long before the birch leaves yellowed and the mists would come, capping the island's piney spires inside another winter. But it would have to wait. The herd was on the move. In the years that followed his dad's departure and in memory of everyone else they'd lost along the way, it had become tradition to go out to the plains each year to watch it.

Cooper's hands clapped hold of the canoe. He hoisted himself up, tossing his head back so ribbons of wet hair lashed his back, and leaned in for a kiss. His blond beard was as coarse as the palms of his hands, but perfectly cut to the jaw now Peter had taken a blade to it.

"Comin' in?" said Cooper.

"Your lips have shrivelled up in the water."

"Int the only thing to have shrivelled up, neither."

"I'm sure," said Peter. "And Becky and Earle really don't have that problem so why don't you leave them to it?"

"I can't feel it."

"Give it time."

"It ain't down there no more."

"It'll grow back."

"When, Pete? When?"

Peter pulled a strand of Cooper's hair from his mouth and rolled it between his fingers. "You're getting split ends."

"Huh?"

"Too much sun. Too much water. Not enough—"

"You!"

Cooper clambered into the canoe, legs flailing about in the hull like a damn salmon, and sprawled across Peter's lap looking up at him. "Kiss me."

"You're a fool."

Cooper blinked once, deeply. "Kiss the fool."

"I love you," said Peter.

"I love you, too."

"But we've got to go."

Cooper shook his head. "Kiss me some more, first."

"But we need to leave for the plains."

"Is it time?"

"Yeah," said Peter. "It's time."

"Then kiss me before it shrivels up for good."

"Later."

"When later?"

"Tonight."

Cooper smiled. "Your hair's gotten curly."

"Yeah," said Peter. "I should probably ask Becky to cut it."

"Nah. Only if you don't like it."

"I don't like it."

"Get it cut, then," said Cooper. "But your shoulders have burned."

"They're OK."

"No, Pete, they ain't. They're as red as the canoe."

"I left my T-shirt on the island."

"Why dint you pull the tarp over you?"

Peter looked at the sheet of tarpaulin at the foot of the canoe and shrugged. Cooper rolled his eyes, planting a kiss on him, then laid out long across Peter's lap in ways that usually indicated very little was about to get done.

Scores of little fish darted beneath the canoe and Peter placed his hand across Cooper's chest. "Your eyebrows have gotten so blond. I can hardly see them."

"Is Junior OK?"

Peter looked across the lake towards Skipping Mouse where Snowball Junior was busy grazing beneath the shadow of the tree house. After Snowball died, three years went by before Cooper had the spirit to break in another horse. Now, they'd built a raft to transport him from the boathouse and back so he didn't have to be left alone on the mainland. But unlike Snowball, who got low when left cooped up for too long, Junior would've been quite happy if he was given a blanket and some snacks in front of the log burner given half the chance. But he needed a stretch on the mainland and besides, the herd was coming.

Cooper lifted his head from Peter's lap. "Well, is he?"

"Yeah. He's fine. He's up on the top deck with a cup of tea, reading Tolstoy."

"*Toy Story*?"

"Tolstoy."

"Huh?"

"Forget it," said Peter. "Why, what's *Toy Story*?"

"Well—"

Peter kissed Cooper on the lips and shoved him forward. "Save it for later. We better get ready."

The canoe rushed through the water, beaching itself on the shore, and Cooper made his way back towards the tree house, threatening to cook something for dinner that night. Peter picked his T-shirt up off the rock but held back at the foot of the rope ladder for a moment. In her first year on the lake, Marge had built a bench up in the tree house for him to remember his dad by. And while he often felt closer to him on the waiting bench beneath the falls where Rider, Emmett and Teddy's names had now been carved, in hope that one day he might emerge through the waterfall having found his way back to him, Cooper rarely passed *Tom's Bench* without having a word.

"Pa," Cooper whispered. "We better have lost them scissors. I like Pete's curls just fine."

Peter smiled to himself. Cooper had taken to calling

Dad their pa some years back now, but it still had the power to move him.

The community left the islands of Wranglestone via the boathouse, travelling on through the forest in single file until they reached the land where golden grasses swayed and the clouds moved as one across the roaming blue. Peter took up the reins, leading Junior and the others uphill to a windy bluff where they could gain good vantage over the plains. And as he secured the reins over the bucking roll, swinging his leg up and over ready to dismount, there they were.

The Dead moved slowly across the plains like the shadow of a cloud passing over land. No one really knew what drove them towards the higher regions when winter threatened to seize their brittle bones. Tokala liked to think the shimmer of the northern lights beckoned them into the afterlife. Others, like Becky, thought they were drawn to follow those streaks of cloud that passed by once in a while. Peter gazed up, noticing the unmistakeable trail of an aeroplane passing overhead and wondered how big their towns and cities were becoming and what would become of the people trapped inside them once the littleness of life took over. Either way, the annual migration of the Dead had come to mean a lot of things to a lot of people in the years since they fled town. Whenever petty differences or the routines of daily life threatened to take over the community, the herd had become that constant reminder that death was coming to us all, and to live. Live now, while you can. But as a pack of wolves broke out in bounding leaps towards the herd, hellbent on picking off the weakest stragglers at the back, the Dead had come to symbolize something else, that people living on the land had been put back in their place, no longer above the planet, or outside of it, but a part of it.

Peter watched Cooper standing there for a while, lost in his thoughts, lost in his hair, lost in the billowing wonder of it all. But as the herd travelled on towards the horizon, Cooper's sights didn't stay with the Dead for long. He turned back, as if seeing even greater journeys inside Peter, and gently took him by the hand.

"Peter?"

Peter wiped a strand of hair from Cooper's lips and smiling said, "What?"

"Oh nothin'. I just needed to hear your name is all."

Cooper held eye contact for a while just to be sure of them. Then he made his way down off the bluff, wafting flies away with the brim of his Stetson, and Junior turned, swishing the sun-soaked dust with his tail for Peter to follow.

And a breeze caught the air,

And the air caught the grass,

And the grass waved hello, bending in golden ribbons on across the plains. *Come*, they seemed to say. *Come.* For they were here, here among those herds of rousing Dead with nothing but the day and the wandering skies all around them, going on and on and on.

ACKNOWLEDGEMENTS

In addition to the acknowledgements already made in *Wranglestone* -

For their support championing Wranglestone during its initial publication, my thanks go to dear George, Daniel at Female First, Starburst magazine, Jim, Uli, and Erica at that most wonderful of emporiums, Gays the Word. Niall and Gary at Foyles Charing Cross, and Gary and Florentyna at Waterstones.

For rescuing *Wranglestone* from the pandemic so Peter & Cooper could go on to have a better shot at finding a wider readership, I extend my deepest gratitude to the 2020 Costa Book Award judges, John, Patrice and Alex, and to that most dedicated armada of booksellers at the Waterstones Children's Book Prize 2021. I wouldn't have had the strength to finish the boys' story without the encouragement you gave me.

At Little Tiger - Lauren, Pip, George and Dannie, heartfelt thanks for your patience, trust in my work and for making the boys shine so brightly in this final outing.

Hannah - this marks the end of a journey that started for us way back in 2015. Thank you for being a friend and a mentor every step of the way.

To my editor, Lucy, who joined me for the last leg of this journey on *Timberdark*. Thank you. It's been a blast and you've been wonderful.

To my illustrator, Karl. You've quite simply put Peter & Cooper's story into so many more reader's hands because of the nuance and wonder you've gifted both books. Thank you for making my dreams come true, your friendship and for inspiring me to do better. It's been an honour.

ABOUT THE AUTHOR

Darren Charlton was born on the South coast of England
where he has returned, dividing his time between East
Sussex and Kent where his partner lives. He studied English
Literature and Theatre at De Montfort University and
currently works part time for the NHS.

Darren's first novel, *Wranglestone*, won the Waterstones
Children's Book Prize for older readers, was shortlisted
for the Costa Book Awards and the YA Book Prize, and
longlisted for the Branford Boase Award.

For more information about Darren Charlton visit:
www.darrencharlton.com

Follow him on Twitter @DarrenRCharlton